WOKE UP LIKE THIS

ALSO BY AMY LEA

Exes and O's

Set on You

PRAISE FOR *WOKE UP LIKE THIS*

"Amy Lea's *Woke Up Like This* reminded me that the exciting and complicated feelings of our teenage years never truly fade away. The book perfectly captures high school nostalgia . . . It's a feel-good story for the young and young at heart."

—Mindy Kaling

"*Woke Up Like This* is witty, earnest, charming, and intensely seventeen. It perfectly captures the highs and lows of being on the brink of big life changes and the thrill of first love (and first hate)."

—Ali Hazelwood, *New York Times* bestselling author of *The Love Hypothesis*

"*Woke Up Like This* charmed me from page one and I never wanted it to end! Perfect for fans of Kasie West and Jenny Han, this book is guaranteed to suck you in and force you to read it in one sitting. Ten out of ten would recommend!"

—Lynn Painter, *New York Times* bestselling author of *Better Than the Movies*

WOKE UP LIKE THIS

A NOVEL

AMY LEA

MINDY'S BOOK STUDIO

This is a work of fiction. Names, characters, organizations, places, events, and incidents are either products of the author's imagination or are used fictitiously. Any resemblance to actual persons, living or dead, or actual events is purely coincidental.

Published by Mindy's Book Studio, New York

www.apub.com

ISBN-13: 9781662511684 (hardcover)
ISBN-13: 9781662511707 (paperback)
ISBN-13: 9781662511691 (digital)

Cover design by Caroline Teagle Johnson
Cover image: © AlexandrBognat, © Erhan Inga, © Squeeb Creative / Shutterstock; © Chuanchai Pundej / EyeEm, © Evgeniia Siiankovskaia, © Somrudee Doikaewkhao / EyeEm / Getty Images

Printed in the United States of America
First edition

To seventeen-year-old me

A NOTE FROM MINDY KALING

I've never been able to resist a coming-of-age story. That's how I fell in love with *Woke Up Like This*, a charming romantic comedy about Charlotte Wu, an overachieving, goal-obsessed high school senior who finds herself in a very strange predicament.

Charlotte is a straight A student, she's landed a solid college acceptance, and she's even almost gotten her crush to notice her. But when she falls off a ladder while putting up prom decorations, Charlotte wakes up in an unfamiliar bed, thirty years old, and realizes she's engaged to her archnemesis. The two opposites are forced to work together to find their way back to seventeen and discover there's more to life than achievement for achievement's sake.

Like *Never Have I Ever* and the classic movie *13 Going on 30*, Amy Lea's novel reminded me that the exciting and complicated feelings we have as teenagers never truly fade away.

Charlotte Wu's High School Bucket List

(Written by Charlotte Wu, age 13—to be completed by Charlotte Wu upon graduation, age 17)

~~-Join student council, student senate, and yearbook committee~~
~~-Honor roll all 4 years—top of list, ideally~~
-Get driver's license (not achieved. don't ask.)
~~-Get invited to Tony Freeman's end-of-year party~~
-Become student council president (ruthlessly sabotaged)
~~-Score at least 1300 on SATs~~
-Do Senior Week with Kassie (in progress)
-Get promposed to (proverbial tumbleweeds . . .)
-Magical senior prom (in progress)

ONE

One month until prom

Prom is the single most important night of a teenager's life, and you can't convince me otherwise. I know what you're thinking—it's overhyped, the same as any other dance. And sure, there are infinite ways it can go horribly wrong:

- Your date could ditch you for their more attractive ex, leaving you to brood in a dark corner while everyone else slow dances to the song *you* requested.
- The cleavage-enhancing silicone inserts you stuffed into your bra could fall out when you get a little too low on the dance floor. (Ask me how I know.)
- A drunk band nerd could projectile vomit cherry punch all over your dress.
- You could spend the entire night chasing down the disease-ridden lab rat someone set loose while everyone watches in horror.

Things can really go from zero to tragic in a millisecond. Trust, I've seen the original *Carrie* movie. But bloodied, telekinetic, murderous prom queen aside, name a better occasion to mark the end of four tireless years of social and academic Olympics. It's the rite of passage we deserve. A fabulous night to trade in those tearstained SAT prep books for outrageously priced formal wear you'll never wear again. One night to forget being unjustly denied from your dream college. Your final night to be a teen, before adulthood drop-kicks you in the privates.

As the student council vice president, executing a magical night to cherish fondly when I'm wrinkled, frail, and demanding a senior discount on my rum raisin ice cream is not something I take lightly.

That's why I've spent all weekend obsessing over my PowerPoint presentation: *Around the World in One Magical Night.* It comes complete with an itemized budget, food vendors, and lists of highly rated DJs and decor items, including translucent globe balloons etched with gold foil that shimmer when the light hits just right.

I'm at the kitchen table agonizing over the font color when Mom shuffles in, disheveled sandy-blonde hair in a french braid from two days ago. She's still in her pajamas, even though she has to be at work at the pharmacy in less than half an hour.

"How long have you been awake?" she asks, popping onto her toes to fetch her red FUTURE BESTSELLING AUTHOR coffee mug from the cabinet. She hasn't published a book yet, but I often find her hunched over her laptop late into the night, guzzling Red Bulls, typing feverishly until her eyes give out.

"I was in bed early. Got up around the same time you went to sleep," I counter, stuffing my face with a spoonful of oatmeal when I catch the time on my computer.

"These bags under my eyes were worth it. Guess what?" I catch the excitement in her expression, and it's not about the fact that I premade her coffee. "I finally untangled that plot bunny in the second act."

"Wanna tell me in the car? We have to leave soon," I remind her as she leisurely pours her coffee. Being late is inevitable with Mom, which is why I usually opt to ride my bike to school. Unfortunately, my bike is still being repaired by the Bike Doctor (a.k.a. the thirteen-year-old computer hacker down the street who also fixes bikes on the cheap).

Mom nonchalantly leans her hip against the counter and begins flicking through her phone. "We have tons of time."

We really don't, but I don't bother arguing. I love Mom, but she's my opposite in nearly every way. She resembles a blonde, blue-eyed shield-maiden straight from the set of *Vikings*, while I'm Asian, vertically challenged, with dark hair and eyes "the color of the abyss" (a deranged and misguided compliment from my ex-boyfriend).

Unlike me, Mom is never in a rush until the eleventh hour and is forever forgetting important things, like a bra, for instance. She's always been this way, even before Dad left. But having single motherhood thrust upon her only worsened her tardiness. At nine years old, I taped a color-coded extracurricular schedule on the refrigerator so she'd stop forgetting to pick me up from swimming lessons. Over the years, making lists and schedules has become my version of meditation. It calms my nerves when things start to feel out of control.

Steaming mug in hand, Mom peeps at my screen over my shoulder, still in no rush. "How's the PowerPoint coming along? You changed the background again, I see."

"Aesthetic is important," I explain nobly.

"You don't think seventeen slides is overkill?"

"Hey, I started at twenty-five. This is the lean version." *Magic is in the details*, after all. Admittedly, I just made that quote up, but I'm sure some wise creative said it at some time in history.

She plops into the seat across from me with a sympathetic, yet puzzled frown. "I can't believe you skipped out on Tony Freeman's big bash."

"Mom, you're the only parent in history who's disappointed her underage daughter didn't get wasted at the biggest party of the year." In fact, Mom actively encourages partying, which she never did at my age. Her parents (my grandparents) were relentlessly strict. So now she tries to live vicariously through me. "Kassie said there were college kids there," I add.

"Last I checked, you're going to be in college in"—she pauses to consult her imaginary wristwatch—"three months."

"Exactly. And I can't close the book on high school until I've planned the perfect prom." Prom is one of the last remaining "to-dos" on my high school bucket list. I won't find peace until it's crossed off.

"Right. The checklist," she drones, sliding down in her chair, long legs extended. She thinks it's ridiculous to pin the success of my high school career on a checklist I made when I was thirteen. Maybe it is. But there is no better feeling than striking out each milestone, one by one.

I move to the sink to rinse my bowl, hopeful she'll get the hint and get dressed.

Instead, she stretches her arms above her head and yawns. "I just hope you're prioritizing fun. You drove yourself into the ground with SAT prep and college applications. Don't you want to enjoy life? Live a little instead of stressing about things you can't control?" She says it like it's an easy choice not to stress. Like I can just opt out on a whim.

"No," I say over the clink of dishes and the burble of water from the faucet. "I much prefer obsessing over everything that could go horribly wrong. Besides, catching grammatical errors in PowerPoints is an underrated thrill."

She chuckles. "My little adrenaline junkie. Seriously, though. Don't be in such a rush to barrel into adulthood."

"Why not? You get to do whatever you want. Eat whatever you want. You can even buy a pet," I point out, blinking away the memory of Mom forgetting to feed my goldfish while I was at summer camp. RIP Herbert.

"Hate to break it to you, but adulthood is just a never-ending cycle of chores, obligations, googling how to fix stuff, and spending money on things you hate. Like sponges and dish detergent." She gestures vaguely to the sink behind me.

Maybe for you. I don't say that out loud, though.

"Hey, that stainless steel sponge has done wonders for us. It was a worthwhile investment."

My statement garners a derisive headshake. "My point is, I spend half the time pretending to know what I'm doing, and the other half ignoring all my problems and hoping they'll disappear. Spoiler alert: they do not. And don't even get me started on your body. One minute you're throwing down chips by the bag, and the next you're stirring Metamucil into your water and using a heating pad on your back." She pretends to crack her back for dramatic effect.

"Wow, Mom. Thanks for painting that bleak picture."

"That's adulting," she says with a knowing *you'll see when you're older* shrug.

Filled with optimism for my uncertain future, I grab my backpack by the door. "I'll take Metamucil and back pain any day over being a teenager with a bedtime. But first—"

"Prom," Mom finishes.

TWO

Unfortunately, other students aren't as invested in executing the perfect teenage rite of passage.

Fifteen minutes into the student council prom-planning meeting and our fair president is nowhere to be seen.

Kassie (secretary and my best friend), Ollie (chief of fundraising), and Nori (creative vision) appear unfazed by our leader's tardiness. Kassie and Nori are too busy hanging on to Ollie's every word. He always has the latest Maplewood High School tea, which is allegedly "piping hot" today.

"Two kids from drama club got caught hooking up in the weight room this morning," he explains, bouncing his thick brows suggestively. "Heard it from Coach Tanner."

Nori perches on the chair like an owl, proverbial popcorn at the ready, layered butter and all. "What kind of *hooking up*?"

Ollie makes a lewd gesture with his hands, which tells me more than I needed to know.

Kassie gasps, as if she and Ollie haven't done much worse—like their bathroom rendezvous at my sixteenth birthday party. I haven't used that bathroom since. "In the weight room? That's ballsy."

I snort. "Literally."

They pass the next twelve minutes sharing other rumors about people boinking on school property (including Principal Proulx's desk).

Meanwhile, I clench my jaw, oversharpen my pencil, and stare at the clock.

I'm about to suggest we begin the meeting without Mr. President when the door whooshes open. Everyone hollers cheerfully, unbothered. Of course they do. Because everybody loves J. T. Renner.

"Track practice went late," he announces unapologetically as he waltzes in, broad chest puffed out like God can't touch him. His navy "smedium" T-shirt is working overtime today, fabric taut around his biceps in a thinly veiled effort to accentuate his muscles. Don't get me wrong, I harbor no ill will toward muscles. As a scrawny nerd with nary an athletic bone in my body, I'm jealous of people who can open water bottle caps with ease and take the stairs without getting winded. I do, however, reserve the right to be petty when those muscles are attached to Renner, whose smug face makes me want to toss myself into a wormhole.

"It's fine, Renner. It's not like we have anywhere else to be." I make my voice sugary sweet as he plunks into the seat beside me, stretching his abnormally long legs under the table. His left sneaker is less than an inch from my mustard patent ballet flat, and I don't like it one bit.

He shoots me the stink eye—he does this whenever I use his last name. Everyone else calls him J. T. "Did I miss anything important?" he asks, extending a tanned arm to swipe one of the nut-free granola bars I generously supplied.

Because I'm a mature seventeen-year-old, I shift the granola bar pile two inches to the left. *If you want it, work for it, sucker.* He still manages to get his grubby paws on one without missing a beat.

"We're only having the most critical meeting to date," I say primly.

He tears the granola bar wrapper open like a chimpanzee as he conducts a stony inspection of my turtleneck T-shirt and matching plaid skirt. "Nice outfit, Char. Diarrhea green really is your color."

"Thanks. I wore it to match your eyes," I retort. For the record, my shirt is olive green.

Nori waves her hand like a wand, casting a pretend hex to dissolve the tension. "Guys, I have a FaceTime with my energy healer in forty minutes. Let's get started."

Ollie turns to a crisp, fresh page in his notebook. "Let's go over the budget after our projected ticket sales," he starts, barely suppressing a giggle when Kassie fondles his thigh under the table.

It was inevitable Kassie would fall for Ollie, a certified hottie (picture Michael B. Jordan but twenty years younger), on the first day of ninth grade. One look at his broad linebacker shoulders and her crush on Renner was but a distant memory.

A bit of important history: Kassie and Renner first met at a beach volleyball charity tournament a few days before high school started. A hot yet meaningless makeout against a tree ensued. But the moment Kassie met Ollie, she promptly forgot about Renner's dopey Noah Centineo vibe, his seafoam-green eyes (that sadly don't resemble diarrhea), and his tousled, wavy locks that look like shaved chocolate.

I'm aware this paints an enticing picture of Renner. But it's just pure fact that he looks like the love child of all the great rom-com jocks. His superpower is bewitching people with his puppy-dog eyes and constant, gleaming smile. It's straight-up sorcery, if you ask me.

There's just something off about people who smile too much. From the get-go, I had a sneaking suspicion he was too good to be true. And he proved me right.

Let me take you back four years to the first week of freshman year. For a total of four and a half days, I may have developed a microscopic crush on Renner (as I said, sorcery). He sat in front of me first period. Every day, he'd turn around, flash me his perfect teeth, and ask to borrow one of my many pencils. I went through an entire package of mechanical pencils in one week, but it was my favorite moment each day.

One morning, instead of asking for a pencil, he slipped me a note that read, *Homecoming? Circle Yes or No.*

Containing my excitement was a task. Inside I was doing mental cartwheels and air-punches. But on the outside, I just lowered my chin in a controlled nod and circled *Yes*.

I regretted being so trigger happy when I told Kassie after class, neck spiking with heat at her blatantly unreadable expression.

"I can totally go back and tell him no," I offered meekly, leaning against the banister for support. "I know I should have asked you first. I just thought you'd be cool with it now that you're with Ollie. But I get it since you hooked up with him and—"

She shook her head, waving my words away before dashing up the stairs. "Technically, you should have. But he's so not my type," she assured as I followed. "Don't get me wrong, I'm happy for you. I'm just . . . surprised."

I never imagined I'd have a date to homecoming (even though it was on my freshman bucket list). I also didn't realize Renner saw me as anything but Kassie's annoyingly uptight friend. Besides, I'm used to being invisible. If our friend group were a rom-com, Kassie would be the main character—the sunshine dream girl with an effervescent laugh. Then you have Nori, who marches to the beat of her own drum, dropping zany one-liners. Then there's me. I'm not sassy, hot, or fun. I'm not even charming enough to be the uptight, sweater vest–wearing heroine who "just needs to let loose once in a while." I'm the tertiary character. The overachieving mom-friend who takes care of everyone in the background but does zero to advance the plot.

But I digress. Back to homecoming. Renner and Ollie planned to pick Kassie and me up from her house. We'd ordered pizza and spent the entire evening in her room getting ready, fantasizing about our future double dates.

"Make sure you bring mints. He's totally gonna kiss you," Kassie declared, dabbing my nose with translucent shimmer powder.

I lit up, picturing my very first kiss under the scattered lights of the disco ball. "You think so?"

"Oh yeah. And he does this thing with his tongue—" And there it was. Another reminder that technically, Renner had been Kassie's first. Comments like this made me uncomfortable, even though she didn't intend it. She was just trying to relate to me. And realistically, it wasn't her fault I was insecure.

Despite feeling eternally second to my best friend, I felt pretty that night in my blossom-pink satin minidress. Kassie said it accentuated my legs. My cheeks were sore from smiling in anticipation. But when Ollie arrived, he was alone, expression solemn. My eyes immediately welled with tears.

"J. T., umm . . . he canceled last minute. Something about plans he forgot," Ollie hastily explained before Kassie whisked me inside.

"Something you should know about J. T. is he's a manwhore. I heard he's been seeing a volleyball girl, Tessa, from Fairfax," Kassie told me, dabbing my smeared mascara with a wad of toilet paper.

"Why didn't you tell me? If I'd known, I never would have agreed to go with him." I sniffed from atop her bathroom counter.

She let out a shaky breath, hesitant. "You were so happy when he asked you . . . I couldn't burst your bubble."

"Ugh, he's such an asshole. I should call him out," I said, fists balled in my lap.

"No." Her tone was firm, eyes wide. "You know what the best revenge is? Having a fabulous night, dancing with all his friends, and forgetting about him entirely." She held her hand out and pulled me off the counter.

Contrary to Kassie's advice, I never forgot. I didn't forgive either.

Renner tried apologizing the following Monday in first period. "I know you're mad," he'd said.

"I'm not. Just disappointed you didn't even have the guts to tell me yourself." I waited for him to reveal the truth—that he was interested in someone else. But he didn't. He didn't offer a single explanation.

"I'm sorry," he said.

I kept my eyes trained on the whiteboard, willing him to turn around and never speak to me again.

"Are you going to accept my apology?" he prodded, drumming his fingers against my desk.

"Honestly, Renner, don't worry about it. I only agreed to go with you because Kassie made me." It was all a lie, of course. He'd humiliated me. I'd cried all weekend in bed in a haze of Cheeto dust. But I'd be damned if I was going to let him know. I'd learned from Dad that disappointment was inevitable. And getting upset when he didn't show up, like to my middle school graduation, never changed anything.

"Wow," was all Renner said, brow furrowed. Then he spun around in a huff.

Served him right. Suffice it to say, we haven't gotten along since.

Kassie mindlessly fluffs her thick, waist-length Blake Lively hair for volume, something she does approximately forty times an hour. "Since we're a month out, we should see about setting up the prom ticket booths at lunchtime," she suggests, unaware that I've already arranged it. I don't say anything, though. She gets pouty when I do things without consulting anyone. "Prom committee is a team effort, not a solo mission," she likes to say.

Renner lifts a lazy hand. "Wait, wait, wait. Did we decide if dinner is included yet?"

I let out a maddening sigh, grip tightening around my mechanical pencil. I see he's stolen one of my three backups. "No, dinner is not included. For the tenth time. You'd know this if you cared to show up to the last two meetings."

"It's not my fault it's track season. Sorry, I actually have a life. I highly recommend it." He throws me one of his smug looks.

Did he really just insinuate I don't have a life? I mean—he's not entirely wrong. I have friends, even if I don't get to hang out with them as often as I'd like. When I'm not scooping ice cream at Two Cows 'N' a Cone or studying, I'm usually in my natural habitat, scrolling through the Netflix home screen, unable to decide between *To All the Boys* I, II, or III for the five hundredth time, only to end up on TikTok for hours. But I'd rather wear my contacts for a week straight than admit that to Renner.

"My sincerest regrets. Between doing your job as president in addition to my own as VP, getting a life slipped my mind. I'll happily take yours, though." I flash a smile.

Ollie, always the referee, waves his notebook like a flag. "Did we settle on the theme yet?"

I take this as my cue to whip out my tablet, which contains all seventeen slides of prom magic. Time to blow some minds.

Technically, Renner and I were supposed to propose a theme jointly to Principal Proulx. But since Renner's been living his best life, I went ahead without him. It probably sounds like I'm a control freak. Maybe I am, but I can't leave prom in the hands of this self-proclaimed "big-picture guy" and his bare-minimum approach to life.

Renner muffles a snicker with his elbow when the projector screen fills with vibrant stock photos of iconic landmarks.

I do my best to blur him out, zeroing in on everyone else's comparatively comforting faces. "Picture this. Guests need a passport to enter prom. We'll get to travel the entire globe in just one magical night. Instead of a sit-down plated dinner, we'll have stations with all kinds of tiny appetizers. Chinese. Mexican. Ethiopian. Italian. And don't even get me started on the possibilities for decor. I'm thinking gigantic cardboard cutouts of all the most famous landmarks, twinkling string lights, shimmery tulle drapery . . ."

When my presentation ends fifteen minutes later, everyone slow claps—except Renner. Kassie is seconds from nodding off on Ollie's shoulder, while Nori has taken to doodling on her wrist.

Renner twirls *my* pencil like a baton. He looks like he's trying to solve a complex algebraic equation, on the cusp of breaking his poor little pea brain. Our eyes snag for a disturbing moment before he simply says, "Nah."

I blink. *"Nah?"*

Nori, Kassie, and Ollie resettle in their seats, like they're audience members at a UFC match, eagerly awaiting a gory bloodbath.

Renner shrugs and leans farther back in his chair. He's practically horizontal, exuding serious dirtbag energy. "I think we can do better than Around the World." He says *around the world* like it's tired and juvenile, as if he's heard it all before. He punctuates it with a half eye roll; he can't be bothered to complete the three sixty.

"And what's wrong with Around the World?" I ask, keeping my tone even.

"How are we supposed to choose what food to order? Which landmarks? I'm Polish and German. I want pierogies and sausages. If we didn't have them, I'd feel jilted."

"Love when white boys get flustered when things aren't all about them," Nori teases.

Renner nods respectfully. "Touché, but my point still stands."

"We won't leave anyone out," I assure. "We'll poll everyone on their backgrounds and—"

Ollie raises his hand. "J. T. makes a good point, Char. It's kinda . . . invasive to go around asking people their ethnicities."

"True," Kassie reluctantly agrees. "I love the idea, but I think it's too broad of a theme. Let's think of something a little more laid-back and fun."

Renner raises his brow in a silent *I told you so*, pleased that he's stolen my thunder. It's one of his favorite pastimes, after worshipping his own reflection and leaving people high and dry on special occasions.

I fold my arms, miffed. They do have a point. I overlooked the glaring privacy bit. But I can't help but feel they've tossed my proposal prematurely without considering ways around it. Traitors. "Then what does Mr. President propose?"

He shrugs. "What about . . ." He looks to the ceiling, as if the answer is up there. "Under the Sea?"

I want to keel over at the thought. Under the Sea means tacky seaweed, bubble machines, anchors, and . . . fish decor. For the most magical night of teenage-hood? Someone hold me. "No. Absolutely not. Over my dead body."

He meets my stare in a challenge. "Let's vote on it."

THREE

Two weeks until prom

You are cordially invited to . . .

Under the Sea

Proudly presented by Maplewood High School's Senior Class

On Saturday, June 15
From 7:00 p.m. to 12:00 a.m.
Maplewood High School Gymnasium A

Tickets:
$40 per person
$75 per couple
$50 at the door

*See Senior social calendar below:

June 3–7—Exams
June 10–12—Prank Days, Senior Symposium, Brick Painting
June 13—Senior Sleepover
June 14—Beach Day
June 15—Prom Night
June 22—Graduation

"Prom is doomed," I grumble at the demented cartoon whale smiling on our freshly laminated prom tickets. Had anyone else proposed Around the World, Renner would have been all for it. But because it was me, he had to derail the idea.

I pretend to sob into a particularly hideous taffeta gown. The saleslady with the tattooed brows frowns at me from across the boutique. She's cranky that Nori, Kassie, and I are disrupting her lunch-break reality television episode. I plop next to Nori on the tufted bench outside the changing rooms.

"This is my best work. It's a certified masterpiece. You're really killing my vibe here." Nori's gold bangles jingle as she holds the prom ticket to the light, admiring her creation from all angles. Her iPad is always at the ready so she can sketch whenever inspiration strikes. She's wicked talented and could probably make a rock from my driveway look visually interesting.

"Prom will be amazing regardless of the theme," Kassie says sternly, voice muffled from behind the dressing room curtain.

"Not with gigantic jellyfish tentacles dangling from the gym ceiling." I shudder at the thought. "Did you know jellyfish don't even have brains?"

"Okay, but they can clone themselves. Us humans—with our big, useless brains—can't do that," Nori points out. The things we learn in biology.

Random jellyfish factoids aside, everyone but me is thrilled about Under the Sea. Even perpetually crusty Principal Proulx.

The past two weeks have been nothing but cramming for exams and elaborate promposals. Most notable was Ollie's. After a choreographed flash mob at the Friday game, the football team stripped their jerseys, one by one, revealing blue painted letters on their chests, collectively spelling PROM, KASSIE? It was inevitable Kassie and Ollie would go together, just like it's inevitable they'll win prom king and queen, get married (with me as maid of honor), and have perfectly symmetrical-faced babies who will go on to procreate with my own children (if my twenty-year plan of marrying a kind-eyed, dependable man who bears a striking resemblance to Charles Melton goes smoothly).

"Char, I say this with love, but maybe you need to sit this one out and let us handle it," Kassie suggests. "I know you're super stressed about exams and—"

"*Sit this one out?* Prom?" I impulsively scratch my neck. The thought of not being in control is hive inducing. "And I'm stressed for exams a very regular amount, thank you."

Nori gives me a knowing look. "She has a point. You've taken the lead on every event this year. Like, you spent the entire Valentine's Day carnival running around, stressed out over the broken cotton candy machine. You didn't even get to ride the Ferris wheel."

Before I can point out that prom is THE MOST IMPORTANT event of all, Kassie parades out of the stall in a floor-length red sequin number that looks like second skin. The dramatic slits up each side flirt dangerously close to her pubic bone. She steps onto the pedestal and sways side to side, channeling the raw star power of J.Lo.

"Steal-your-man red," Kassie says in a faux British accent. "As my mom calls it. Does it make my boobs look big or no?"

Nori pretends to shield her eyes. "I dunno about your boobs, but that color is offensive. My eyes are watering just looking at it." Her tone is a little clipped. She and Kassie are frenemies at best. I'm the glue that somehow makes our unlikely threesome work. To Nori's credit, Kassie is like a boomerang, always bringing the conversation back to her. Like when Nori broke up with her first girlfriend two years ago, Kassie decided it was an appropriate time to complain about how Ollie didn't invite her on his family's vacation to Disney World.

Despite Kassie's vapid tendencies, I also know a totally different side of her. The Kassie I met at camp when we were nine who took me under her wing when home was the last place I wanted to be. She gave me her polka-dot scrunchie, claiming it was the perfect accessory for my "retro Britney Spears" outfit. The Kassie who picks me up after my hellishly long summer shifts at Two Cows 'N' a Cone to drive around aimlessly while scream-singing love ballads. The Kassie who gives me clothes on the regular, claiming they don't fit her anymore even though I know that's not true.

Kassie knows my mom juggles two jobs—her begrudged day job as a pharmacy assistant and twilight shifts as an aspiring novelist. I'm not poor by any means, but unlike most of my peers at MHS, I can't afford the newest clothes and electronic devices. Kassie knows all this and has never said a word about it to anyone. Sometimes I feel like I owe her for that.

"The color is nice," I say defensively, turning back to Kassie. "You could go in a burlap sack and shoes made of Kleenex boxes and still win prom queen."

"I don't think I'm feeling it. Doesn't go with the theme," Kassie decides, running a hand over the tight bodice.

"The theme," I mumble bitterly, following Nori into the dressing room. "Renner ruins everything. He's like that marinara sauce stain on my white Keds that won't go away no matter how many times my mom bleaches them."

"I know you guys hate each other. But for your own sanity, you've gotta stop letting him under your skin. It only encourages him," Kassie warns, like it's all my fault he's the bane of my existence.

"Lest we forget what he did," I shout from behind the curtain.

"We were fourteen. And still obsessed with Shawn Mendes. You really need to forgive and forget," she says as I step into a satin, purple dress.

For the record, I'm still obsessed with Shawn Mendes. I also have the memory of a dolphin.

And it extends far beyond homecoming.

J. T. Renner's transgressions against me: a complete history

-9th grade—ditched me at homecoming
-9th grade—called me a "kiss ass" and "teacher's pet"

-9th grade—made a penis joke during my biology presentation
-10th grade—invited entire sophomore class to his garage party except me
-10th grade—loudly pointed out a spelling error in my Civil War history PowerPoint presentation
-11th grade—accused me of ripping a potent fart at Lucy H.'s New Year's party
-11th grade—made fun of me for being the only girl who didn't receive a Valentine's Day carnation and candy gram in homeroom
-11th grade—mocked my driving in driver's ed
-11th grade—unfairly beat me in a law class debate
-12th grade—still brags about last year's law class debate
-12th grade—emotional trauma from his bullying caused me to fail my driver's test—twice
-12th grade- claims to have beaten my SAT score (no evidence of claim provided)
-12th grade—THE STUDENT COUNCIL ELECTION

Of all Renner's transgressions, student council was the cherry on top. I'd been the ninth, tenth, and eleventh grade rep, and the entire student body of Maplewood High School knew the president position was mine. I'd worked tirelessly for the past three years for this.

Extracurriculars are key for graduate school, which I'll need to become a school counselor. They're also important for scholarships, which I spent all of spring break applying to. In fact, I have an interview next week for a $20,000 scholarship from the Katrina Zellars Foundation—a nonprofit that funds aspiring educators. Mom has saved as much as she can for my college fund, but it's still barely enough to cover one semester in the dorms.

Anyway, I was high on endorphins, practicing my victory speech because I was running unopposed. Then, two days before the election,

Renner decided to toss his name in with zero forethought, despite having no student council experience whatsoever.

When I confronted him about why he was running, he just said, "Because I knew it would piss you off. And I thought it would be fun."

Fun. That's how Renner lives his life. *Lover of all things fun* is even his social media bio.

Unlike me, Renner had no official election platform. I spent countless hours hunched over my laptop, surveying peers, developing a list of goals I was passionate about, including increased support for diverse clubs, adding a deli and salad bar in the cafeteria, and equality for girls' sports programs.

Meanwhile, Renner spouted off fifteen minutes' worth of unpracticed, somehow eloquent nonsense about collective school spirit and ensuring all voices are heard, channeling the effortless charisma of Obama.

And because everyone loves J. T. Renner, he won the presidency with a 75 percent majority.

I still can't talk about it without ugly crying. Renner's obsession with ruining my life cost me my dream college on the West Coast. The admissions counselor never said it outright, but I think he was less than impressed by my status as vice president—not president. The only benefit is that now I'm going to college in the city, with Nori.

I emerge from the dressing room in the purple gown, hoisting myself onto the pedestal with an ungraceful grunt. I feel like a bride on *Say Yes to the Dress*, minus twelve nearest and dearest bystanders in varying degrees of bitter over my upcoming nuptials.

This satin, royal-purple number does absolutely nothing for my five-foot body. My flat chest occupies only about half of the laughably huge cups. I look more like a five-year-old playing dress-up in her mom's clothes than a teenager one year shy of adulthood.

Nori hops onto the pedestal next to mine in a bumblebee-yellow trumpet-style two-piece and frowns like a hungry couture model at Paris Fashion Week.

"Only you can pull off a color like that. You look amazing," I assure her before her doubt creeps in.

The saleslady saunters over with the emerald-green dress I was eyeing in the window draped over her arms. "Still want to try this on, dear?" she asks Nori.

Nori blinks and points at me, confused. "Uh, my friend is the one who wanted to try it."

The saleslady's hawk eyes cut to me, surely judging my uncanny resemblance to Barney in this purple number. "Oh, right." Flustered and embarrassed, she shuffles into my changing room and hangs the emerald gown on the knob.

Nori flashes me a funny look. This isn't the first time people have mixed us up, even though we look nothing alike. Nori is Korean, tall, and pale, with unicorn-dyed hair that grazes her shoulders. And I'm half-Chinese, half-white, with long, dark hair. It's not like Maplewood isn't diverse (sort of), but there's always the odd person who stares, or kids who crack stupid Asian jokes about being good at math. Apparently, by simple virtue of being Asian, your spot on the honor roll is guaranteed.

Once I reemerge in the green dress, Kassie circles my pedestal to capture it on video. Nori nods vigorously in the mirror, signaling her approval as I turn to inspect my side profile.

Strangely, the halter neckline actually elongates my short torso and legs.

"I might even have the perfect heels to match," I say. I found orthopedic nude heels with specially padded insoles last month for graduation.

Kassie rolls her eyes. "Not those old-lady church shoes."

I gasp, feigning offense. I spent weeks scouring the depths of the internet for them. "They are not church shoes. They're functional. Optimal arch support is important. I'll just need to break them in."

Disclaimer: me and high-heeled shoes have a troubled history. The first time I wore heels at a middle school dance, the left heel wedged itself into the front lawn and I fell face-first into a bed of thorny roses. Fast-forward to the tenth grade Spring Fling: the ambitious red stilettos I ordered online turned out to be literal stripper shoes (not that I'm judging). I looked like Bambi on stilts, towering over my five-foot-tall date—Jamie Nemi.

If I could do one thing in this life, it would be to bring justice to flip-flops. They get a seriously bad rap for being tacky. But they're functional as heck. Unfortunately, I doubt I'll be able to revolutionize flip-flops before prom. So I've succumbed to geriatric heels.

Nori straightens the train behind me. "Forget the ugly shoes. This gown is everything. If you don't buy this right now, I'm buying it for you. End of story."

"You have five minutes to decide. We're gonna be late for class," Kassie warns. She pulls a tube of shimmery lip gloss from her bag and applies it generously, smacking her lips in the mirror.

I stare at my reflection and hold my hair up the way I've always imagined it, a soft, romantic low bun. I'm reminded of how confident I felt getting ready for freshman homecoming, staring into Kassie's hair-spray-smeared bedroom mirror. Though I'm determined prom will have a better outcome. If I'm spending half my savings on one night, I'd better look fire. "Okay. This is it. I'm saying yes to the dress!"

Nori squeals and claps. "See? Prom is gonna be perfect. Fish or no fish."

I snort. "Ew. Never put *fish* and *prom* in the same sentence again."

Kassie shakes her head like a disgruntled mom of five children brawling in the back of a minivan. "Please just don't rip J. T.'s head off at prom. Let us have one last drama-free night, okay?"

"I can do that," I agree. "So long as he sits on the opposite end of the limo. Far away from me."

FOUR

Four days until prom

Clay Diaz is walking past my lunch table.

You know those teen movie scenes where the sexy love interest saunters slo-mo down the hallway? That's him right now. Cue "Watermelon Sugar" by Harry Styles. All five feet, ten inches of his cross-country runner bod are backlit by the heavenly white beam of light streaming through the cafeteria window. His floppy charcoal hair blows in the nonexistent breeze, like a windswept actor in a luxury car commercial.

I white-knuckle my lunch tray as the distance between us closes. Suddenly, I'm questioning all my life decisions. Does my topknot make my head look gigantic? Renner once said my head is "humongous," and ever since, I've been paranoid that wearing my hair up accentuates its bigness. Am I eating my Subway sandwich too suggestively? What the hell do I do with my hands? Can he hear my heart thrashing against my chest?

Guys don't usually render me catatonic, but then again, no other guy at MHS has Clay's whip-smart intelligence, soulful brown eyes, steel-cut jaw, and singular left dimple.

As he passes me in the narrow space between the cafeteria tables, I do a weirdly formal, slow head bob, like he's British royalty or something. His lips spread into a smile that nearly catapults me into the spirit realm. "Hey, Canada," he says. He's called me Canada since February, our last Model UN.

"Uh, hi, Clay—I mean, Turkey—" By the time I remember how to speak, let alone which country he represented, Clay has already beelined it to his usual table with the Model UN and debate kids, most of whom will surely go on to run the country.

This is how it always goes. Since joining Model UN freshman year, we've barely spoken more than two sentences. To be fair, Clay has tried striking up a few conversations here and there. But because I'm too awkward for multiword responses, the exchange pretty much dies instantly. One time, he even sat next to me on the bus to a summit and I promptly forgot how to breathe. I also got sweat pitters, which I had no choice but to hide under a thick wool blazer. It was an off day for me, to say the least.

Why am I like this? I wish I had Kassie's effortless confidence with guys.

Kassie pulls her eyes from her phone and gives me a smirk.

"Are you still coming over tonight?" I ask through a bite of my sandwich. Nori and Kassie had planned to come over to celebrate the end of exams and my scholarship interview (scheduled for after school today), but Nori bailed because her mysteriously rich aunt is in town. Secretly, I'm happy it's just Kassie and me. We rarely do things alone anymore.

Kassie gives me a hesitant look, partially distracted by the rowdy sophomore table next to us. "Crap . . . Ollie asked me to film his football practice for his college coach."

How did I know this was coming? "No worries," I say quickly, forcing an appeasing smile.

What else can I say? I can't force my best friend to hang out with me. It still sucks to lose out on time together, especially since we'll be separated by eight hundred miles in only three months. Kassie is following Ollie to Chicago, where he got a full football scholarship. She's taking a year off, which is probably for the better. Three days ago, she was still flip-flopping between majoring in criminology or business. Though if we're being honest, Kassie's true dream is to become a rich WAG (a wife and/or girlfriend of a pro athlete), which I respect, because that life isn't for the faint of heart.

"You're the best." Kassie blows me a sideways kiss before turning her nose at Nori's latest smoothie concoction. "What the hell are you drinking? It looks like mud."

Nori chugs half of it as fast as humanly possible, nose plugged. "It's carrot juice, kale, blueberries, a shot of plant-based protein powder, and a healthy dose of male tears," she says nonchalantly.

Kassie makes a grabby-hand motion. "Sounds right up my alley. Gimme."

Nori hands over her smoothie cup and turns to me. "Oh, by the way, the rest of the deposit for the limo is due in a few days. Do you think you'll have a date by then?"

I can tell she feels bad asking, yet again. Admittedly, I'm making the bill complicated. I'm the lone person in the limo without a date, even though there's a spot reserved for one. I've stubbornly held out hope someone would ask me by now. Along with executing the perfect prom, being "promposed to" is sadly still outstanding on my high school bucket list.

"Of course she'll get a date. Don't rush her," Kassie says before I have the chance. "Are you gonna put on your big-girl panties and finally ask Clay? You have no excuse now that he's single."

Clay dated Marielle MacDonald—MHS's resident horse girl—for years. They used to come to the ice cream shop on my shifts and share a two-scoop mint and butterscotch ripple cone. One time, I saw Clay lick ice cream off the side of her face and audibly gagged behind the counter. They heard me and I had to awkwardly pretend I was coughing.

"But is his singleness actually confirmed?" I probe, delaying.

"Yup. He changed his display pic on all his accounts," Nori informs, even though I already knew that.

If there's one thing Kassie and Nori agree on, it's that I should ask Clay to prom (because screw gender norms). Normally I'd agree. I don't want to sit around like a demure little daisy waiting for Clay to look in my direction. But how am I supposed to ask him to prom when he makes me forget my own name? I've put serious thought into asking him in a handwritten letter, dropping it in his lap, and running away. But apparently my inability to communicate with him isn't just oral—every time I try to write that letter, my mind blanks.

"FYI, Mercury is in retrograde. I'd be careful how you approach it," Nori adds.

"It's fine. I've accepted my fate as the thirteenth wheel." I slouch, wincing at the prospect of being the only single one in the limo.

Kassie rolls her eyes. "Stop it. You're asking him today." She says it like it's so easy. Then again, it is for her. Even without Ollie, she'd have a line of guys who'd jump at the chance to take her to prom.

"I'm too busy to face rejection this week," I whine. It's Senior Week, after all. And as VP, I'm overseeing all the activities. Most notable is the Senior Sleepover, where all the seniors bring their sleeping bags and spend the night in the gym. Then there's Beach Day—where we skip class Friday to hit the beach the day before prom. The lead-up week is one of epic pranks, both on faculty and fellow students. Last year, the hallways were filled with approximately 3,493,483 red Solo Cups, balloons, and "napping" seniors.

It's only Tuesday and pranks have already begun. Yesterday, during the track meet, three students in Gollum masks ran nude across the field. Their antics are now forever preserved on YouTube.

Kassie levels me with a look. "All I'm hearing are excuses. Come on. Imagine you two, side by side in your prom photos. He looks like that telenovela star, doesn't he? With the shaggy hair? He's sort of sexy, in a hipster, I-love-obscure-bands kinda way." She casts an admiring look at him over her shoulder.

An obnoxious voice sounds nearby: "Who's sexy?"

Midbite of my sandwich, I clamp my eyes shut, hoping that Renner sliding into the next seat is but a nightmarish mirage.

His lemony scent confirms it is not.

"None of your business," I snap, too flustered to verbally roast his essence. I shoot Kassie and Nori a look, silently warning them not to mention Clay in front of Renner, of all people. He is not to be trusted with such top-secret intelligence.

"Anyone want an extra fry?" he asks, holding up a second cardboard container overflowing with salty fries.

"Why do you have two?" Nori asks, plucking a fry. She's the vulture of our group, always poised to polish off our leftovers.

"The lunch lady loves me," he says with a casual shrug, despite the known fact that crotchety Lunch Lady Libby despises all living beings, especially humans. She's known for muttering vague insults under her breath as kids roll through with their trays.

"Anyway, we're trying to find Charlotte a prom date," Kassie says, like I'm a pitiful charity case.

Renner's face lights up as he slides the extra fries across the table. "Ha! That's a *task*. You sure you wanna take that on pro bono?"

"Anyone would be lucky to go with a hot piece of ass like Char," Nori retorts, not-so-discreetly jabbing her thumb in Clay's direction.

Renner is unfortunately more observant than he looks, eyes tracing Nori's thumb. He raises his brow. "Clay Diaz? That's who you wanna go with?"

Before I can deny it, Kassie jumps in. "If Clay doesn't pan out, I started a list of other possibilities. I know you like your Plan B's," she adds, eyeing me knowingly.

Renner's eyes light up.

Prickles of heat crest my cheeks. So much for keeping my crush on Clay on the DL. I begrudgingly lean in to peer at the list of more realistic options, hoping this will distract Renner.

Kassie clears her throat. "Curtis Carlson?"

"Nope. Jasmine will cut me." Curtis is my friend Jasmine's most recent ex. And after spending the better part of a sleepover performing a ceremonial exorcism wherein we burned Curtis's hoodie, slippers, photos, and all the gifts he ever gave Jasmine in a firepit, going to prom with him just wouldn't sit right with my soul.

"Moe Khalifa?"

I tilt my head. "I did a group project with him in Law. He's a decent guy. Did his portion of the work. Made me somewhat regain my trust in humanity. Unlike some people." I flash Renner a pointed look.

He grins like a deranged clown from that Stephen King book. "Khalifa is asking Naomi. I heard him bragging about it in the locker room."

Kassie continues down her dwindling list of potentials. "Okay, how about Kiefer Barry?"

Before I can decline, Renner snorts. "Barry? Dude's a snooze. Next."

Sadly, Renner is right. Barry is one of those guys who tries to impress people by bringing up Nietzsche and Voltaire in casual conversation. My dryer lint trap is probably more interesting than him.

"Damian Mackey?"

I shush Kassie. Damian is sitting a mere three tables away. "Too immature," I whisper at the precise moment he launches a spitball through a plastic straw.

Kassie sighs and turns her phone over. "No offense, but you can't afford to be this picky only four days out. There aren't any more single, half-decent-looking Maplewood guys."

Thanks for the reminder, Kass, I want to say. But I don't. I know she means well.

Nori slaps the table with her palm. "Wait, Char. You want a mature guy, right?"

I raise my brow. "Do specimens of that variety even exist?"

"What about my cousin Mike?" Nori suggests. "He's a college freshman. He's super mature. His favorite book is *A Handmaid's Tale.*"

A momentary flutter tickles my stomach. A dude who's into feminist literature? Praise be. I've only met Mike once at Nori's family reunion. He's super nice and cute in a discreet, nonthreatening way—definitely the type who'd hold the door for you and still say *thank you.*

Renner's lips perk in amusement. "A college guy, huh?"

"I think I'm done with high school guys," I decide.

This elicits an eye roll from Renner. I'm shocked his eyeballs aren't lodged in the back of his head. "Oh, right. You're too mature for us. Because a frat boy who does keg stands every weekend is much more on your level."

"First, my type would never be caught dead doing a keg stand," I point out. "They'd be in the library, studying, taking their future seriously. And second, don't act like you're not diving headfirst into the frat life the moment your toe hits campus. That'll be you in a year and a half, getting your stomach pumped after ten Coronas too many."

Nori snorts. It's far too easy to visualize.

Renner looks slightly wounded. "You really think I'll be some sketchy frat guy in college?"

"It's your destiny, as one of the most popular guys in school," I confirm.

"Last time I checked, I had free will. But okay."

"Come on, Renner. Most girls would eat their own arm for a chance to make out with you, and you're too weak to resist the power that comes with that," Kassie points out.

A shiver rolls down my spine as I zero in on his perfectly shaped lips. For a split second, I wonder if he's really as good a kisser as Kassie said.

He lets out a deep laugh and the thought vanishes. "You really think girls would dabble in cannibalism for a shot at this?" He gestures dramatically at his bod with a french fry.

"Yes," I reluctantly admit. "For god knows what reason, everyone loves you."

"Except for you." He pretend frowns at his lunch tray.

I don't bother to correct him.

"I'll have you know, I've been turned down by many girls."

I open my mouth in pretend shock. "Who turned you down? I'll need to get their autographs."

"Carrie-Anne Johnson in seventh grade. Nathalia Green, just last month, actually. And—"

"You've been turned down by two whole girls in your entire seventeen years of life. The pain!" I clutch my chest in faux agony as Nori and Kassie snicker.

"Hey! My ego is very fragile."

"I'm aware of that. Anyways, Nori, Mike is a potential. It could be a good opportunity to get some advice on meal plans," I say, drumming my chin.

Renner looks at me like I'm an extraterrestrial. "You're really gonna spend prom night talking about college meal plans? Talk about a buzzkill."

I poke a mental pin into my imaginary J. T.-shaped pin doll. "Sorry, I didn't realize talking about our immediate future was so boring."

He shrugs. "We have less than two weeks left until graduation. I'm not wasting it thinking about college."

"So anyway . . . ," Nori pipes in, trying to steer us away from another brawl. "J. T., who's your lucky prom date?"

"Why? You wanna go with me?" He gives her his stupid wink, which strangely, only he can pull off without looking like a raging pervert. He's kidding, obviously, because everyone knows Nori is going with Tayshia. They're back together after a monthlong breakup.

Nori gives him a sympathetic pat on the shoulder. "You're not equipped to handle me. Sorry, bud."

"J. T., I told you in the group chat that Andie is waiting for you to ask her," Kassie says, examining her leopard-print fingernails that she spent all of last period painting. Her voice trails when she realizes her mistake. They have a separate group chat, without Nori and me. I found out last year when she asked me to take pictures for her photo shoot at the park. I haven't admitted I know about it, because I'm fairly certain someone else must have started it. Kassie wouldn't intentionally leave me out.

"Wait—Andie? She's not still with that Travis kid from St. Ben's?" Renner asks.

Andie has been Kassie's second best friend for longer than the usual—around six months now, since they started working together at Kassie's parents' store. Andie has the IQ of a Twinkie (though I don't hold that against her), but she's an effortless kind of cool. The girl who can rock a baseball hat and her boyfriend's flannel and still look dainty and cute. Meanwhile, the rest of us look like Home Depot trainees. She's also supermodel tall and confident enough to flaunt her midriff on the regular. Basically, the opposite of me.

My relationship with Andie is similar to Kassie and Nori's. We're friends, according to the niceties of high school, but I can guarantee we won't stay in contact after graduation. Don't get me wrong, she's not a bad person. She's just one of those people I don't want to be left alone with because we'd have nothing to say to each other.

"She and Trav were never official. He was too clingy," Kassie explains. He also showed up to every party a six-pack deep, wasted to the point of peeing in Ollie's pool. But she leaves that part out. "Andie needs someone to match her energy. Someone with more confidence," Kassie explains, winking at Renner.

I snort. "No shortage of confidence over there."

"Hey, nothing wrong with confidence." Renner's eyes sparkle with interest, as they always do when someone pads his ego. "I'd be into Andie. She's pretty hot."

Kassie squeals, delighted that she's made at least one suitable match. "Oh my god. You two would have beautiful babies."

I'm overcome by a heaving gag, triggered by the thought of Renner in action, no matter how many abs he has (six, but who's counting?). The scent of someone's microwaved fish lunch a few tables over isn't helping.

And that's when I spot Clay exiting the cafeteria. In a rare turn of events, he's alone, not surrounded by all his supersmart friends. Maybe this is my chance.

Besides, Kassie's right. I've nursed this pathetic crush on Clay for all of high school and I've done absolutely nothing about it, which is so unlike me. I'm a go-getter. I make things happen, headfirst, elbows out. I can prompose to a guy my damn self. Screw the bucket list.

I stand up and follow him out.

FIVE

Clay is nowhere to be seen by the time I amble out of the cafeteria, baby toes pinched in my prom heels.

Nori thought it would be a good idea to "break them in." But I'm about ready to toss them in the trash. So much for "orthopedist approved." I'm convinced high heels are the devil's footwear.

The rainbow smattering of freshly painted bricks catches my eye as I limp to my locker to get my books for next period, defeated. It's tradition that each graduating student paints one brick with their name, immortalizing themself on the MHS walls. I've already reserved mine next to Kassie's and Ollie's joint brick, though I haven't started painting yet—mostly because putting brush to wall feels so final.

I still remember walking these halls for the first time. Kassie and I busted through the doors giggling, arms linked, ready to take on the world. We were buzzing with anticipation, swapping gossip about all the kids from other feeder middle schools.

Of course, my confidence was a facade, unlike Kassie's. Truthfully, my gut was more twisted than a plate of lo mein noodles when we entered the noisy gymnasium for the freshman welcome assembly. Kassie gripped my wrist and whispered, "Straighten your posture and smile." I followed close behind as she led us up the bleachers, past a sea of anxious faces. I'd pulled us left when I spotted an empty row, but she yanked me to the right, conveniently smack-dab in front of Ollie and Renner.

I was envious of Kassie's ability to waltz up to the dude she'd made out with days before like it was no big deal. Turns out, the smile wasn't for Renner. She'd zeroed right in on Ollie.

Renner flashed me a megawatt smile that nearly sent me sideways off the bleachers and said, "I'm J. T." Just as I went to shake his hand, Kassie flashed me a warning look, reminding me not be one of those "basic girls" who falls for his cult-leader charisma.

In return, I smiled shyly and turned away, just in case Kassie still liked him. She had him first, after all.

I veer left into a relatively empty hallway, and a pair of heavy, Paul Bunyan–style footsteps gain on me. Renner. He narrows his gaze as he passes like one of those professional speed walkers. He has one goal, as do I: to get to our locker first.

Unlike the beautiful, shiny, full-length lockers in the movies, Maplewood High lockers are those obnoxious half-size stacked ones, one on top, one on the bottom. And because life has it out for me, mine is directly below Renner's. We can't comfortably be at our lockers at the same time without my head winding up somewhere near his crotch.

Every day it's a mad dash to see who will claim the territory first. I've beaten him about 70 percent of the time, not that I'm counting or anything.

I channel *Emily in Paris* charging through cobblestone streets in her four-inch stilettos, even though I look more like a severely injured crab missing a leg.

Triumphantly, Renner arrives first. At nearly a foot taller, he has an unfair advantage.

"By the way," he starts, stance wide as he takes his sweet time with his combination. "I'm planning on going to the party rental store after school to grab the prom decor. Wanna come with?" It's tradition that student council decorates in the mornings so we get to participate in Senior Week fun.

I slow blink. "Why are you inviting *me*? Shouldn't the *president* have it under control?"

"I do. I was supposed to go with Ollie but he bailed like usual. Like Kassie does with you," he says knowingly.

I'm shocked that he's even picked up on my issues with Kassie. I never complain to anyone about her, not even Nori.

"Ollie ditches you all the time too?" I ask.

He arrows a hard stare at his lock. "Sure does. It's really freakin' annoying, actually. Sometimes it feels like they just don't care about anyone but themselves." He pauses for a moment as he finally opens the lock and resets, like he regrets talking badly about them. "Anyway, wanna come? The last thing I need is you on my ass about something dumb like the napkin color."

I try to hide my smile. This is his backward way of asking for help because, in the depths of his pea brain, he knows he's clueless. "Napkin color is important. The last thing we need is that tacky blue color messing up the look."

"May I ask what *tacky blue* is?"

I snap my fingers, fumbling for the words. "That ugly bright blue. Like the Facebook logo."

He takes a sharp breath, looking offended. "What do you have against Facebook blue?"

"It's the color of depression."

"Good to know. I'll put in a rush order for a bulk pack of Depression Blue napkins."

I can't tell if he's being serious or not. "Actually, don't worry about it. I'll just go alone," I say, waving him off.

He gives me a lingering stare. "As president, I should be there to supervise."

"That would be a first," I sneer. "Trust, I've planned many a school dance without you. I'm fine to take over."

"How are you going to transport all the decor on your own? Your bike basket ain't gonna cut it."

I glare at him. He has a point. And my bike is out of commission.

He sees the gears turning in my head and pounces. "Meet me on the steps after fourth period."

"I have the Katrina Zellars Foundation scholarship interview. Tomorrow after school?"

"Nope. I have plans," he brags.

"Shotgunning beers behind the Sundown Diner with Pete? Please. You can reschedule." Something about his statement digs at me. I'm suspicious that the group is hanging out without me, again. Just last week, I found out they'd all had a barbecue at Andie's. Kassie ignored my text earlier that day asking what she was up to.

Sometimes it feels like our group is like a jawbreaker. There's the core—Kassie, Ollie, and Renner. Then there are the outer layers. The people who are progressively less and less integral to the greater group, like Andie and Pete, then Nori and me.

I wonder if I'd be friends with them at all if it weren't for Kassie (not that I'm "friends" with Renner). Probably not. They're all jocks, and I can't even dribble a basketball without it nearly breaking my nose. (Don't ask.) The only reason I ever got a decent grade in PE was because of the health portion.

His jaw tightens. "No, actually. Real plans. I can't cancel them."

I don't have the energy to guess, so I just shrug. "How about Friday morning?"

"Not gonna work. That's Beach Day."

I sigh. He has a point. It's tradition to complete prom setup in advance of the sleepover and the beach. No one wants to be stuck on decor duty while everyone else is soaking up the sun.

"Fine. I can ask the rental person if we can come early tomorrow morning before class?" he offers. "We both have spare first period anyway. We can start decorating early."

The mere thought of spending all morning with Renner makes me want to stress clean. But I also don't trust him anywhere near the napkin colors. "Fine."

I lean against the next locker, heels in hand, watching as students hustle in from lunch break. "Accidentally in Love" by Counting Crows blasts over the PA. It's one of twelve ancient tunes the teachers play between periods to signal that it's time for class.

Meanwhile, Renner just stands there, idly texting in front of his open locker. I take great pains to regulate my breathing. *I will not choose violence today. I will not choose violence today.*

"Ticktock, Renner," I warn, voice trailing as I spot Clay's mop of hair coming around the corner. He's striding toward me, looking far too fine for my mere mortal eyes. Our gazes lock from a distance and I remember what Kassie said in the cafeteria. *Put on your big-girl panties.*

What's the worst that can happen if I ask him to prom? Even if he says no, I won't see him after graduation anyways. He's moving across the country for Stanford, after all. I'd be in no worse position than I am right now (aside from the cold wrath of humiliation, but let's not get ahead of ourselves).

It isn't my imagination that he holds eye contact as he passes by. And I'm certainly not imagining his cheeky over-the-shoulder look my way before he stops to chat with Joey Mathison.

This is it. This is my moment. It's now or never.

I start to devise a plan: I'll grab my books and backpack, then approach cool and casual, like I'm just heading to class, even though calculus is in the opposite direction.

Before I can talk myself out of it, I elbow Renner's legs out of the way to grab my bag.

He gapes down at me. "Jeez. Your elbows are bony. I bruise easily, you know."

"Didn't realize you're such a delicate little peach," I say, pulling the door as far as it'll open against Renner's shin. The thunk gives me a momentary high. I don't make a habit of reveling in the pain of my adversaries, but he makes it so darn easy. Like the dirtbag he is, he widens his stance farther, leaving the narrowest space to pull out my backpack and toss my heels in.

"Renner, seriously. Stop being a dingus for two seconds and move," I demand.

"*Dingus.* That's a new one. More original than *donkey*, at least."

"There's a lot more where that came from." I run through the catalog of vicious insults I've banked for moments such as this. But as usual, I fail to come up with anything else under pressure. I settle for a growl. "Move. Now."

His face twists with confusion. "Chill. I'm not even blocking you."

And that's when I see it. The thin fabric of the front pocket of my bag has snagged on a jagged piece of metal in the door.

Evidently annoyed that I'm breathing down his neck, Renner yanks my bag free. With one swift movement, the threadbare fabric rips like tissue paper. My spare tampons, all *ten* (yes, ten, I like to be prepared), stream out like an avalanche, sprinkling onto the hallway floor. I'm frozen in blatant horror as they roll in all directions at people's feet like a spilled container of marbles.

At that exact moment, the rowdy group of freshman boys stampeding by quite literally screech at the sight. They dramatically jump out of the way, body-slamming into lockers, dodging them like an active land mine site.

Even Renner is speechless for once, probably committing my humiliation to memory for future use.

I have half a mind to pull a Forrest Gump and run, barefoot. Out of the school, out of Maplewood entirely. I could adopt a whole new identity, even get a wig. I've always wanted blonde hair. But because I'm me, I'm compelled to clean my mess. At least, I try to.

I drop to my hands and knees, scrambling between people's legs in a sad attempt to retrieve the tampons before anyone else sees. It's like a sick version of Frogger (which, by the way, is an awful game for children), trying to cross the road without being flattened by traffic. No wonder I don't drive. I yelp when Sylvester Brock's chunky running shoe crushes my hand in the process. And again, when I almost get kicked in the forehead by a freshman running at full tilt. I start to wonder what

I did to deserve such a harsh fate. I must have done something really egregious in a past life. At least, that's what Nori would say.

By the time I pop back to my feet, crimson faced, I've collected exactly eight tampons. Everyone—even Judy Holloway, the girl who wears cat ears and hisses at her enemies—is judging me. Clay and Joey are gawking, mouths hanging open. And worse, one rogue tampon is rolling directly toward Clay's shoes.

"Um. Hi. Hello. Sorry about that," I word vomit, busting out a graceless wave. Unlike the cute, shy-girl wave I'd imagined, I'm wielding eight tampons between my fingers like Edward Scissorhands.

Clay is stone-faced, evidently appalled. I didn't think there could be anything more ego-crushing than the prospect of him turning me down for prom. I was dead wrong.

He kicks the rogue tampon toward me like it's a live grenade. Then he turns away and heads in the opposite direction with Joey. I bend down to collect it—and will myself to disintegrate into the floor. *Goodbye, cruel world.* At least I had a semidecent run.

Renner is leaning against the lockers when I return, the tenth tampon pinched between his fingers.

I take a sharp breath, bracing for his taunting. But when he hands it over, I catch a brief flash of what looks like pity in his expression. Even worse.

By the time I zip my torn bag and close my locker, Clay is long gone, as is the prospect of asking him to prom.

SIX

Three days until prom

Renner is late. Shocker.

We made special arrangements to pick up the decor at 6:00 a.m. for prom decorating. It's now 6:05.

It's cool. No one else's time is important or anything. Not that I really want to leave the house.

I'm sprawled on the couch lopsidedly, awaiting his arrival. Frankly, I'm still unwell. When I close my eyes, I'm tormented by the memory of Clay Diaz's face when he saw my tampon. He was disgusted (and somehow still incredibly handsome). *Disgusted* is probably too generous—more generous than the portions at IHOP.

It's not quite as mortifying as when a gust of wind blew my skirt up in sixth grade, revealing my period panties and superabsorbent pad to the entire class—but it's nearly as bad.

Kassie and Nori tried to convince me periods aren't embarrassing, that it's natural, yada yada. Logically, I agree. But spilling a pharmacy's worth of feminine products in front of the entire student body (including your crush) is flat-out humiliating, no matter how you slice it.

To make matters worse, the whole debacle caused me to bomb my scholarship interview. And by *bomb*, I mean I rambled incoherently about the double standard for women versus men. For the record,

Cynthia, the foundation chairwoman, had merely asked me to outline my biggest academic accomplishments.

Renner is to blame, obviously. If he hadn't blocked me and subsequently ripped my bag pocket like an ape, this never would have happened.

Nori is adamant that I slide into Clay's DMs for damage control. *It's weirder NOT to acknowledge the tampon explosion.* Kassie agrees and says it gives me an excuse to strike up a conversation instead of my first choice: disappear into obscurity.

After much back-and-forth in our girls' chat, I fired off a casual peer-reviewed Instagram DM this morning.

Me: Hey Clay. Sorry about what happened in the hallway yesterday. Hope you weren't too traumatized.

And then it began. The staring contest with my phone. It's like watching boiling water under the delusion that my eye lasers will speed up the process.

I've grown weary of the lack of response, and send an SOS in the group chat, which only heightens my anxiety. Whenever my phone buzzes with *Calm down* texts, I'm overcome with false hope that it's Clay.

I've restarted my phone twice now, paranoid that it's not receiving correspondence of any sort. I can only conclude that Clay thinks I'm a freak. (He'd be correct.)

My phone vibrates and my heart kicks into double time.

My Fair Leader: sry, gimme 5.

I grumble like a curmudgeon. Since ninth grade, Renner has made an annoying habit of stealing my phone and changing his contact name. Since the student council election, he's gotten cockier with the names.

Sexy President

Commander & Chief

Your Worst Nightmare

The Right Honorable JTR

J. T.

In my opinion, *Twit* or *Satan* would be more fitting. I promptly switch his name back to the latter, with the purple devil emoji.

Footsteps in the hall jolt me out of my trance. Mom's up.

"Rachael is draining me today," she announces through a yawn. Rachael is a fictional psychopath who has a habit of poisoning her husbands. It's part of Mom's "process" to speak about her characters as if they're real people.

"Sorry to hear. Maybe Rachael should see a therapist," I croak.

"Oh, she'd love the attention, the narcissist." Mom's rooting around in her purse, juggling her phone, sunglasses, wallet, and keys in a way that triggers my anxiety. She finally tosses a pack of Band-Aids toward me. "Grabbed these last night at work. For your blisters."

"Thanks," I say, grateful.

She plunks onto the couch beside me, pulling my battered feet onto her lap to inspect. "Orthopedic shoes, my ass. Why don't you just wear flats?"

"Kassie says flats are basic."

Mom rolls her eyes. "Of course she does. Anyways, how was school? Don't you have your big scholarship interview today?"

"That was yesterday."

"How'd it go?"

My future just dove headfirst down the drain. Clay Diaz also thinks I'm a freak. I'm going to be dateless at prom. My best friend is moving far, far away in a matter of months. Life as I know it is changing. It's cool. It's fine. No big deal. Of course, I'm too drained to say all this out loud, so I settle for a grumpy, "I don't have the strength to talk about it."

"Well, I'm here when you're ready," she says, though the dark circles under her blue eyes tell me she doesn't have the bandwidth for emotional labor.

"Thanks. I appreciate it."

"Weren't you supposed to celebrate the interview and end of exams with Kassie? She wasn't over last night." She pulls my legs on her lap, settling next to me on the couch.

"She was with Ollie. Where else?" I mumble.

I can read her look. She's about to launch into the same speech she's given me since ninth grade—about how I need to be honest with Kassie that it hurts my feelings when she ditches me. "You know that baby photo of you in those crocheted overalls?"

I crinkle my forehead, unsure what this has to do with Kassie. "The ones that make me look like I have a saggy butt?"

"Georgia made those as a gift for my baby shower," she says, giving me an affectionate nudge in the ribs.

"Who's Georgia?"

"Exactly. Georgia was my best friend. All through school. We were attached at the hip, like you and Kassie. Grandma used to say she was her second daughter because she basically lived at my house."

"How come I've never heard of her?" Mom has a small circle of girlfriends she gets wine-drunk with at monthly book club, and none of them are named Georgia.

"Because we're not friends anymore," she says simply.

"What happened?" I frown, running down the list of grisly potential best friend betrayals.

She drums her fingers over my legs, eyes misty. "We grew apart. After college, she went backpacking around the world. I moved to Maplewood, married your dad, had you. We talked on the phone every single day for a while. Then it was once a week, once a month, and then we started dodging each other's calls . . . only calling back because we felt obligated to, you know?"

"Obligated? But wasn't she your best friend?"

"She was. There was no bad blood. No fight. No real reason why we stopped talking. I guess we just ended up living two completely different lives that no longer intersected." Mom lets out a soft chuckle. "Actually, we're not even friends on Facebook anymore."

"No one uses Facebook anymore, Mom." I eye her warily, shaking my head. I know where she's going with this. "And that won't happen to me and Kassie." We're supposed to be maid of honor at each other's weddings and godmothers to our future children.

Mom sighs and gives me a weak smile. "I'm not saying you and Kassie won't be best friends in twenty years. But friendships can change. Sometimes people drift apart. That's just life. It doesn't make it any less painful, though."

I swat her words away like pesky houseflies. I don't mean to be a brat, but Mom is out to lunch. I can't imagine a reality where Kassie isn't blowing up my phone, asking how hot she looks on a scale of her grandma to Kylie Jenner in certain outfits, or whether she's wearing too much bronzer. And then there're the serious texts when she vents about how much she wishes her parents would just divorce already, because they're both checked out.

Mom can tell I'm over the conversation and starts scrolling on her cracked iPhone. "Want to order pizza for dinner tonight?"

"We ordered pizza last week," I remind her.

It's been just Mom and me for years now. We aren't a family who breaks bread at the table every night, rehashing our days. We usually eat on the couch. Ever since Dad left, Mom thinks sitting at our six-person dining table, just the two of us, is "depressing." She's probably right. I have vivid memories of sitting at the table with Dad. At the beginning of each meal, he'd ask what I learned in school that day. Mouth full, I'd jump at the opportunity to show off all my newfound knowledge, reciting facts from every subject. Bonus if I had a good grade to report. Dinner was when Dad and I bonded most, probably because he'd spend most of his evenings working. Sitting at the dining table across from his empty seat just feels . . . wrong, like a stark reminder of what I no longer have.

Mom props her bare feet on the table. "What about Subway? Oh, before I forget—I got a voice mail last night."

"A voice mail? From who?"

"Your dad."

My stomach plummets. "Oh." That's strange. Dad never calls just to talk. He prefers to text intermittently, only asking about school, as though my grades are the only thing he cares about. We only have formal phone calls on Christmas and my birthday, which happen to fall within a month of each other.

"He left a rambling voice mail. Asked me to ask you to give him a call, if you want." Mom has that forced neutral tone she uses when she doesn't want to persuade me either way.

"If I want?" I repeat, hesitant.

"I know he's not Dad of the Year, but I think you should give him a call." There's something odd about her tone. A weird, nervous lilt, like there's something more going on.

"Why should I?" I don't bother to mask my saltiness.

Dad left for the city when I was nine. Mom fell into a depression for months afterward. Camp with Kassie that summer was my solace—a place I could decorate myself into oblivion with stickers and temporary tattoos, fill up on candy and white freeze pops, and forget about how much I missed Dad and the way things used to be.

For the longest time, his calls were the highlight of my week. I couldn't wait to tell him about my latest test grade, or the elementary school speech I rocked, just like our dinner table conversations. He would get all warm and affectionate when I told him good news.

By middle school, things had changed. He started climbing the corporate ladder and married a woman named Shaina, who he's currently in the process of divorcing. She was pleasant in a Stepford kind of way and owned multiple frilly aprons in different colors for every occasion. She also abided by the hashtag #happinessishomemade, which is the clear opposite of Mom, whose idea of homemade is a dry Betty Crocker box cake. She smiled a lot, but she already had three kids of her own, so she wasn't particularly interested in me. After they married, my calls with Dad became distant and less frequent. They mostly consisted of me rambling while he put me on speakerphone and tapped away on his laptop. No matter how good my grades were, his responses were clipped, delayed, and often completely unrelated.

Things went downhill in ninth grade. I called to tell him I'd been elected freshman student council rep and he didn't even remember that I was running in the first place. That was the moment I gave up seeking his approval. The moment I stopped visiting him in the city. What was the point? He was never coming back anyways, no matter how much I accomplished.

Mom fiddles with a loose thread on my sweater, reminding me that I need to ask her to sew my ripped backpack. "Well, he's still seeing that new woman. Maybe he wants you to meet her."

I crinkle my nose. "Which one? The assistant?" Since announcing his divorce from Shaina, he's had a couple girlfriends, all of whom are in their twenties.

"Nope. She doesn't work for your dad. She's a publicist. Her name is Alexandra. I creeped her on social media and she's totally out of his league," Mom adds, scrolling through her phone for a photo. She turns it toward me.

Dad definitely has a type: young. Alexandra is no exception. She's tanned, sun-kissed, and posing in a black one-piece on the balcony of what appears to be a tropical resort. Her sharp cheekbones and slender build remind me of one of those dark-haired Victoria's Secret models.

"Good for him, I guess," I mutter. Though I still have no interest in meeting her, regardless of how nice a person she probably is, especially if he'll be on to someone new next month.

"You need to make more of an effort with him too, you know. Maybe go visit this summer. You could have a hot-girl summer in the city."

I shoot her a poisonous look as I type an SOS text to Kassie about Dad and his new girlfriend. "Mom, don't say *hot-girl summer*."

"I'm just sayin'. You don't want to end up with daddy issues like me, or Rachael."

Too late, Mom, I think, just as a whirl of red pulls into the driveway. It's Renner. Finally.

SEVEN

Renner's cherry-red mom-van is infamous. It has a few different names. Sometimes it's the Cherry Blaster, or the DILF Mobile. Really, it depends on Renner's mood. He confidently drives it around town, chauffeuring everyone to and from parties when he's not drinking.

The fresh-laundry scent of his air freshener hits me as I hoist myself into the passenger seat. I cringe, kicking a jock strap out of the way.

Before I can open the Maps app, he whips us out of the driveway like a Hollywood stunt driver—in the complete wrong direction. I death-grip the edge of the seat. "Do you even know where we're going?"

He lifts one shoulder, arm draped over the wheel. Definitely not ten and two like we learned in driver's ed. "Eh. I know the general direction."

"You obviously don't, because it's that way," I say, jerking my thumb backward.

He keeps course while Siri shouts at us to turn around. After the fourth block, he finally pulls over to do a U-turn. "You, of all people, have no right to back seat drive me."

It brings Renner a disturbing level of joy to remind me that I failed my driver's test—twice. The first time, I couldn't parallel park, even after five attempts. The second time, my bumper just barely kissed the side of a very pregnant woman in the DMV parking lot. I cried about it and basically offered her my future firstborn child in apology. (She did not want my unborn baby and looked appalled by my offer.) But in my defense, she was wearing the exact same color dress as the pavement.

"Okay, no one parallel parks," I remind him.

"Everyone parallel parks."

"You sit on a throne of lies." I huff, anxious to get out of the van. His mere proximity feels detrimental to my well-being. "Take a right at the light."

"So, did you ask Clay Diaz to prom yet?" he asks, fiddling with the volume on a Kane Brown song.

The mention of Clay makes me want to punch something. "None of your business."

"I'll take that as a no."

"As if I'm going to ask him after *yesterday*," I snap.

Renner lifts a shoulder. "I don't really get what the big deal is. You dropped a couple tampons in front of him. So what?"

I don't have the patience to explain the rules of the patriarchy to him. I stiffen and avert my gaze out the passenger window. We're ripping through downtown at least ten miles over the speed limit. "It's not just the tampons. The whole thing threw me off. I bombed my scholarship interview."

"And that's my fault too, I suppose?"

"Yes. Yes, it was."

"Relax. I'm sure it wasn't half as bad as you think."

"Easy for you to say. You just breeze through life willy-nilly, with no regard for other people's time, and everyone still loves you no matter how much you mess up."

"Look, I'm sorry," he says so quickly I second-guess whether I've heard him correctly.

My body stiffens, unsure how to react. A mea culpa? From Renner? It's a weak, slightly backhanded one, but it's an apology nonetheless. This is new. "Is J. T. Renner actually apologizing? I must be hallucinating."

"To be clear, I'm only apologizing for ripping your bag. Not for standing in front of my locker, where I had every right to stand."

I remain unconvinced. "Is this some sort of trick? This just isn't . . . a *you* thing to do."

He lifts both brows. "Maybe there's a lot you don't know about me."

"Doubtful."

I know Renner well. Too well, in fact. Every good leader must know their enemy. Knowledge is power. Over the past four years, I've collected intel via personal observation, trusted human sources, and straight-up social media stalking. If we're being honest, I could probably write his autobiography. I know he eats the toppings and cheese first on his pizza (a serious red flag). He has a small scar on the left side of his chin from a brutal football hit in ninth grade. While generally adventurous, he has extreme phobias of heights and germs. In fact, he will never share a utensil or a drink with anyone. Admittedly, he's also a good friend (to people he likes, at least). He goes out of his way to make sure everyone's included in plans (well, except for me).

He bumbles on when I don't respond. "I can . . . uh . . . buy you a new bag?"

"It's fine. I don't need a new one," I assure him.

He scratches his head. "Well, I feel like I owe you."

"You definitely do. And you can repay me by not letting prom go up in flames."

"Yeah, 'cause that's my master plan: organize a shit senior prom and ruin everyone's night, just to spite you."

I shift in my seat. "I'm not ready to count that possibility out. Spiting me is your modus operandi. And you've already made your first move by strong-arming me over the theme."

"You really need to let that go. Your idea sucked. Deal with it. And everyone else loves Under the Sea," he brags.

"Not me."

"This sounds like a good villain origin story," he says.

"It is pretty good," I agree, drumming my chin, then flicking my gaze back to him. "You'll be my first victim."

"Wouldn't expect anything less. Just don't ruin my face. I'd like to have an open-casket funeral."

"Of course you would. And a horse-drawn carriage to cart your body through town too, right?"

"A gold stagecoach could work, yes." I bask in silence for a solid minute until he breaks it. "Still no prom date, huh?"

"None of your business."

He grumbles something unintelligible under his breath and cranks the volume on "Every Morning" by Sugar Ray. It's always a thrill when I can silence him.

"Every morning there's a halo hovering around the top of my beddddd," he belts at the top of his lungs.

"Those aren't the lyrics," I point out.

He shrugs. "What are you? The lyrics police? It's the gist of the song."

"It's his girlfriend's *four-post bed*," I inform him, enunciating slowly.

"I won't believe it if you don't sing it."

"Absolutely not."

"Fine. Suit yourself," he says, continuing to bellow his incorrect lyrics.

Lucky for my eardrums, we pull into the parking lot a few minutes later, thanks to my Maps app. Brenda, the owner of the party store, greets us with a harsh frown. I think she's bothered we're late. But after a few moments of small talk with Renner, she's charmed. He casts dark magic, I'm sure of it.

"Your collection is fantastic, Brenda," Renner says, taking a gander around the warehouse. "How long have you been in business?"

"It's been in the family for ages. My grandfather opened it in the early fifties," she responds, eyes resting on Renner.

He lets out an impressed whistle.

"That's amazing. So much history," I say eagerly. Still, Brenda's gaze stays fixed on Renner, like I'm a dust particle.

Renner tosses her another smile. "We really appreciate you letting us take a look around so early in the morning."

Her ample chest vibrates with giddiness. She waves a hand, like it's no bother. "Anytime you need to come back, just give me a call. I live close, so I can always swing by," she offers enthusiastically.

While I pick out all the necessary prom items—drapery, tablecloths, and chair covers—Renner acts like a five-year-old in a toy store, distracted by all kinds of items we don't need. He even tries to convince me to switch to a Mardi Gras theme because of a wall mount in the shape of a giant playing card that catches his eye.

I would have happily chosen Mardi Gras over Under the Sea a month ago, but it's too late to go back now. If he took his role as president seriously, he would know that.

We end up with ten jellyfish lanterns, an array of cardboard aquatic animals, a fisher's net, shells, and streamers. Nori requested balloons both for a photo booth arch, and ones to drop from the ceiling when the prom court is announced, so we get an obscene number of those too.

Our selection process involves various disagreements, like which shade of blue napkins is less tacky—aqua or cyan. He's also far too keen to rent a cardboard cutout of *Jaws*.

I wait beside the van, shifting my weight to relieve my feet while Renner loads the back with decor. I catch the flex of his muscly arms straining against his cotton T-shirt, and a single bead of sweat rolls down my temple. It must be the heat.

I tear my eyes away as my phone vibrates in my hand.

It's Dad.

EIGHT

Odd. Dad never calls me directly. He prefers to go through Mom like I'm a small child.

Against my better judgment, I pick up. "Hello?"

"Charlotte. It's Dad." It seems ridiculous that he needs to clarify, but I guess we hardly speak.

"Hi?" I say, hoping he'll just skip right to the point.

Pregnant pause. Something is up. "Did your mother tell you I called?"

"She did. Sorry I didn't call you back. I've just been really busy with school and stuff."

"No worries. Listen, I was wondering if you wanted to have lunch with me in the city." His tone is stilted. Almost robotic, as if he's reading from a script.

I'm momentarily distracted by Renner attempting to Tetris a clownfish cutout into the van bed. He's going to scrape the paint if I don't intervene soon. "Uh, I'm a little busy right now with prom and grad. I don't think I can make it. Maybe in the summer?" I offer, purely out of guilt. Should I be more excited at the prospect of seeing my father? Probably.

"That's actually exactly what I was hoping to discuss with you."

Renner manages to wedge the clownfish in, wiping his dirty hands on his jeans.

"Charlotte?" Dad repeats.

I shake my head, willing myself to focus. "Sorry. I really don't think I can make it to the city till after school ends."

"Oh, okay." He actually sounds disappointed.

Guilt takes hold of my insides, squeezing tighter and tighter, until I remember how heartbroken I was when he basically disappeared from my life. He's missed almost everything important since, like every holiday, middle school grad, when I received an award for my work on the student senate, and every single Model UN summit except for one. "Can't you just say what you wanted on the phone?"

"I—I suppose so," he says, unsure of himself. "Alexandra and I are pregnant." He says her name with an undeserved air of familiarity, as though she's part of our family. As though I've met her and we're besties or something.

"Pregnant?" I narrowly manage to avoid choking on my saliva. Dad's having a baby? With a woman he's only been dating a couple of months?

"She's due in November. We're really excited."

I'm stunned as he rambles on about Alexandra's cravings, how they'll be staying at Alexandra's family lake house in Fairfax, a quaint, Shakespearean-themed town half an hour from Maplewood, and how he's going to slow things down at work, maybe even work from the lake house when the baby comes. That last statement catches me off guard. Work has always been Dad's number-one priority. Never me. Now he's slowing down? For his future child?

"I was also wondering . . . Well, Alexandra and I were wondering if you'd be interested in staying at the lake house for the summer. We have a spare bedroom and the beach is barely a minute away—"

Stay with them at their lake house? For the whole summer? This is completely out of left field. Out of this universe. I could understand if he invited me for a weekend—and even that would be out of character. But an entire summer? Where is this coming from?

Renner flashes me a brief look of concern from where he's loading things into the trunk. I avoid his eyes, casting my stare at the gravel under my feet.

I think about all the years Dad and I have been estranged. All the times I wished my dad had shown up, when all my friends had theirs.

Tears threaten my lash line, but I manage to hold them at bay. I want to yell at him and tell him how I feel. How unfair it is to spring this on me. How angry I am at him for missing all this time with me when he'll be with his new child every day, bearing witness to every milestone. But all that comes out is, "Dad, I don't know. I'll have to call you back."

A pause. "I know it's last minute. I wanted to reach out earlier, but we wanted to make sure the spare room would be ready."

"I just—I don't know if I can come."

Another pause. "Well, give it some thought and let me know, okay, kiddo?"

"Yeah. Okay."

Dad starts rambling nervously about how busy I must be with the end of the school year, but I barely hear a word.

Renner clears his throat, reminding me again of his pesky presence. He has one leg propped behind him against the van. His brow is furrowed in an expression that vaguely resembles concern. This is just crap-tastic. He is the last person I want around when I'm having a personal crisis. It's too much. I can't deal. Impulsively, I hit "End" on the call.

Renner backs away slightly as I hobble toward the van on account of my blisters from yesterday. "Uh, you okay?"

"It was my dad. He's having a baby. With his girlfriend of a couple months," I say tersely. He already heard my conversation anyway.

Renner settles into the driver's seat. "Um, I take it that's not exactly good news?"

I fasten my seat belt, eyes glued on the windshield for a minute before I finally take a breath. "I don't know," I say, already feeling guilty for not being thrilled for him and Alexandra. Objectively I know a baby is happy news. But why does it make me feel so awful?

"Maybe it could be fun. To have a little sister or brother," he offers. "Especially since you're an only child—"

"My dad and I don't speak. And I've never even met his girlfriend," I cut in, hoping he'll drop it.

And he does.

~

The gym is empty except for me and Renner, who is currently outside grabbing the decor from the van. School doesn't start for another hour.

I'm brainstorming how I'll assign the tasks when everyone else arrives when my phone vibrates again.

Dad: I forgot to add on the phone, Alexandra wants to know what your favorite color is. She wants to have the spare room painted this weekend.

As I read the text, my brain pummels me with images of children being hugged and adored by their dads. I fumble for the wall behind me.

Feeling faint, I starfish down on the mat and cover my face with my hands. My cheeks are wet and my fingers blacken with mascara. The sight of my hands ignites a full-body sob.

Through my tears, I vaguely make out Renner hauling an old, rickety ladder from the storage room. He comes to an abrupt stop when he sees me.

"I—uhm . . . I can go, if you want?"

I eye him warily, not bothering to sit up. With one hand, Renner gives me three awkward pats on the shoulder. He wouldn't dare touch me unless I were in dire straits, which only makes the whole situation feel even more pathetic. The last thing I need is pity comfort from J. T. Renner. He's seen far too much of my life today.

When my tears return, he leaves the gym. For a moment, I assume he's left entirely. But he returns with a handful of one-ply toilet paper from the bathroom and drops it in my lap.

“Thanks,” I manage before blowing my nose.

He props the ladder and stands over me. “Can I help you up?”

“I guess so.”

His mouth curls disarmingly and he tugs me by the arm without an ounce of delicacy, pulling me into a reluctant standing position. We’re mere inches from each other, almost chest to chest. I don’t think I’ve ever been so close to Renner. Two hits of his lemony scent and I’m stable on my feet.

I note the golden ring around his irises. His lush lash line. The tiny half-moon scar above his brow. His lips look soft, almost pillowy.

Suddenly, I’m aware of the scratchy tag of my sweater, my saggy bun, and the clench of my jaw. I’m also mindful that he’s staring right back at me. His eyes fiercely search my face, probably judging my swollen eyes and puffy cheeks. He’s now seen me ugly cry. Before he can razz me about it, I take a stride backward and brush the dirt from my sweatpants.

He clears his throat and rocks on the balls of his feet, shoving his hands in his jean pockets. “So, uh, what can I do?”

I blink, making a concerted effort to push Dad and his do-over baby from my mind. I don’t have time to think about him. Over the years, I’ve learned that tucking these thoughts away is just easier. If I think about him for too long, it becomes overwhelming. Too heavy. Like a sharp ache that knocks the wind out of me.

“You can start securing the cardboard seaweed around the walls,” I instruct.

I expect him to give me a hard time. That’s just how he is. But he spins on his heel and dutifully starts on the opposite wall.

We work in silence for a good half hour, just the two of us, which is more comforting than I expected. I relish in the tranquility, knowing it’ll get rowdy when Kassie, Ollie, and Nori arrive.

“Kassie texted. She and Ollie are gonna be late,” I announce. She still hasn’t acknowledged my SOS text about Dad’s new girlfriend from this morning. No response. As usual. Meanwhile, I’m at her door with all her favorite snacks practically the moment she has the smallest fight with Ollie. The least she could do is respond to a text, especially since she's been through it all with me. Since the summer Dad left. She saw how hurt I was when her dad snapped endless pictures at our middle school graduation while mine was nowhere to be seen, despite his promises.

Renner peers at me as he struggles to rip off a piece of tape with his teeth.

"This would go faster if we had scissors," I note, heading for the supply closet.

Renner follows me inside, arrowing his chin toward the cobweb-laden boxes piled in the corner "I saw some in one of those boxes earlier."

I almost rip the dusty flaps of a box as I slide it away from a corner, nearly throwing out my back in the process. It's heavier than expected. Inside sits a shiny, cylindrical steel object.

Time Capsule—Class of 2024 is engraved in script across the front.

It's tradition that each MHS graduating class buries a time capsule after the graduation ceremony filled with handwritten letters to ourselves at age thirty.

"It's our time capsule," I say. The moment I touch the cool metal, the pads of my fingers zing with electricity. Pinpricks roll from my neck down my back. "Ouch. Static shock." I lift my hand for a moment, and when I run my finger over it again, the metal suddenly feels warm.

Of course, Renner doesn't listen. Like a child shoving a fork into an outlet, he runs his hand along the metal, pulling back with a jolt.

"Told you," I taunt, lifting my hand to massage my temple. I'm feeling weirdly light-headed all of a sudden.

He ignores me, setting it back in the box with a slight wobble of his own. "I assume you finished your letter already?"

"Not yet." I retighten my bun, making a mental note to do that tonight. "Where will you be at thirty, Joshua Taylor Renner? Eating insta noodles in your underwear and rotting in your parents' basement?" I venture, tamping down the urge to evil laugh. Last I heard, Renner was going to school in Boston. I haven't the foggiest idea what he's planning to major in. Probably something useless like underwater basket weaving or puppet entertainment arts.

He runs a calloused finger over his jaw as he heads back to the gym. Still light-headed, I follow at his heels, abandoning the time capsule in the supply closet.

We're working on the same wall now, nearly side by side, when he finally answers my question. "I was thinking of majoring in business. Or maybe law. Though I've always wanted to coach a varsity team." Renner spends his summers volunteering at the children's rugby and track camp as an assistant coach. A far cry from the major league.

"Varsity? Please. Gym teacher, maybe."

His eyes light up. "That's high on my list of possibilities too, if the others don't work out."

"Convenient," I say, snickering at the thought of a balding Renner with a wispy comb-over, donning an Adidas tracksuit that stretches over his beer gut, whistle around his neck, hell-bent on reliving his youth.

He furrows his brow. "What's convenient?"

"That you want to be a teacher too." I've always wanted to work with kids. In first grade, my grandparents bought me a sticker set, and I used all my parents' printer paper making fake homework, slapping on stickers and pretending to grade them with a red pen.

My goals have changed throughout the years. I've gone from wanting to teach first grade, to being a principal, to high school English lit. After peer tutoring sophomore year, I found my true calling as a school counselor. What better way to flex my compulsion for planning than helping others find their paths?

One corner of his mouth tugs upward, amused. "Here we go again with the conspiracy theories. It's really funny how you think I spend so much time thinking about you that I'd go so far as to copy your future career."

I toss an empty roll of duct tape on the floor, setting a hand on my hip. "You never gave a crap about student council in the first three years of high school. You knew it was my thing and you just had to go for it. And you've known for years I want to be a teacher. And suddenly, you're all about becoming a gym teacher. Coincidence? I think not."

His cheeks turn pink and his chest heaves. I've hit a nerve. Victory. "Did you ever stop to consider that maybe we have more in common than you think?" He pauses, shooting me a pointed glare. "No, you didn't. Because you've never bothered to get to know me."

It's on the tip of my tongue to inform Renner that I did intend to get to know him. That I even liked him, just a tiny bit—until he stood me up for another girl before homecoming. But nothing comes out aside from a huffy, "It's highly convenient is all I'm saying."

"Get over yourself, Char. Your dreams aren't unique," he says with a patronizing expression as he runs a hand over the seaweed to adhere it to the wall. My nostrils flare, but I manage to control my anger until he asks, "How many cats do you plan to own by thirty? Nine? Ten?"

"First, I like dogs. Not cats. And why is success measured by my relationship status? You didn't even ask about where I'd be in my thriving career," I point out. "If you were asking Ollie the same question, you'd never ask whether he lived with cats."

"Because I already know Ollie will be married to Kassie," Renner retorts.

I tilt my head, a little surprised by that admission. "True. Ollie is future-husband material."

"Future-husband material? And I'm not?"

I keep my lips pressed into a thin line. "You sound bothered. I'm sensing jealousy."

He makes a perplexed face. "Of who? Ollie?"

"Why not? You really liked Kassie. That summer before we went into high school."

He shrugs. "If that's how you wanna describe it. I was also fourteen years old. My mom still picked out my outfits for school. Besides, Kassie likes Ollie way more than she ever liked me. I've always been happy for him." His response catches me off guard. I've always assumed he felt some type of way about his best friend stealing the girl he liked, as anyone would.

I'm about to call him on it, but his face hardens again and it feels like the moment has passed. We work in a heavy silence for another few minutes.

"Can you pass me the blue streamers?" I ask from the top of the ladder.

He fetches the roll at a glacial pace.

"Make it snappy," I say, holding myself steady on the ladder. My blistered feet are aching in my sneakers.

He rests an arm on one of the middle steps, causing it to wobble. Probably on purpose. Is Renner trying to *kill me* when I'm at my most vulnerable? "I don't understand what makes Ollie future-husband material and not me," he reflects, still miffed. "Not that I want that with Kassie. Not at all. She and Ollie are great together. I just don't understand why others don't see me that way . . ."

"I can't understand what makes you think you're deserving of the title," I scoff. "Just look at it objectively. Ollie has been with Kassie for four whole years. Meanwhile, you'd already been through at least half of the female population of MHS by tenth grade." I'm not exaggerating. Nearly every girl I know has dated Renner at some point in the past four years.

"That doesn't mean I'm not going to settle down eventually. Besides, I have a lot to offer."

"Like what?"

"For starters, I can drive, unlike some. And I make damned good Kraft Mac and Cheese," he adds.

"Doubtful."

He shakes his head, and I catch a mischievous tug at the right side of his lip. "Even the mac and cheese doesn't intrigue you?"

A laugh comes from deep in my stomach, echoing around the gym. I clutch the sides of the ladder so I don't topple off. "Hard pass."

"Okay, but picture this. A zombie apocalypse. Everyone dies. Except us."

"Jesus take me." I close my eyes for a split second and press my hand to my chest at the thought. "Besides, women don't require a husband to complete them in life," I point out, yet again. "If anything, you'd weigh me down in an apocalypse. I wouldn't have time to babysit."

He trucks on like I haven't spoken. "We're the only two humans left on Earth. You'd rather carry on alone and get mauled by zombies than team up with me for survival?" His eyes pierce mine, awaiting a response.

Would I really rather go it alone? It's hard to say. But my brain is a little too frazzled for ridiculous hypotheticals. So I settle for a simple, "Yes. Now hand me the streamers, please."

He holds out the roll, expression stony, not bothering to stretch his arm any farther than necessary. Given I just went off about being a fiercely independent woman, I'm not about to ask him to bring it closer.

I take my left foot off the ladder to tilt my body weight just so. In that precise moment, one of the cardboard seaweeds falls off the wall across the gym.

It all happens so fast. Renner is startled and turns his body toward the noise, inadvertently moving the streamer roll farther out of my reach. I lean a smidge too far to make up the distance. Before I know it, everything is sideways.

The last thing I see is Renner's horrified expression as I crash directly into his face.

NINE

A high-pitched, siren-like wail cuts the air, snapping me to consciousness.

There's a jagged, throbbing ache threatening to slice straight through my eyes. I pinch them shut to minimize the pain, but the torment shifts to my eardrums. *What is that sound?* Maybe they're testing the fire alarms. It's getting louder and louder by the second, as if someone is precipitously turning up the volume on the school PA system.

Something faintly tickles my left cheek. When I try to scratch it, my hand brushes against something warm pressed into my shoulder. Another person, perhaps?

The memory of toppling off the ladder face-first into Renner blazes through my mind in high definition. I clench my jaw, remembering that moment of panic, bracing for impact, before it all went black.

When I find the strength to open my eyes, a beam of sunlight blinds me. Odd. There's zero natural light in this dingy gym, which is why graduation is always held on the football field (weather permitting).

Vision spotty, I accidentally dig my elbow into the floppy body underneath mine. I assume it's Renner. For a millisecond, I feel bad for landing on top of him.

He lets out a strangled groan, confirming that he too is in pain.

We're a tangle of arms and legs. His chest is bare for some strange reason. My eyes trace the swell of his tanned biceps. Sheesh. I knew Renner was lean and ripped for a seventeen-year-old. But I've never seen these thick, ropy muscles before. How has he been hiding these in his smedium T-shirts?

Speaking of shirts, where did his go? Maybe I broke a bone and he ripped his clothes off, Hulk-style, and used them for a tourniquet? Unlikely. Renner wouldn't sacrifice fashion on my account, even in a medical emergency.

I flex my toes and fingers, ensuring all are still functioning, before rolling over. But instead of being greeted by the cold, hard gym floor, my face presses into something impossibly soft and white, like a cloud. A blanket of some sort.

When my palm indents a cushiony padding, my arm hair stands on end. I'm in a bed. Have I been hospitalized? Am I in some sort of fancy hospital king-size bed for rich people? And if so, why is Renner here too?

I pull myself into a sitting position to get a better look. It's certainly not a hospital. It appears to be a sunlit bedroom, painted the prettiest shade of robin's-egg blue. A wide, white, distressed dresser sits on the wall opposite the bed near a bay window. Vacuum lines streak the plush cream carpet.

The blanket is soft against my skin, and I realize I'm no longer wearing my sweatpants and hoodie. Whoever dressed me had some style. I'm in a cute sleep set. One of those fancy, silky tank-and-shorts combos I've only seen on television. This is weird.

My mind starts to spitfire possibilities. Did Renner and I drunkenly hook up? No. There's no way. It's a Wednesday morning. We weren't drinking. And I would never, ever skip school to boink, especially with Renner. But why else would we be in bed together?

"Where am I?" I realize I've said this aloud when Renner stirs and rolls toward me, his warm arm pressing against mine.

When I shift to put a comfortable distance between us, the mattress creaks and his eyes snap open. At the sight of me, he jolts like I'm a sinister creature from a dark dimension, barrel-rolling off the opposite side of the bed. His body hits the floor with a hard thud.

"Char?" He pops his head up like a gopher in one of those carnival games, and I let out an impassioned shriek.

It's Renner. Same striking seafoam eyes. Same small scar on his forehead. Same crooked, resting smirk. But it's not. He's different. His face is broader somehow. A few new creases line his forehead. And his usually clean-shaven, criminally sharp jaw is specked with . . . facial hair? He has a beard. I didn't know he could grow a beard.

When he stands at full height, my eyes traitorously follow the light dusting of hair trailing down his sculpted abs and V-line, down to . . . I cover my eyes like they've been burned. I just saw Renner's package. The image will be seared into my retinas forevermore. I need eye bleach ASAP.

I've seen Renner's naked torso enough times at Ollie's summer parties. I know he has an effortless six-pack. But this chest is broader. Manlier. Like his face.

This can't be J. T. Renner.

Have I been kidnapped by a murderer who looks remarkably like Renner? Maybe this is his psychotic, secret older brother? I grope for the nearest object I can find. It's a framed photo on the bedside table.

"Don't come any closer!" I screech as he rounds the end of the bed. In my mind, I'm channeling some hard-core secret-agent vibes. But in reality, I come across like a cartoon character, swinging a picture frame with rounded, smooth edges like it's a sword.

Unamused, he swipes the picture from my hand and carelessly tosses it on the bed. "Were you really going to hit me with a picture frame? It's me. Renner." His voice—it's the same. Deep, but with a bit of a lazy, can't-be-bothered lilt.

I shake my head, but it only heightens the throbbing behind my eyes. "You're not Renner." It's not possible. But somehow, it is. "Why do you look like that?"

He knits his brow. "Why do *you* look like that?" he demands, taking a gander at my chest. His eyes are basically dinner plates.

My gaze follows his. Holy moly. What were barely B cups are now at least Cs. I take them in my hands to confirm. The flesh spills over the sides of my fingers. Yup. Definitely no longer Bs. Maybe all my prayers for bigger boobs have finally been answered.

I swiftly hoist the duvet over my braless boobs. "Did we . . . um . . . do—"

"Are you asking if we hooked up?" he clarifies.

I nod silently.

He runs a large hand through his messy hair. "No. I mean, I don't think so? I'd remember *that*. I'd have to be really wrecked to go there," he adds, waving a vague hand in my direction.

I should be offended, but the feeling is mutual. And to be honest, I'm comforted that we're both utterly confused. I grimace at the thought of his naked body on mine. I need a memory wipe, back to factory default. "Is this your house?" I whisper conspiratorially, even though I already know the answer. I've been to Renner's house multiple times over the years. I once took care of a very drunk Kassie in his parents' bedroom. Unless they did a full remodel in the past few months, this ain't it.

He shakes his head, eyes scanning like a hawk. "I have no idea where we are."

I'm about to ask whether he remembers me falling on top of him, but there are more pressing matters. Like his beard. "When was the last time you shaved?" I blurt, fixated on his jaw.

"Before I went to school this morning." He runs his hand over his jaw to confirm. His lips part slightly before he turns to the full-length mirror, next to what appears to be a walk-in closet. "What the . . . ," he mutters, groping at his face.

I scramble out of bed and follow him, duvet still wrapped around me like a protective cloak. "It's fake." I reach and give the wiry hairs a yank. They don't budge.

"Ouch! What the hell?" He smacks my hand away.

"Okay. Not fake." I turn, hands pressed to my temples. Mid-tizzy, my eye catches the framed photo Renner tossed on the bed.

It's a photo of a couple. The woman is in a delicate lace, lilac-colored dress. Her dark, shiny hair is swept back in an updo with wavy barrel curls framing her angular face. The man is in a deep-indigo button-down. He's kissing her forehead, staring at her like she's his forever. It's an I'd-rather-die-a-grisly-death-than-go-two-seconds-without-you kind of love, by the looks of it.

They look weirdly familiar upon closer inspection.

The longer I stare at it, tilting my head like a dog to view it from every angle, the more it sets in.

The couple is us.

TEN

I toss the framed photo on the floor like it's a heaping pile of dog poo. "This is a prank."

"It would have to be one elaborate senior prank," he says in disbelief, unable to stop combing his fingers through his very real beard.

My cheeks heat. "This looks like Nori's work. She's always playing around with Photoshop. Remember that time she pasted all our heads on that *Riverdale* picture? It looked so real." I was aggrieved because she made me Betty and Renner Jughead. Even a totally pointless, photoshopped pairing doesn't sit right.

"But how could Nori . . . how could *anyone* do . . . all of that?" He makes a faint gesture toward my chest again, but quickly thinks better of it when he meets my scowl.

My left boob threatens to flop out of these weird silky pajamas. I bolt into the walk-in closet for literally anything to cover myself.

The closet is full, but seemingly organized, split in two with his-and-her shelving. There's a laundry basket on the floor, and a gray hoodie that reads MAPLEWOOD HIGH SCHOOL across the chest rests on top. I grab it and pull it over my head.

When I emerge from the closet, Renner is in the en suite bathroom. Like a child distracted by shiny objects, he runs a hand along the marbled countertop and touchless tap, while admiring his bearded face in the mirror. He's making that pouty face models make when they're trying to be all sensual. That's how I know it's really him. His ego is unmatchable.

The hallway outside the bedroom (our bedroom?) is lit with a rosy hue from the morning sun. We appear to be on the second floor of a home. There's a carpeted staircase directly to the left of the master bedroom and two other bedroom doors down the hallway, along with another bathroom.

The larger of the two bedrooms is fairly nondescript. There's a neatly made oak-framed twin bed and clutter-free furniture. The smaller room appears to be a home office. Near the landing above the stairs, a collection of framed photos sits atop a floating shelf.

The photos depict Renner and me in nauseatingly romantic poses in random places, including an apple orchard. Who takes photos like this and why? Nori really went to great lengths to photoshop these. I idly wonder if I'm on camera, if I'm unknowingly starring in one of those YouTube prank shows.

"*Ha ha*, very funny. You got us. You can all come out now," I say, waving my arms toward the ceiling, examining it for cameras.

Nothing.

I head downstairs, arms crossed, bracing myself for Nori, Kassie, and Ollie to jump out from behind a closed door and scare the crap out of me. The kitchen and living area are long and open with a nautical vibe. Strangely, it's exactly how I've always imagined styling my future home. I'm a little jealous of whoever owns this house. I rack my brain, trying to figure out who could convince their parents to loan their home for such a prank.

A couple dirty, free-form ceramic plates are stacked on the coffee table. The pantry is sparse, aside from approximately a year's worth of peanut butter and some boxed macaroni. Whoever owns this house must love peanut butter. The fridge isn't much better. There's a half-empty carton of eggs, a brick of marbled cheese, a nearly empty jar of dill pickles, and jumbo bottles of condiments.

I head for the front door, again bracing myself for the pranksters to reveal themselves. Either that, or I'm locked in by some deranged kidnapper who's wearing Renner's face and imitating his voice. I turn the knob as the chilling possibility sets in. It's open. I'm not being kept in this adorable home against my will. That's a good sign. I squint into the sunlight as my bare feet hit the cool concrete of the shaded front porch.

I recognize the Craftsman style of the surrounding homes with their cute little porches and posh blend of siding and stone. Shiny, gleaming cars line each driveway.

I walk into the grass, relishing the cool morning dew against my blistered feet. It's only then that I realize my feet aren't aching anymore. In fact, the massive blisters on both baby toes are nonexistent. I lift my right foot, running a finger over what was previously a bloody, wounded heel. It's perfectly smooth. My blisters are gone, even though I was cringing when I put my shoes on this morning. Unless . . . unless it's no longer Wednesday? What day is it?

A man with a tiny Yorkie wearing bright-yellow booties strolls by and eyes me sideways, probably because I'm examining my feet in public while sporting silk short-shorts. I ignore him and head to the edge of the lawn to get a better look at the street sign. Bois Court. I'm in Kassie's neighborhood. We're in the cul-de-sac down the street from Renner's place.

Nothing makes sense except my overwhelming urge to go home, crawl into bed, and avoid reality. So I run. Barefoot.

I only make it a couple strides before I hear Renner. "Where are you going?" he calls from the end of the driveway. He's wearing joggers now, though he's still shirtless.

"Home!" I shout into the wind, not bothering to linger.

I know this route well. I've been to and from Kassie's a million times. I break into a jog whenever I pass by Old Lady Brown's house on the next corner. She's a miserable woman who spends her days screeching at passersby and journaling life's injustices in her "disappointments diary," which she's requested to have published after her death. A massive oak tree has practically eaten up her entire yard. The shadow of the spindly branches scares the shit out of me at night.

As I round the corner toward the house, I come to a full stop in the middle of the street. The tree is gone. Am I losing it? Am I forgetting which house had the scary tree? I question my sanity until I spot the disturbing cloth doll that always sat in the window. It's definitely the same house. As much as that tree spooked me, the lawn looks like a barren wasteland without it.

A horn pierces the air and a fancy car lurches to a stop a few feet from flattening me. "Watch where you're going, lady!" a red-faced old man hollers out the window.

Lady? Who does he think he's talking to?

As Mr. Road Rage peels off, I note that there's barely any sound. No loud revving of an engine. Now that I think of it, the cars in the driveways look different—sleeker, somehow. This is a middle-class neighborhood, not a high-end, luxury-car kind of neighborhood.

Even more confused, I pick up the pace to a full tilt.

I'm a sweaty mess when my street comes into view. It's lined with smaller, older brick bungalows.

Mom's sedan isn't in the driveway. A collection of wilted red and yellow spring tulips catches my eye. Those weren't there before. I try to open the door, but it's locked. I peer through the window into the living room, but the blinds are drawn.

Maybe she's at work. The pharmacy is at least a fifteen-minute walk and I've sufficiently tired myself out. I head to the backyard to grab Mom's bike since mine is still being repaired.

The shed leans slightly. I don't recall it being in such rough shape. Maybe the recent windstorm knocked it over. I peer in. Mom's silver bike is propped against the shed wall. Upon closer inspection, it's almost rusted over. I wheel it into the driveway and timidly hop on, bracing for it to collapse under my weight. When it doesn't, I pedal as fast as my legs will take me.

I don't even bother to lock the bike when I get to the pharmacy. Stacey, Mom's longtime coworker, is behind the counter, rooting through the prescription bags in the pickup bin. She's changed her hairstyle since last week. What used to be a brunette angled bob is now a sassy pixie cut streaked with gray.

"Stacey, it's you," I huff, resting both elbows on the counter.

She leans back slightly, probably scared I'll drip sweat on her. Then she peers over the counter, appraising my PJ shorts, as well as my bare feet, which are now black from my journey here. "Are you okay, Charlotte? Do you need to sit down?"

I'm tempted to start sobbing right here in the pharmacy. I'm desperate to tell someone, anyone, that I fell off a ladder in the gym and woke up in an unfamiliar house with huge boobs.

But alas. There are people around, including an elderly woman with a poodle perm impatiently tapping her foot in line behind me. I must play it cool. "Uh, yeah. I'm fine. Never better. I'm just looking for my mom," I say, feigning calm and collected.

Her stare is perplexed. She gives my hand a pitiful pat. "Dear, your mom doesn't work here." She can see I'm confused. "She hasn't worked here in five years. She's back at the uptown pharmacy now over on Oak. Are you sure you're feeling okay? Why are you still in pajamas?"

I squint at her, trying to understand. Mom definitely still works here. I hung out here the other day and organized the shampoo aisle, waiting for her shift to end so she could drive me home. "Can I just ask . . . what day is it?"

"Friday, June 12, 2037," she says, like it's obvious. It's certainly June 12. But 2024, not 2037.

If it really were 2037, that would mean I'm . . . No. It can't be.

Mystified, I lean closer, peering over my shoulder to ensure the woman behind me isn't eavesdropping. She definitely is. "How old am I?" I whisper for confirmation.

Stacey does the mental math. "You were born the same year my Teddy was born . . . so that would put you at thirty?" She smiles sweetly.

Thirty. THIRTY?

A hot flash besieges me. Spikes of heat radiate up my back and neck. My entire body is a scorching inferno. My vision is blurring. I need to lie down. What the hell is happening to me?

Stacey prattles on, unaware of my utter confusion. "Seems like just yesterday you were in here buying candy with your friends for your movie nights." No shit. Because it was last week. Kassie ditched Saturday night. Shocker. But Nori and I watched a horror movie about a girl who gets sucked inside a Ouija board. I slept with the lights on. I'm certainly no thirty-year-old.

Stacey chatters away about how she still remembers my zombie-cheerleader Halloween costume from when I was seven, but my brain zeroes in on the last bit. "And now you're getting married next week. I hear you're having quite the shindig. A joint bachelor/bachelorette if the rumor mill is true?"

"Married?" I rasp. "Excuse me?" I stare at her intensely, waiting for her to laugh and cop to the prank. And that's when I see it. Sitting there on my finger. A sparkling oval diamond sitting atop a thin, yellow-gold band. It's stunning. And heavy.

Before I can give it more thought, a tall woman with a giant black purse over her forearm approaches. "Charlotte Wu?" She extends her hand. "I don't know if you remember me. I'm Ivory's mom."

I stare at her, blank-faced. I've never seen this woman in my life. "Ivory?"

"Ivory Eckhart? You're her school counselor."

I freeze entirely. A school counselor? For real?

When I don't confirm nor deny, she plows forth, eyes darting to my bare feet. "It looks like you're a bit busy, but I wanted to say how much Ivory has benefited from your help with her college applications."

I'm going insane. Either that, or this is some Captain America shit. I went to sleep, somehow got lodged and preserved in the ice, and woke up a billion years later, only I'm not a mega-ripped supersoldier.

Then again, if this woman is telling the truth, I've achieved even more. I'm a school counselor. A good one, apparently.

I'm not entirely sure how to respond, given I have no idea who this Ivory person is, so I open my mouth as wide as possible, force a smile, and nod.

My Joker smile must scare her, because she takes a step back. "Oh, I hope you and J. T. have the best wedding day," she says before heading down the aisle.

J. T.?

I blink. If falling off a ladder, hitting my head, and waking up thirteen years in the future isn't traumatic enough, now I'm getting MARRIED? To Renner?

The photos of us plastered around the house cycle through my mind like a slideshow.

Sweet baby Jesus.

I'm marrying Joshua Taylor Renner.

I don't know how this happened. But one thing is certain: I am officially in the pits of hell.

ELEVEN

This is a nightmare. I'm sure of it. There's no way I time traveled. That's absurd.

If this truly is a nightmare, I should be able to wake up. Delighted at the prospect, I slap myself hard across the cheek as I book it out of the pharmacy. *Ouch.* Maybe a measly slap won't suffice.

Time for more drastic measures. I pedal furiously into a residential area and hurl myself off my bike (into a bush to cushion my fall). A man with gardening shears looks down on me. He's not overly pleased. I briefly entertain diving in front of an oncoming vehicle. But wouldn't that be suicide? What if I'm *not* dreaming?

Resigned—and a bit bruised—I decide that the only logical step is to return to the house for more information. Renner is still there, man-splaying on the front porch, hair disheveled, unsure which way it wants to flop.

"You have a branch in your hair," he says, voice deep and gravelly—like a thirty-year-old's . . .

I set my bike in the driveway so I can fish the branch out. "Why are you still here?"

"I went home." There's a weird look on his face that tells me there's more to the story.

"And?" I already know what he's going to say, but I need to hear it.

"It's 2037," he tells me, like he's already accepted this strange fact.

"So I've heard." I finally let out a deep exhale. I park myself on the step next to him and stare out at the street. Another one of those fancy cars drives by. I guess that's why everyone has one. We're in the future. "And we're . . . getting married next week." I hold up my ring finger.

"Yeah. My mom told me." He runs both hands down either side of his face.

"You saw your parents?"

"I saw my mom," he says definitively, jaw ticking with unease.

A lump forms in my throat at his expression. "Your dad . . . wasn't home?"

His eyes flick to his shoes. "They're divorced."

"Oh my god. How is she?"

"She's . . ." He pauses, flinching. "She's . . . different. Happy." His eyes widen and he shakes his head regretfully, as though he's said too much. This Renner, disheveled and slumped over, is a far cry from the cocky, smirking one I'm used to.

"Anyway, my mom thinks I've lost it. She tried calling you." He dangles a phone over my lap.

I blink at him. Renner's parents' divorce feels like too big a topic to just gloss over. I want him to elaborate, to ask if he's okay. I want to assure him he *will* be okay, even if it doesn't feel like it now.

But do I really expect him to cry on my shoulder and divulge his family problems to me? If the tables were turned, I'd seek support from a grizzly bear before Renner.

"She tried calling you," Renner repeats, snapping me back to reality.

I have four missed calls. Two from Dorothy, Renner's mom, one from my mom, and one from Nori.

"What the hell is happening?"

Renner starts pacing around the porch. He folds his arms over his chest, and my eyes flare at the sight of his biceps. Yup. He definitely didn't have those at school this morning. "Okay, let's think about this logically. What's the last thing you remember?"

"It was Wednesday, June 12, 2024. We were decorating for prom and arguing," I tell him. "The seaweed fell off the wall and you made me fall off the ladder. What's the last thing you remember?"

"Exactly that. Mostly your boobs crushing my face," he says, the faintest smile on his lips. "And for the record, it's not my fault you fell. You're not blaming me for this."

"Good to know you're still immature." I shake my head. "Anyways, that's a good sign. We both remember being seventeen, decorating for prom, and the ladder."

"But what happened to us? To everyone else? How is it now Friday, June 12, 2037?"

I take in a deep breath. "We know this isn't a prank. There's no way the entire town of Maplewood could pull this off. What are our other possibilities?"

"Death. We could be dead. This could be purgatory," he suggests. "Or maybe we hit our heads and got amnesia? What if we have brain damage? Or what if we somehow fell into an alternate dimension? Into the Upside Down?"

I twist my lips. "Do you realize how that sounds?"

He hands me his phone. "Look. Scroll all the way up."

I flip through the photos. There are at least a thousand. All of Renner and me throughout the years. The earliest is dated 2029, five years after high school graduation. These photos seem foreign, an in-depth look at someone else's life, someone else's memories and travels. Logically, I know it's me in the photos, but I have no memory of any of it, especially not the trip to Paris and what looks like a tropical vacation on a white sandy beach.

"There's no way Nori had the time to photoshop all of these," he says.

"Why would we be engaged? Of all people? Were there really no other options?" I ask. He doesn't respond.

I scan my recent texts. One from *Pain in my ass* ❤, and others from Nori, Mom, and a bunch of random names I don't recognize.

Renner plucks my phone and holds it out of reach. I grab for it, to no avail. I wish I could say I'm taller than my seventeen-year-old self, but apparently not.

He holds his arm out, blocking me from another attempt. "Wait!"

"What?"

"We can't just go around telling people we've jumped into the future. Everyone's gonna think we've lost our minds."

I inhale a labored breath. He has a point. "You're right. No one is ever going to believe this."

He shifts his gaze from his feet to my face, like he's just had a light bulb moment. "We both know someone who might."

I nod, a little disturbed I didn't think of it first. Of course. "Nori."

~

Adult Nori is a trip. The first thing she does is grab a piece of licorice from the pantry. "Breakfast of champions," she calls it, practically dive-bombing the armchair in the living area. She looks quite comfortable here. More so than Renner and me as we awkwardly shift on the couch.

Her previously shoulder-length unicorn hair is now streaked with blue and falls around the waistline of her skinny jeans. They remind me of the ones Mom always wears.

"Being old really is the tits," she says, tearing off a bite of licorice. "I can't drink sugary drinks anymore. My body can't handle it. And I didn't even drink nearly as much as you two. I'm shocked you're even awake right now."

Renner leans forward. "We drank last night?"

She juts her chin forward. "Are you kidding me? You threw up on Mitch's lawn. It was like grad party all over again. Honestly, I thought you'd need a stomach pump—"

"Mitch? Mitch who?" I cut in.

"Mitch Wong."

"That little freshman?" I clarify. Mitch is so tiny, he was duct-taped to the cafeteria wall for freshman initiation day.

Nori narrows her gaze, confused. "Uh, well, he's twenty-six, but yes, I suppose he was small as a freshman."

I shift to the edge of the couch and look her dead in the eye. "Okay, Nori, we're about to get weird."

She leans into the couch and gives Renner a brief glance. "What do you mean by *weird*? Should I be frightened? Because you're doing that wonky eye thing."

I hold my stare as she frantically chews the last chunk of licorice. "We're going to tell you something. Something huge. And you need to promise you won't tell anyone."

Her jaw hinges open. "Oh my god. You guys are pregnant! No wonder you moved up your wedding date."

I wretch at the thought of procreating with Renner. "God no. Eww."

A flash of confusion falls over her face.

"This is going to sound bizarre," Renner interrupts. "But we woke up not remembering how we got here."

Strangely, Nori takes this in stride. "That's because Ollie drove you guys home. He fireman carried you to your bed, J. T. He even sent me a video."

I shake my head. "No, you don't understand. We had an accident. In the school gym. I fell off a ladder—"

"She fell on my face," Renner clarifies.

"We were seventeen," I continue. "Decorating for prom. Everything went black when I fell off the ladder. And then we woke up . . . here. This morning."

Nori closes her eyes and shakes her head like a wet dog. "Okay, wait, what?"

I lean closer. "We don't remember anything from the past thirteen years."

Nori searches my face, trying to gauge whether I'm screwing with her. When I don't crack, she starts laughing nervously. "You two drank way too much. Honestly. Maybe you just need a hot shower, or a personal day. You should totally skip work."

"Nori, I'm serious. The last thing I remember is being upset over the Under the Sea theme," I say.

"The prom theme?" she asks, eyes widening in realization. "Oh my god. Do you remember my dress? That weird one that accentuated all my worst angles? I untagged myself in all of those photos. As if you could forget that. Oh, and that's the night you two first hooked up. Remember?"

Renner and I simultaneously bust a gut. "Hooked up? We hooked up? As in me and Renner?" I'm not certain I want to know the answer.

She snorts like the answer is obvious. "At least, I think it was prom night."

"We don't remember that. Or anything else," Renner says, a little more forcefully.

She blinks. "You're being serious? You're not playing some ridiculous prank?"

"Cross my heart." I make an *X* over my chest. "We need to know what's happened in the past thirteen years."

Still a little unsure, she gives us the basics. It's all out of order, as per usual when Nori tells a story. But I manage to get the gist.

Renner and I first hooked up on prom night and dated for the first year of college. I can't help but laugh because it sounds so outlandish. Renner just rests his head in his hands like his life is over. We broke up in our second year, dated other people, and got back together when we both moved back to Maplewood to work at MHS. We got engaged this winter on a Hawaiian vacation.

Engagement aside, I think about the unlikely reality that both of us would become educators. At the same high school. How could that even happen? Of everyone in our friend group, Renner was the person I was most looking forward to never seeing again after high school.

"Everyone knew you two were meant to be," Nori tells us, all starry eyed. She explains that Renner moved back to be a PE teacher. He coaches both the rugby and track teams.

"I'm a gym teacher," Renner notes under his breath.

I can't help but snort.

"What's so funny?"

"I just can't imagine you demonstrating how to put a condom over a banana with a straight face."

"I dunno why you're shaming me about teaching kids to stay physically active while educating them about safe sex." I dry cough when he says *sex* all deep and authoritative. I feel like I'm in middle school sex ed all over again, chuckling over the word *vulva.* He continues on when I don't respond. "Puberty is no joke. Kids need someone to teach them about body odor."

"You would know," I sneer, desperately scraping my memory for a time Renner had BO, to no avail.

"You're just pissed because I'm probably the cool teacher everyone loves, and you're the terrifying one rumored to lock kids in an underground dungeon as punishment for being a half second late to class." I wouldn't be shocked. Renner would still manage to upstage me in a weird alternate universe.

"First, I'd have a candlelit lair. Not a dungeon. It would be sacred. And for the record, I'd rather be terrifying than ridiculous," I shoot back.

Nori clears her throat. "J. T., you were assistant coaching a college rugby team in Boston for a while. But you wanted to come back home to be with Char."

He runs both hands down his face, looking disturbed. I am equally concerned for both of us. Renner actually gave up his dream of coaching college rugby for me? What was he thinking?

Apparently, I'm the school counselor at MHS, and Nori's a freelance graphic designer.

She goes on a tangent about how she couldn't transfer to Rhode Island School of Design because the world wasn't ready for her brand of talent. (She still seems bitter.) But it worked out for the best because we went to college together, where she met her girlfriend, Sasha.

"What about everyone else?" I ask. "What happened to Kassie and Ollie? Are they married?"

Nori looks at me in disbelief. "Kassie and Ollie broke up after high school grad. I can't believe you don't remember. It was a huge blowout. Ollie is engaged to Lainey now."

I blink. Kassie and Ollie broke up? How? Why? My brain is fuzzy from information overload, settling on the more digestible tidbit of information. "Ollie is with Lainey Henderson? The curly-haired kid I used to babysit?" I clarify. "She's . . . a ten-year-old."

"She's twenty-three. He hired her at the office. He's a Realtor," Nori informs us.

"This is . . . insane." My head feels unusually heavy. This is too much new information. "We lost thirteen years. *Thirteen.* Did I make dean's list? Was I valedictorian?"

"Relax, girl. You made dean's list and you were valedictorian and gave a big speech. It was a good one—at least, I think it was. Pete and I got buzzed in the coatroom right before the ceremony so my memory is a little fuzzy but—"

"There's gotta be an explanation for this," Renner mutters.

Nori starts tapping on her phone. "Okay, hold up, I'm googling."

Renner and I crowd the back of her chair, watching as she types, I woke up in the future.

There are thousands of hits. A song by some band called The Intangibles. An old movie called *13 Going on 30* with Jennifer Garner that Mom always loved. And a bunch of news articles about amnesia and severe head trauma.

Nori taps on the screen with her matte-black nails. "Oh, look at this." It's a news article about a woman who woke up at thirty-two believing she was a teenager. "It says she was diagnosed with *transient global amnesia*. Apparently, you remember how to do basic things, but you forget qualitative memories. It says you'll remember them eventually."

"Okay, but look. It also says it's incredibly rare," I point out. "Why would *both* Renner and I have it?"

"True." Nori bites her lip. "Wait, what if you two have been sent to the future to change something? Prevent some sort of disastrous event?"

Renner hangs his head. "Like our apparent marriage next week? I can't believe we're getting hitched."

I nod vigorously. For once, I agree with Renner. "There's no way we're actually getting married."

Nori stands, shaking her head. "Are you guys really doing this again? Your bickering is *so* high school. You better get a grip before your bachelor/bachelorette party tonight."

Renner coughs. "What party?"

"My mom's coworker mentioned it," I grumble.

"Ollie and Lainey are hosting. Everyone's going," Nori says, buzzing with excitement.

"Who's *everyone*?" I ask, hesitant.

"Literally everyone. Even your mom. Trust, I tried to steer you away from a family-oriented party toward the genitals-and-strippers variety. But you two were very insistent on keeping things wholesome to preserve your reputations as educators and community leaders."

Renner rolls his eyes, resting his hands behind his head. "Sounds like Char."

Nori ignores him. "Like I said, everyone is going. Including you two, obviously."

I shake my head and stand up. "No. We're not going. At least, *I'm* not going. Tell Ollie we have to cancel."

She gives me an icy look. "You're not *not* going to your own bachelorette."

"We're not getting married. We have to call it off."

She looks at me like I'm a Martian. "After all the hours we spent designing invitations and place cards? No way! Besides, guests are coming from out of town and your parents will be so upset."

"Let them be upset. We're not getting married, period," I say stubbornly.

Renner nods in agreement.

That's probably the first thing we've ever wholeheartedly agreed on.

TWELVE

Before Nori leaves, she crafts a "foolproof" plan. Renner and I will go to school (otherwise known as work) and re-create the ladder fall in the gym in hopes of somehow propelling ourselves back to seventeen.

"Purposely chucking myself off a ladder is the opposite of foolproof," I point out, already wincing from the phantom pain. Though . . . at least it's a plan. And it's the only thing that remotely makes sense.

Nori ignores my reluctance. "Make sure to do it in the exact same place, exactly the same way. I bet my left boob you'll wake up back in 2024." She pauses, grinning like a Cheshire cat. "Oh, and if it works, you have to tell my seventeen-year-old self not to cut my own bangs before college. It wasn't a good look."

"And if it doesn't work? What if we're still stuck here in 2037?" Renner asks, a desperate look on his face.

"You have to come to your joint bachelor/bachelorette at Ollie's tonight and pretend everything is normal until we find out what's going on," she says, not blinking. "I'm not letting your underdeveloped teen brains ruin your adult lives. Besides, maybe seeing more people you know will help spark your memories."

Doubtful.

Re-creating the ladder fall sounds ridiculous, but what other option do we have? I'm willing to do anything to save my future self from making the biggest mistake of my life.

~

"You're delusional if you think you're driving," Renner says, nudging me away from the driver's side as I stride toward the car, fob in hand, channeling Vin Diesel in *The Fast and the Furious.*

"Why not? I have a license. See?" I pull my perfectly legitimate driver's license from my bag and brandish it in his face. Believe it or not, I passed my driver's test somewhere along the way. I truly don't know how it happened, but I'm damn proud. Besides, if future me has a cool, sleek, futuristic car, I'm not passing up an opportunity to take it for a joyride. There have to be some perks for being robbed of my youth and forced to marry Renner.

He leans in, scrutinizing it like an eighty-five-year-old with cataracts. "Char, you're a liability on the road."

I shove the ID back in my purse but keep the fob tight. "I am not. You can't hold one tiny incident against me. Lots of people fail their driver's test. You're unfairly targeting me because I'm an Asian woman." Yes, I'm aware I've perpetuated the ridiculous stereotype that Asian women can't drive. I'm not proud of it.

He levels me with his look, running a hand through his hair, exasperated. "First, this has nothing to do with stereotypes. I'm going by the facts. It wasn't just one incident, it was multiple. We were in the same driver's ed class. And if I remember correctly, you almost backed over a pregnant woman."

"You're being so dramatic. I merely tapped her. She walked away without a scratch. And maybe she should look where she's going before she walks into a car."

He tosses his hands in the air and heads for the passenger side. "Fine. Drive. Maybe you'll kill us and put us out of our misery," he adds.

To be fair, our "relationship" is flat-out insufferable. Not that I expected anything less. I've tried to give him some grace after his parents' divorce bomb. But it's proving a herculean task. We've been bickering all morning, ever since he used all the hot water, claiming he needed extra time to wash his beard. He also ate the last piece of bread in our pantry without even asking if I wanted half. If my future entails living with a man with the emotional intelligence of a ten-year-old, I don't want any part of it.

I attempt to open the car door, but there's no handle. Instead, there's a little sliver of chrome. After much inspection, I realize the chrome rectangle is a button, which opens the door.

The interior of the car is about as familiar as an intergalactic spaceship. There are no buttons or dials. Instead, there's a massive, shiny touchscreen down the middle of the console.

Renner clears his throat. "Um, are we going? Or are we just gonna sit in the driveway all day?"

"Relax, Renner. I'm just taking it all in." Frankly, I have no idea how to start the car. But I'm certainly not about to admit that.

As if he can read my mind, he leans over and presses a button near the triangular-shaped steering wheel, which starts the engine. It's impossibly quiet as it purrs to a start, just like the car that nearly crushed me this morning. A backup camera pops up at the bottom of the screen. Unlike Mom's sedan, it's not grainy and covered in dirt. It's clear as day, like an HD movie.

When I tighten my grip on the steering wheel, a pleasant voice filters through the speakers. "Good morning. Are you on your way to work?"

Renner and I stare at each other, startled. "Uh, yes?" I squeak. "Are you . . . a person?"

"I am Raina. Your vehicle's software. Would you like to drive yourself today?"

Renner runs his hand over the dash, eyes sparkling like he's discovered a pile of gold. "Holy crap, it's a self-driving car. This is so freakin' cool. This makes the DILF Mobile look like a steaming pile of junk."

I death-grip the steering wheel. "No. Give me the mom-van over this any day. This is terrifying," I whisper. "Drive myself," I yell, panicked at handing my life over to a robot. I once watched a YouTube documentary about artificial intelligence taking over the world. I've been haunted ever since.

Renner pouts. "You're such a killjoy. It's probably a hundred times safer to have the robot drive."

I ignore him, trying to figure out how to adjust all the mirrors and the seat. After ten minutes of scrolling, we realize the car has two profiles, mine and Renner's, which automatically adjust to our customized settings. Satisfied and comfortable behind the wheel, I tap the button to put the car into reverse.

As we roll out of the driveway, Renner lets out a shriek. *"Stop."*

I brake, and we come to a grinding halt as a tomato-red car whizzes by behind us.

"You almost T-boned that car! Even with a huge backup camera," he says, gesturing to the massive screen.

"I'm sorry! I'm not used to this!" I shriek, heart hammering. "There are so many things to look at and—"

He unfastens his seat belt and opens his door. "Nope. Nope. Nope. I decided I don't wanna die today. Get out, I'm driving."

~

We manage to get to the school in one piece, thanks to Renner. He handles the new car like a boss, managing the interior lights, the AC, and the music while driving. The music is difficult to digest. I barely recognize anything other than a Justin Bieber song on a "throwback hits" playlist. Disturbing, to say the least.

Maplewood High looks exactly the same. Unlike the rest of Maplewood's charming historical aesthetic, the high school is drab. There are few distinguishing features, unless you count the spray-paint graffiti along the front wall that magically changes every few months. No one knows who the culprit is.

I'm halfway out of the car when I notice that Renner's hands are still locked on the wheel.

"You coming?" I ask.

His lip twitches and he fumbles to unfasten his seat belt. "I, uh . . . we work here. And we have no idea what we're doing." His face is all red, and I'm fairly certain there's a bead of sweat on his forehead. I don't know that I've ever seen Renner flustered before. He's usually maddeningly calm in every situation.

"Look. Maybe we won't have to see anyone. School doesn't start for half an hour. All we need to do is get to the gym before anyone sees us. Nori's plan will work," I say. It has to.

He nods silently and gets out of the car like he's heading down death row. But his mood lifts when we pass the marquee sign that reads:

CONGRATULATIONS GRADUATING CLASS OF '37.
ANAL EXAMS—JUNE 1–5

Renner can't help but snicker at the typo and missing letters. Of course he does. He can't resist a butt joke.

"I can't believe you work here. In a position of authority," I mutter, entering ahead of him.

"Only the best of minds for the next generation," he says, whistling. Nothing like teenage humor to shift his dour mood.

As the heavy doors close behind us, a mixture of antiseptic, rubber erasers, and BO hits my nostrils. At least it smells exactly the same.

Thankfully, the hallway is empty as we creep toward the gym like the Grinch who stole Christmas. Halfway down the corridor, Renner stops to look at a wall of large framed graduation composites. I follow his line of vision. The Class of 2024.

My grad photo is just cruel. I don't know who selected it, but they obviously had a grudge against me. I'm stiff and awkward. One eye is wonky, nearly half-closed in a blink. Renner's photo makes me seethe. His should be used as the stock photo for the photography company's advertisements. He's got that effortless sideways grin that never fails to charm.

I peruse the rest of my classmates' eager smiles, wondering what's become of them in this strange future. Have they stayed in Maplewood? Are they living fabulous lives in the city? Are any of them wealthy tech billionaires in Silicon Valley?

"Hey, there's that plug Garrett you used to date," Renner says, pointing to Garrett's photo.

Garrett Hogan and I dated for a hot second last year. Nori planted the seed that we were soulmates because we're both list-obsessed type As. As it turns out, dating another version of me, someone who second-guesses everything and overplans every meticulous detail (including how we were going to lose our virginities) was painful. Spending forty-five minutes in the contraceptive aisle at the pharmacy where Mom works, weighing the pros and cons of ribbed vs. smooth vs. sensation condoms, really put a damper on what was supposed to be the most romantic moment of my life. 0/10 do not recommend.

When I don't react, he prods. "Why haven't you dated anyone since him?"

"I'm too busy to date," I say. He gives me his skeptical side-eye. "Senior year is a lot! AP classes. Student council. Model UN. SATs. College visits. I can't even keep my barrel cactus, Frank, alive—and he only needs watering once a month. There's no time left to cater to a needy boyfriend."

"Sounds like you're making excuses," he says. He's not wrong. It all sounds so trivial now . . . as a thirty-year-old.

"Come on, let's go find our bricks," I cut in. The last thing I need is a lecture on my dating life from my alleged husband-to-be.

I've painted mine red with little daisies around the edges. My name is in what looks like Times New Roman font, and I've written initials along the bottom. I see *KL* for Kassie, *NW* for Nori, *OI* for Ollie, and last, *JTR* with a little heart.

Renner's brick is next to mine, painted forest green. His name is in simple block letters. He has way more initials than me, which makes sense because he's friends with the entire student body. But my initials are there too, at the end, with a matching heart.

"That's . . . interesting," he notes, pointing to my initials.

"Yup. Very." How could we possibly go from being enemies to immortalizing each other's initials on our grad bricks a mere two weeks later? It doesn't add up. "Let's get to the gym and make this all go away." I spin on my heel and a red-haired woman in a sky-blue sundress comes barreling around the corner. "Hey! I've been looking for you guys." I don't recognize her, but she certainly recognizes us. Her eyes are wide, bright, and full of good intention. At least, I think so.

So much for dashing in unnoticed.

"Oh, well, you've found us," I say with a nervous laugh. I try leaning against the wall, but I look like I'm doing awkward wall push-ups.

"I noticed the assignment list in the teacher's lounge," she says.

"Assignment list?" Renner asks, not-so-casually slinging his arm over my shoulder and pulling me into his side a little too forcefully. He may smell delightful, like a Bounce dryer sheet, but I'm hella uncomfortable. When I stiffen, he gets the hint and loosens his grip.

"The one for prom. Charlotte made the list?" she says, as though we should just *know*.

A list. This sounds like something adult me would do. "Prom assignment list. Yes," I repeat with fake enthusiasm.

"You assigned me for the early shift tomorrow night, but I'd need to find a sitter for Rudy until Chuck gets home. Rudy's got a bit of a cold and it's a whole thing. Can you switch me to the late shift?"

"Uh, yeah. Sure. Kids come first," I chirp.

Her shoulders lower with relief. Seems we've just done her a huge solid. "Thanks for understanding. He's been difficult lately with food. I think we need to switch his brand of kibble."

Renner raises his brows. "Kibble?"

"The vet recommended a new brand. Said most hedgehogs thrive on this one but—"

"Rudy is a hedgehog," I clarify, tamping down my laughter.

"Of course he is. You babysat him a couple weeks ago. Are you two okay? Pre-wedding jitters melting your brains?" she asks, eyeing us with playful suspicion.

I don't have a chance to answer, because Renner starts asking all sorts of questions about Rudy, how old he is, his feeding schedule, and whether he can do tricks like a dog. Hedgehog Lady delights in the opportunity to discuss Rudy's aversion to baths. I flash him a look, silently daring him to ask yet another question.

"Um, we better get going. We're gonna be late for—um, we're gonna be late," he says, wrapping his arm around my shoulder and guiding me away.

The moment we turn the corner, I shrug myself out of Renner's grip. "Please don't touch me."

"Sorry. But everyone thinks we're engaged. Wouldn't it be weird if we never touched?"

"We're at work. We have to stay professional," I grumble, walking ahead.

"Who was that? And why does she have a hedgehog and treat it like her child?"

"I don't even want to know. And had we gone straight to the gym like we planned, we wouldn't have had to deal with it," I hiss.

He lets out a heavy sigh, fixing me with a tormented expression when we reach the gym. "You're not blaming me for this."

"Of course I am," I whisper.

The gym is quiet, just as it was earlier this morning, before I fell off the ladder—thirteen years ago. Only, instead of Under the Sea decor, it's decked out like Mardi Gras. There's a big deck of cards illuminated on the far wall, as well as tables with royal-purple linens and large feather centerpieces filled with silver beaded necklaces. There are even gold sheets of fabric draped from the ceiling.

"I can't believe *we* are supposed to chaperone this thing tomorrow. We didn't even get to go to our own prom," I say.

"Well, with any luck, we won't have to chaperone. I'm gonna fetch the ladder," he says and heads for the storage room.

Just as he turns the knob, we hear voices approaching, followed by the squeak of the door. A group of bright-eyed students funnels in, one after another.

My first thought is to dive behind Renner and hide.

"Hi, Mr. Renner." A girl in a yellow cardigan greets him cheerfully, the glimmer in her eyes fading when she pans to me. "Ms. Wu."

"See? Dungeon teacher," Renner whispers before turning back to the student. "Oh, hi. What are you doing in here?" he asks, his voice comically low. He sounds like a Marvel villain.

"Decorating for prom," Yellow Cardigan Girl says with perky confidence. I'd bet money she's student council president.

"Right. Um, well, carry on." Renner dips his chin and pulls me into the hallway.

"Where are we going?" I groan, clasping a hand on the doorframe. I can envision soaring off that ladder, out of this nightmare and back to my seventeen-year-old self. "We're so close."

"We can't do this with a bunch of people around," he says matter-of-factly. "We'll have to come back after hours."

He has a point. We certainly don't need witnesses to our ridiculous attempt at time travel. "Fine."

"I'm hungry. Wanna grab breakfast at the breakfast club?" he asks casually.

I use my last morsel of strength to pull myself upright, arrowing my wrath in his direction. "Seriously? That food is for kids in need. And how can you think about food at a time like this? We're stuck here. In the future."

For some reason, I was convinced our plan would work. I'm not sure I could eat until we're back to normal.

"We *are* in need. And we haven't eaten all morning. I'm starved."

"Correction, I didn't eat. You ate the last piece of bread." I leave out the fact that he got toast crumbs all over the counter and just left them there. I'll bank that grievance for another time.

"That hardly counts as a balanced breakfast. I won't make it the rest of the day on toast," he says.

"Get something from the vending machine," I snap, brushing the dirt off my argyle tights.

He flashes me a disappointed look, then pulls his phone from the pocket of his chinos. "Just got a text from Ollie."

"Ollie? What does it say?" I ask, leaning in.

"He's asking what time we're coming for our party tonight."

"Shoot. The epic bachelor/bachelorette." I groan, on the brink of panic. "No, no, no. We can't go. We're coming right back here after work today and returning to 2024."

"Well, yeah, obviously. But if that doesn't work, what then?" He lowers his voice as a couple more students walk toward the gym, arms laden with Mardi Gras decor.

Renner kindly holds the door for them, and I run both hands down my cheeks. Panic is setting in. "We—we keep trying. Until it works."

He levels me with a knowing look. "The party is for us. Besides, aren't you the tiniest bit curious to see everyone?"

I wave him off. Seeing people is dead last on my list of priorities. "We can't go to a party as an engaged couple, Renner. We'll just have to break up."

His face contorts, as though I've suggested we commit mass murder. "You just wanna break up? A week before our wedding?"

"We're not actually engaged!" I peer over at a student with a bowl cut coming toward the gym. Based on his skeptical look and slowing stride, he must have heard me.

Renner flashes his infectious smile. "She's just joking," he says, playfully swinging his arm over my shoulder. He waits for the suspicious student to disappear before whispering, "Char, we can't bail on our own party. Everyone's gonna be there. And remember what Nori said. We need to act as normal as possible until we figure out what's going on. We can't meddle with the future."

He's right. I know he's right. And the last thing I want to do is disappoint Adult Ollie, who was kind enough to throw us this party. Besides, if everyone we love is in the same place, it'll be a good opportunity to collect information. The more information we gather, the better chance we'll have of getting out of this mess.

I emit a labored sigh. "Fine. We'll go. We just have to get through the day," I say, resigned. "Ask Ollie if we need to bring anything."

"He and Lainey have all the food covered."

"Lainey . . . ," I repeat, reminded once again of how much has changed. "How are we about to be married, but Ollie and Kassie broke up?"

Renner shrugs. "Dunno. But we really are in the Upside Down."

THIRTEEN

Future me is a lovesick fool.

Cluttering my desk in the guidance center are seven framed photos of Renner and me. There's another 8 x 10 of us cheesing on the beach affixed to the wall next to my master's in counseling diploma. There's even a Valentine's Day card from 2036 with a cartoon illustration of a single macaroni noodle holding hands with a triangular piece of cheese that reads, *You are the cheese to my macaroni*. The inside of the card is even worse:

> *Happy Valentine's Day, Char. Every year gets better and better with you. I am so thankful to have you in my life. Thanks for putting up with me. Love, J. T.*

This is just obnoxiously extra. What exactly am I trying to prove by displaying all these love tokens in my professional work space?

I pile the particularly nauseating photos into a random drawer in my desk, catching a glimpse of my ring sparkling in the sunlight. I thought about not wearing the ring out of protest today. But it is stunning. I've never owned a piece of jewelry like this—neither has Mom—so I'm wearing the crap out of it, regardless of what it symbolizes.

While I shudder for turning into *that* girl, the one who takes kissing photos and brags about how great her relationship is, at least I have good taste in snacks. I'm about to gorge a Halloween-size Snickers bar and scroll through the unhelpful results of my Google search, Help I've fallen into a wormhole and can't get out, when Leigh, the student administrative assistant, pokes her head in. We met when I needed help signing into my computer. Apparently, future computers rely on iris recognition.

"Ms. Wu? Your nine o'clock appointment is here." She sounds like a Pixar character, not a high school student volunteering for community service hours.

I cough, swallowing a hunk of stale chocolate. "My what?"

"Your nine o'clock appointment," Leigh says sheepishly, adjusting her plaid headband.

Appointment? Shoot. There goes my plan to barricade my office door, hide under my desk all day, and self soothe by eating my way through my stockpile of snacks.

"Uh, sure. Send them in," I say, nervously straightening a pile of papers next to the computer.

Before I have the chance to confess that I'm a fraud, a dude wearing frayed denim shorts and a T-shirt three sizes too large with a photo of his own face across the belly collapses into the chair opposite my desk. "Hi, Ms. Wu."

~

Kyle, my nine o'clock, tells me his name about five times before I remember it. Just like the hedgehog-loving teacher, he asks if I'm okay. He seems like a nice guy, despite his questionable fashion sense and the fact that he smells like he bathed in Axe body spray. Boys of the future still haven't learned.

Turns out, he needs help planning his class schedule for his sophomore year. I have no idea how to pull up the list of potential classes. But Leigh saves the day, working her magic to project Kyle's schedule on the wall.

Luckily, the curriculum is essentially the same. Kyle says he wants to be a welder when he grows up, so I convince him to take all the shop classes he can, as well as math. He leaves the appointment hopeful and optimistic about next year, which makes me feel marginally better about my general ignorance. Maybe I am good at my job, after all.

My eleven o'clock appointment never shows, which gives me ample time to root through my phone. It's full of unanswered texts and emails from wedding vendors. I really should have invested in a wedding planner. Then again, I'm not surprised my adult self doesn't trust anyone else with the logistics.

One text from yesterday catches my eye. It's from Alexandra, Dad's girlfriend.

Alexandra: Hi Charlotte. I just wanted to let you know we won't be able to join you for your party tomorrow night. Both Marianne and Lily caught a nasty bug that's going around at school. We're recovering, but not fully healed. I'm really sorry. We really wanted to be there. But can't wait to see photos and will see you on the wedding day.

I'm shocked. Dad is still with Alexandra after all these years? After his second marriage imploded, I pegged him as a noncommittal guy. But what's even more shocking is that I have sisters. Two, from the sounds of it. And while I knew Alexandra was pregnant, seeing their names in text is entirely different. They're real. They're living, breathing humans.

As I digest that information, it occurs to me that Alexandra is the one texting me. Not Dad. From my phone's history, it looks like Dad and I don't text at all. I guess I shouldn't be shocked that he won't be at my party either. I wonder how many other life events he's missed out on. Frankly, it would be a miracle if he came to my wedding. Not that I'm having one.

Before I can formulate a response, another young teacher slips into my office to vent. Apparently, a nasty girl in her English class created a social media post about her that went viral. She had unknowingly spent an entire class teaching with the back of her dress tucked into her period panties. The girl caught it all on her phone.

"She even hashtagged #missperiodpanties. I swear, I'm at the end of my rope with these little twits."

Her candor catches me off guard. I've never witnessed a teacher reveal their honest feelings about students before.

Before I can offer adequate sympathy, she begins explaining (in detail) the proper technique to express her hairless cat's anal glands with piercing eye contact. What is with teachers at MHS and their strange pets? Then she quickly pivots, asking if I want to go out for lunch since she "owes me" for taking her after-school detention duties all last week. To be fair, she seems cool (despite said cat details), but I politely decline to avoid embarrassing myself or ruining my reputation and rush out to find Renner.

He's in the gym, running drills with a freshman class. Turns out, Gym Teacher Renner is not some chump in a tracksuit with a whistle trying to relive his glory days. In fact, he appears to be living his best life right now. He looks like an A-list actor playing a teacher in a movie. He fills out his button-down and chinos nicely, iPad in hand, brows knitted in concentration as he encourages his students across the gym.

The sight of him makes something inside me flutter. Gym Teacher Renner is kind of, sort of, attractive.

"You look like you were born to do this," I admit, sidling up next to him.

He startles at my presence before giving me a flirty smile. "You think?"

There's a nagging in my gut that makes me wonder if he's disappointed in how his life turned out. Does he regret giving up his dream of coaching a college team to come home and teach high school kids?

"I really couldn't picture you in an authoritative position, but it looks like you've got this coaching thing down," I say, cringing at the sight of a guy doubled over, ready to hurl after running drills.

He abruptly blows his whistle before he can respond. "Hey, man." He points to a kid in red gym shorts. "Your speed is fantastic right out of the gate. But I notice you lose steam a bit at the twenty-yard mark. Let's focus on your endurance," he tells him encouragingly.

The student nods and says, "Thanks, Mr. Renner."

A satisfied smile plays across his lips, like a puppy awaiting approval after learning to sit. "See? They're listening to me."

I clap my hand to my chest. "Wow. I'm surprised you didn't let them run feral and smoke dope behind the bleachers."

He chokes out a laugh. "Dope? You sound like my police officer dad."

"I know." I shrug, owning it. "Hey, wanna have lunch together? Talk strategy for tonight? Apparently, I hoard snacks in my desk . . . along with knitting needles, yarn, and a container of Tums." Adult me is a rip-roaring good time.

This piques his interest. "What kind of snacks?"

"Lots of candy bars. And jumbo bags of chips."

"Flavor?"

"Plain."

He makes a face. "Plain? What kind of sicko are you?"

"Wow. The slander. Plain is delicious, thank you very much."

His lips curve, teasing. "Well, you get to enjoy them all to yourself. I actually need the hour to prep for my health class after lunch."

I raise a brow. This is very unlike Renner. I don't know if I've ever seen him crack open a book. And somehow, he still manages to pull off decent grades.

"It's the STI unit," he clarifies.

"You're teaching sex ed today?" I can barely contain my giggle. I'd give my left arm to sit in on Renner's sex ed class.

He rolls his eyes. "Yeah, yeah, very funny. I'm petrified, I'll have you know."

I snort. "Do they still have the sex ed treasure chest?"

"Oh yeah. It's in my office. It was the first thing I saw when I walked in. It's filled to the brim with condoms. And some dental dams," he adds matter-of-factly. "I'm in over my head."

I pat him on the shoulder sympathetically. For a flash, I think about offering to look over his lesson plan, until I remember we do not have that kind of relationship. We don't help each other. We're enemies, after all. So I settle for, "You'll do just fine."

He cringes. "But what if they have . . . questions?"

"Well, luckily you have a lot of experience," I point out. As rumor has it, Renner lost his V-card in tenth grade to an eleventh grader named Harley at a tent party. Since then, he's practically made his way through the female population of our class, as well as the class below. Not that I care.

He gives me a look. "Are you slut shaming me?"

"Not at all. It's simply a fact."

He squeezes his eyes shut. "Okay, can we not talk about my sex life? I'm freaking out. I'm not qualified to teach shit. This feels illegal."

"More illegal than giving a student advice on their educational future? Probably not. Let's just get through the day without drawing suspicion. Do you have a lesson plan?"

"Yeah. It's in a binder. I'm really into consent and protection, I guess, because I wrote pages' worth of notes," he adds.

"Just read straight from your lesson plan. They won't even notice."

"If only it were that easy . . ."

"Best of luck, Renner. Remember, the sexual health of the next generation rests on your shoulders!" I call back at him before exiting the gym.

FOURTEEN

Renner is like a golden retriever who magically turned human. On our drive to Ollie's, he has his arm out the window, belting all the wrong lyrics to a Glass Animals song (on a 2020s station).

We were never supposed to go to Ollie's. But the gym was occupied all day with students setting up for prom, leaving little privacy for our attempt at time travel. We plan to come back tonight after Ollie's, when all the staff and students are gone.

I flash him a dirty look when he sings, "Sometimes all I do is love youuu," instead of the correct lyrics, though it does nothing to dim his mood.

He's still high from his sex ed class, which was a smashing success. In fact, he proudly declared it a "slam dunk" when he picked me up in the guidance office.

I don't know why I'm surprised. Renner has the uncanny ability to pull everything off regardless of how much effort he puts in. Every time a big test or exam rolls around, I spend every waking hour studying, and he takes pleasure in "winging it." Just like his student council speech.

"I think I got through to them, you know? They seemed like they really wanted to learn," he says for the fourth time in the last three blocks. "Maybe teaching really is what I was meant to do."

"Guess you've found your calling," I say, cringing at the thought of Renner demonstrating how to place a condom on a banana. At the same time, I'm glad he's in better spirits after his parents' divorce news. I could tell that was a real blow.

"Hey, it's a noble one at least," he points out as we pull onto Ollie's crowded street. My heart drops at the sight of his packed driveway and the cars lining up on either side of the road. I'd assumed this was an intimate gathering, despite what Nori said, but it appears she wasn't exaggerating. Ollie invited the entire town.

What used to be a neighborhood full of eighties homes has undergone a makeover. Most of the old houses have been replaced with minimalist, boxy white and gray exteriors. Ollie's place is no exception.

Renner stares through the windshield in awe. "Holy crap. Ollie's rich."

Before I can respond, Renner bolts from the car and starts up the driveway, clearly eager for a reunion with his best friend.

I groan and sprint after him. Just before he unlocks the gate, I yank him back by his veiny forearm. "Wait, wait, wait. We need to talk."

"About what?" He shoots me a quizzical look, eyes flickering to my grip on his arm. His excitement literally radiates through his veins. He's a quintessential extrovert, and the prospect of entering a party gives him life.

I drop his arm. "About how we're going to act?" I shouldn't have to pose this like a question. A question he should certainly have considered by this point.

He slowly blinks. "I'm not following."

I take a step closer, close enough to envy the density of his lash line. "Renner, we're supposedly engaged. Don't you think we should figure out how to act like a couple? We can't just avoid each other at our own party." I hate myself for saying it, but it's true. If we're going to carry on as normal, like Nori suggested, we can't change our behavior too drastically.

"Oh." He feigns disappointment. "Because I was planning to stay six feet apart from you. At all times."

I arrow him with a *get real* look.

"It's funny you mention this, because I recall saying the exact same thing this morning."

I relent. "Fine. You were right. Happy?"

"Yes." He runs a hand through his hair, scanning Ollie's perfectly manicured shrubs. "So what are we talking here? Holding hands? Closed-mouth kissing? A little bit of tongue?"

When he says it like that, so breezy, a thick lump forms in my throat. "Well, no. We don't need to be all over each other. And definitely no kissing. Closed mouth or otherwise."

"No, no," he says, his expression ultraserious. "If we're sticking with the status quo, we don't want anyone to get suspicious. We have to act like we would normally—like we're in love," he advises, a cheeky grin spreading over his face. He holds his hand out. "Come on, wifey."

I mentally face-palm. I shouldn't have said anything at all. Renner loves a challenge. He also takes great pleasure in my embarrassment. This is a lethal combination.

Before I can take the last two minutes of my life back, he's already swung his muscly arm over my shoulder, tucking me snugly into his side. "All right, sugarplum. It's showtime."

I squirm out of his grip. "Please don't call me sugarplum. I'm not a child."

"Honey pie? Honey buns?"

"That sounds geriatric."

"Well, we are thirty. But okay." He resets. "Snookums?"

I fire a warning glare. "Where are you getting these pet names? And no cuddles. Let's just . . . hold hands."

He rolls his eyes, extending his hand again. "Fine." When I slide my fingers between his, he yanks it back, flexing his fingers. "Ouch, is this really how you hold hands?"

"What are you talking about? I hold hands completely normal." I grasp for his hand again, but he pulls it out of my reach.

"No. You have an iron grip."

"My dad says you're supposed to have a strong handshake." This mention of my dad slips out before my brain even registers it. I think Renner is surprised too, because he immediately looks down at his shoes.

I wonder if Dad is here tonight, or if he's buried in a mountain of work and obligations to his new family. Probably the latter. I shove that tiny pang of hope deep, where it belongs. Hoping has never done me any good with Dad.

Renner registers the look on my face and softens his expression. Our eye contact holds for a blink before he shakes his head. "A handshake is different from hand-holding, Char. Just relax for once." He takes my hand again, softly threading his fingers through mine in a way that actually doesn't feel awful. His touch is maybe the tiniest bit comforting given that we're about to enter a party filled with our nearest and dearest—after missing the last thirteen years of our lives.

We walk up the small, groomed path leading to the gated backyard. Awaiting us behind the gate are at least twenty people, who erupt in cheers, whistles, and inappropriate catcalls (mostly from Nori).

Renner tightens his grip on my hand and puts on his charming act as he waves hello.

"There's the couple of the hour," Nori shouts. She's the first to rush forward for a hug before the mob descends.

It's mind-boggling, being face-to-face with everyone you know. Only, everyone's older, including Mom, who's the second to approach with a hearty hug. She looks a mess, as usual, and her long, wavy hair is now streaked with gray. The years have weathered her skin, particularly around her eyes. Renner's dad has aged too. His hair is thinner on top and completely salt and pepper.

"How are you?" Renner asks, embracing him in a weirdly long hug.

His dad shrugs away, seemingly confused by his son's affection. "I'm great. Why wouldn't I be?"

Before Renner can respond, Ollie greets us with two cerulean blue drinks topped with tiny umbrellas. He's still taller than Renner with a wide, tapered athletic frame that Kassie used to fawn over. Only now, he's a little less lean and slightly bulkier. His easy, toothy grin hasn't changed, though. "You two look like you need a drink. Rough day shaping young minds?"

"You could say that," I say with a forced smile. This is so, so weird.

"It's been an interesting one. But I rocked my sex ed class today, so that's a win," Renner announces.

"Right on, man." Ollie gives him a high five.

"Thank you, by the way. You didn't have to do all of this for us," I say, gesturing at the white balloons and lights strung along the fence, and the Mr. and Mrs.–themed plates and napkins on the food table. While Ollie has always been an excellent host, it's clear he really put a lot of thought into tonight.

"Hey, no need to thank me. You guys are my oldest friends. I'd do anything for you, you know that." Ollie's sentimental tone nearly makes me tear up. He and I have always been friendly, but we've never been super close. Part of me wonders if my resentment toward him for taking so much of Kassie's time has gotten in the way of that.

I wish I could say that to him. But instead, I just pull him in for a hug, careful not to spill my blue drink. "You're the best, seriously."

"I did fail on one thing, though. Couldn't get that shrimp dip you like. My dad went rogue and made buffalo chicken dip instead." He gives me an affectionate hair tousle before getting distracted by Renner's uncle Larry, who is desperate to talk to him about the physics of home building. Renner whispers that he's a retired physics professor at Cal Tech and has the world's largest collection of Star Wars memorabilia.

Soon Renner's lost to the crowd, wading through like a member of BTS after a concert. He seems to be having the time of his life chatting with everyone. Meanwhile, I'm awkwardly chilling on the sidelines, eavesdropping on Renner's aunt Lynn telling someone about how she plans to divide her ashes in Mason jars for her family to display on their fireplace mantels. Is this what adults talk about on the regular? I feel like an awkward grade-schooler at recess, walking around the perimeter with no friends to play with.

I pounce when Nori finishes her conversation with Heidi, a girl a grade below us (who I was never even friends with). "Going back to the scene of the crime didn't work?" she asks quietly, offering me a carrot from her plate.

"The gym was occupied all day with students. They're decorating for prom. We're gonna go back tonight when everyone is gone."

"I have a feeling it'll work," she says with confidence. "And if it doesn't, maybe this is all a dream. Maybe you'll wake up tomorrow in your regular life."

Wouldn't that be nice . . .

"Or maybe your memories will come back," she says as though it's that simple. Like at any given moment, more than a decade's worth of memories will return.

I steal another carrot from her plate. "Either way, I don't know how long I can pretend, nodding when people talk to me about anal gland expression."

She doesn't bother to inquire about that one. "You know, when you two first walked in, I thought things had gone back to normal."

"Why would you think that?" I ask, stealing a glance at Renner. He's standing on Ollie's deck, delighting in the attention.

"The way you guys came in holding hands, staring into each other's eyes adoringly. It kind of looked like you wanted to suck his face off." Her eyes are all starry and wistful.

I nearly gag. "Adoringly? No. That was a carefully planned act we agreed upon two seconds before walking in."

She winks at me, crunching a celery stick loaded with ranch dip. "All I'm sayin' is, you coulda fooled me. You looked blissfully engaged."

I see what she's getting at and I won't be lured. "I won't be marrying that man," I say, holding stubborn.

"Suit yourself. But if I had someone who looked at me like that, I wouldn't be in a rush to ditch them, even if I were trapped in an AU—" Nori stops, eyes widening over my shoulder.

When I turn around, everyone is staring at me. Renner is beside Ollie, waving me over.

"What's going on?" I ask through clenched teeth, approaching tentatively.

"They want us to give a speech," he whispers, tugging me by the hand.

Oh no.

My knees instantly weaken. See, I'm good at public speaking. Speeches are my bitch. But I cannot speak off the cuff. Speeches take planning. Forethought. Word-for-word memorization. I can't cope without my color-coded cue cards.

Before I have the chance to spiral and run away, Renner kicks things off. "Char and I just wanted to thank each and every one of you for being here tonight. Especially Ollie and Lainey for generously hosting. It's rare to have everyone we love in one place, but Char and I are so thankful to have you all in our lives."

My fingers, which were locked tightly between his, loosen ever so slightly as he begins speaking with surprising ease. How is he so relaxed right now?

"To be honest, I'm just as surprised as you all are to be standing here tonight. As many of you may recall, Char hated me in high school. And I mean *hated*." Everyone laughs good-naturedly as Renner gives me a wink. I swear his eyes are sparkling. "Many hours were dedicated to pissing each other off. I learned very quickly that there are three surefire ways to annoy Char. First, being tardy. In fact, half the time she's not even satisfied with being on time. If you're not early, you're late. Second, singing the wrong lyrics with any ounce of confidence. Third, losing. She cannot stand to lose. Board games. Bets. Student council elections." He lets that one linger, smirking at me when I shoot him a look.

"Shit. Thirteen years still too soon for that joke," he says, garnering more laughs and a loud snort from Mom. "I'm shocked I'm still alive after that election. Anyway, I never really knew what started it all . . . and still don't. I never told her this, but the truth is, I was in awe of her from the moment we met. She's always the smartest, most driven, most beautiful person in any room. And maybe my teenage self felt intimidated.

"Either way, no one could get under my skin like Char. And she still does to this day, let's be honest. There've been days where I thought I couldn't stand her, but I found myself thinking about her when we were apart. All the time. Somehow, through all the fighting, she wormed her way into my heart." He tightens his grip around my hand and looks directly into my eyes. "Ever since then, my life has been fuller, happier, and infinitely better with you by my side instead of against me. Together, we're infinite. Beyond. And I think I just plagiarized *Toy Story*. But the point is, Char, I cannot wait to spend the rest of my life with you."

The crowd goes wild for his speech. I'm having déjà vu of the applause after Renner's student council campaign speech. Maybe Renner's calling isn't teaching gym. Maybe he should be a professional speechwriter. Or a motivational speaker.

I don't know who started shouting "Kiss her," though I suspect it was Ollie. But soon, everyone is cheering us on, clinking their cups, and demanding a kiss.

"Come on, give her a kiss," Renner's aunt yells, phone poised to capture the moment on video.

My eyes meet Renner's, and we exchange a look that silently says, *Shit*. But then the corner of his lip raises in that signature smile and my breath hitches. My head whirls with a foreign feeling, something I don't quite recognize.

"We don't have to . . . if you don't want to," he whispers.

"Um, I—" He loosens his hand around my waist, sensing my reluctance. Every logical, rational part of me says that J. T. Renner is the absolute last person in the world I want to kiss. But not kissing him at our own engagement party, in front of all our friends and family, would only lead to suspicion. Right?

For a hot second, I'm entranced. Hoodwinked by his unnatural gift with words. By the way the orange sky has illuminated the tiny gold flecks in his green eyes like tiny, fiery beacons. I imagine I'm character in a movie. The main character who withstands a torrential downpour and subsequent pneumonia, all for that grand gesture. The character who throws caution to the wind and accepts another's love.

And I do it. I kiss him.

FIFTEEN

I've kissed three guys in my life, but I've never been the kisser. The one who leans in and makes first contact.

And now I know why.

Renner isn't expecting my lips to crash into him like a Mack Truck. As I close in, his eyes widen like saucers in abject terror.

But it's too late. I've propelled myself forward with too much momentum. Our noses smash together, punctuated by the hard clank of my teeth against his upper lip. And there it is, the faintest metallic taste of blood.

Ouch.

Nonetheless, we've done it. We've kissed, at least in the technical sense.

"There," I say through an epic sigh of relief, the tips of my fingers zipping with adrenaline as I pull back.

I expect anger or frustration for ruining the show. But instead, the corners of his eyes crinkle in amusement. "Was that . . . a kiss?" he whispers, eyes trained on mine, as though we're the only people in this backyard. As if all eyes aren't on us.

"I think so?"

He pulls me in and chuckles softly, chest rising against mine. "Somehow that's worse than your hand-holding. You nearly knocked my teeth out." He touches his front teeth, feigning concern that they're still there.

If I had to kiss Renner, why did I do it so poorly? In front of a crowd, no less. He doesn't have anything else to razz me about.

He leans in to try again, forehead grazing mine. From this angle, I can see the thick swoop of his lashes. The slight cluster of freckles dusting the bridge of his nose. The way his lips quiver as I inch closer.

He tilts his head to the left, running his thumb over my jawline to cup my chin, leaving me breathless. His lips slide into an earnest grin that nearly sends me adrift. It reminds me of that very first day of school. For that moment on the bleachers, I'd been charmed by his sunlight. His effortless smile. That intoxicating lemony scent.

I only realize I'm shaking when he squeezes my hand, which manages to slow the wild thrash of my heart.

Unlike me, he comes in slow and tentative. *This is how it's done,* his body says, catching my bottom lip with a softness I didn't know him capable of. His lips draw apart, then slide back together, a little deeper than before. His beard hair tickles the side of my face ever so slightly, lighting up every cell in my body. Our lips melt together seamlessly in a way I've never felt. Like opposites colliding. It feels safe, yet electrifying.

A part of me, a part I didn't know existed, is desperate to pull him closer, run my fingers through his thick, silky hair, recapture his lips with mine. But he pulls back.

Before I can register what the hell just happened, he's lapping up praise from the party guests. He shouts something to my mom that I can't hear over my ringing ears.

And then he leans in and says, "Nice show, huh?"

Whoop, there it is. None of what just happened was real. It was all for show. The speech. The kiss. Because of course it was.

Renner deserves an Oscar for that performance.

~

For the rest of the night, our guests ogle us like we're some famous penguin couple in a zoo. Renner's speech fooled everyone.

Since our kiss, there's a heightened awareness between us. It's like whenever Clay enters the classroom and my heart cartwheels. I get a little clammy, my hands clench in my lap, and I can't help but wonder if everyone notices how freakin' weird I'm acting.

Not that I have a crush, by any means, but Renner is in my peripheral vision no matter where I go in Ollie's backyard. Maybe I'm just being paranoid, but I keep catching his eyes lingering on me too. When I'm not being awkward, stuffing my face with Tostitos and heaping buffalo chicken dip, I master the art of evasion. I deflect difficult questions like, *Are you excited for the wedding? Do you think you'll cry when you walk down the aisle?* It's easy enough, so long as I remain vague and avoid the temptation to tell everyone it's canceled. And after seeing the joy on my mom's face, we'll need to think of a gentle way to drop that bomb.

Unfortunately, Renner is making me look like a total nitwit. I overhear him telling everyone about our elaborate five-hundred-guest wedding. He includes oddly specific tidbits, claiming Pizza Hut is catering the affair, that we're having a chocolate fondue fountain, a rose archway, a ten-piece live band, a skating rink, fireworks, Cirque du Soleil acrobats, and exotic animals casually moseying around the premises. I've seen enough reality TV to know that most of the time, husbands remain aloof and uninterested in wedding planning. Renner is not one of those men.

I corner him near the hot tub. "Why do you keep telling everyone we're having an elaborate wedding?" I whisper, glancing over my shoulder to ensure no one is eavesdropping. According to Nori, we have a strict budget for our 150-person wedding at a resort near Fairfax, near Dad and Alexandra's lake house.

He shrugs, leaning his weight against the hot tub. "Why not? Go big or go home."

"We aren't getting married, first of all. And even if we were, which we aren't, I'm not blowing my life savings on one day."

"The most special day of your life," he corrects.

"Nope. If anything, we should have chosen to elope."

He covers his mouth like I've confessed to murder. "Eloping isn't my style."

"This is so typical. Tossing out my ideas without consideration. What's so wrong with a small, intimate wedding? It's romantic. Not that we're aiming for romance here, but—"

He furrows his brow. "You're saying you don't want to be surrounded by friends and family on your big day?"

"I mean, a handful. Not the entire town." I don't know why I'm even arguing. Of course Renner would be foaming at the prospect of a day all about him. He wouldn't give up that opportunity.

He tips his head to the side. "Why are you trying to convince me to elope when you just said we're canceling?"

I blink, coming to my senses. "Right. We aren't actually getting married. We're getting out of here. Tonight," I remind him. But he doesn't hear me. He's distracted by a new arrival, his mom.

He was right when he said there was something different about her, aside from being more than a decade older. I've only seen Renner's mom a handful of times. She was always naturally stunning, but a little worn with dark circles under her eyes, like a woman weighed down by life.

That isn't the woman I see today. Her face has filled out, her skin practically glows, and she radiates joy, from her eyes to her smile.

A slightly balding man in a polo shirt with a lumberjack frame follows close behind her. It's only when the crowd parts that I see they're holding hands. Renner's mom is holding hands with . . . a man who isn't his dad.

Renner looks like he's seen a ghost, eyes darting from them to his dad at the other end of the yard, who waves casually as they enter. I can tell from Renner's expression that he didn't know about this new guy.

An ache settles deep at the base of my stomach. Instinctively, I place my hand on his shoulder, but he heads inside through the sliding door.

Against my better judgment, I follow him into Ollie's gleaming white kitchen. Renner's making himself busy, collecting random soda cans and tossing them into the blue bin with excessive force.

"I'm sorry, Renner. Your mom didn't mention him this morning?"

His lips tighten as he tosses another can in the bin. "Nope." His eyes pierce through the kitchen window toward his mom and her new boyfriend on the deck.

I think this is the first time I've ever seen Renner not smiling, not the life of the party, at an event. Even when he's arguing with me, he's usually emitting an aura of nonchalance that makes me want to slap him. He's never shown weakness, no matter what hurtful words I toss at him. But right now, sagged over the counter, he seems stripped of all that Renner-like energy. He looks flat-out sad. I don't like it. At all.

"For what it's worth, your mom seems really happy," I say gently.

"She does. Happier than I've ever seen her, actually." His eyes are a little misty as he watches her through the window. "I guess I can't really be upset."

I inch closer. "You can be. I get it," I say, surprised at the words coming out of my mouth. I never thought I could really relate to Renner. "My parents never really fought in front of me, or if they did, they hid it well. So when my dad left, it felt so . . . out of the blue."

He lowers his shoulders and gives me a sympathetic glance. "That must have been really hard."

"It was." My body eases as a new, unfamiliar energy passes between us. It's not hatred or judgment or annoyance. It feels a little bit like understanding.

The sound of the sliding door interrupts my thoughts. Nori and Lainey come charging into the kitchen—a little tipsy—in search of hot dog buns.

Renner slips back into the yard and I take refuge in the washroom, sitting atop Ollie's sleek toilet that doubles as a high-tech bidet. The water-pressure options are endless. It even illuminates the water in your choice of color.

Just as I begin to relish the solitude and cool tiles on my feet, there's a knock on the bathroom door.

"Hon? You in there?"

"Mom?" I call.

"It's me. Let me in. I need to pee!"

I open the door and she waltzes in, all smiles, a little flushed from the alcohol. "Gosh, this is the tenth time I've peed in an hour."

"I think you just really love the bidet."

She smirks. "I have a love-hate relationship with it. The first time I tried, I got splashed directly in the mouth. But it has a heated seat so I think I can forgive." She rattles on about the various features for the entire length of her pee before pausing to study my face. "You seem a little . . . overwhelmed tonight. All the attention getting to you?"

"I just . . . I don't know," I say, dazed, afraid to say too much.

"You don't know about what?"

"Everything. The wedding . . ."

She peers at me. "You're not getting cold feet, are you?"

You could say that. "What if I was? I mean, do you really think I'm ready for marriage? I'm only seven—" I stop myself. "Thirty."

"You've always been more mature than everyone your age." She sighs. "I'm not one to talk when it comes to marriage advice, but I do know this. I've never seen you happier than when you're with J. T."

"You say that like I was never happy without him."

"It's just . . . you've always been so careful. Grounded. Unwilling to let loose and have fun." Her expression darkens. "I know it's because of me. That you aways felt like you had to keep things together. But he brings out a side of you I haven't seen since before Dad left."

There's a lot to unpack there, too much for this moment, so I settle for, "Speaking of Dad . . . he's not here. Shocker."

She levels me with her look. "You know he would be here if he could."

Would he, though?

"Speaking of the wedding, do you still want me to come by your room early for hair and makeup?" she asks. "I know they're doing the bridal party first but—"

My mind snags on her words. "Bridal party," I repeat, flooded with the memory of Kassie and me tanning on her deck that first summer we met, scrolling through wedding dress photos on her mom's tablet.

"As my future maid of honor, you're obligated to tell me if the dress I pick is as atrocious as this one," she'd said, cringing at a couture dress made exclusively of feathers.

"Wait. You want me to be your maid of honor?" I asked, eyes wide and hopeful. We'd only been friends for a month.

Being her friend already felt like winning the lottery. But being her designated future maid of honor was something entirely different. I felt like a teen hero in a fantasy novel who was prophesied to save the world. The chosen one.

And that's when it hits me. Kassie isn't here tonight. Where is she?

"Mom? Who's in my wedding party?" I ask.

"Your wedding party?" she repeats, bewildered. "You decided to have one person each, remember? J. T. has Ollie, you have Nori."

I shake my head. "No. I wouldn't leave Kassie out."

She shoots me a funny look. "Kassie? You haven't spoken to Kassie in years. You aren't friends anymore."

"We're not?" I blink, unable to compute.

"At least, not that I'm aware of. You drifted apart. Are you sure you're okay?"

My mouth dries and my stomach twists and turns, as though someone's wrung it like a dishcloth.

Drifted apart. The words grate, refusing to settle in my gut. There must be a reason. Some sort of falling-out. Bad blood. A fight or disagreement that knocked us off course. Drifting apart is neutral, almost cold. Did we really just apathetically decide not to put any more effort in? That our friendship was no longer worth it? Somehow apathy hurts more than any theoretical fight we could ever have. Because here's the thing. You fight with people you love. You ignore people you don't care about. Kind of like Dad.

I clutch my gut, afraid I might hurl.

How could this even happen? I don't believe for one moment that I'd just let us "drift apart" for no solid reason.

Mom keeps talking, but her words are echoey and garbled, as though we're stuck in a fishbowl. All I can hear is the blood rushing through my ears. I repeat the words again silently. *Kassie and I haven't spoken in years. We aren't friends anymore.* Everything has changed.

I need to get out of here. Now.

SIXTEEN

Please work. Please work," I plead to whatever cosmic force is to blame for this mess. Beads of sweat pour down my forehead as I scan my pass on the school door for the fifth time. No dice.

Renner sighs from his perch, slumped against the door. "It's locked, Char."

After the bathroom at Ollie's, Renner and I went straight to the school with an unspoken urgency, entirely forgetting that it's locked after hours for security purposes. I learned this when Ms. Chouloub and I got locked out after Halloween dance prep. We had to store the leftover decor in her car overnight.

I rattle the door again, kicking it for good measure, as if it will magically open with my rage.

"We'll have to come back tomorrow morning. Students will be here to finish decorating before prom," Renner says.

"But we can't wait until tomorrow morning. I can't stay here!" My voice echoes into the dark night.

I can't stay in a world where I've lost thirteen years and I'm marrying Renner. And I can't stay in a world where Kassie isn't my friend. It feels criminal that she wasn't at my bachelorette. And even more criminal that I didn't choose her as my maid of honor. She should be by my side, taking pictures with me, holding my bouquet during the ceremony, telling me to straighten my back, and giving a charming speech about how she's my *real* other half.

"You think I want to stay here?" Renner counters.

"There has to be another way. We could go through an open window."

"All the windows are closed. I already looked," he says.

"Well, if we can't go through . . ." Panicked, I hastily scan our surroundings for anything. Literally anything. My sight zeroes in on a large rock in the garden along the pathway. I like to think I'm the opposite of impulsive. I always think before acting, probably too much. But right now, that cautious side of me is drowned out by desperation. Before I know it, the rock is in my hand and I'm flinging it toward the window.

Renner screams something I can't hear as the glass shatters into a million pieces, shards of all sizes clattering to the pavement.

Holy crap. I just shattered a window and tried to break into the school like a common criminal.

Who am I?

A piercing alarm sounds, and we both cover our ears to block the screeching.

Renner is taken aback, his eyes wide and body still until he snaps into action. *"Run!"* he bellows before sprinting away from the school premises.

We're off like a pair of bats from hell, tearing down the dimly lit street at full tilt. The cool night air stings my lungs. As we round the corner for our car, a police cruiser comes out of nowhere, speeding down the street toward us.

We have a split second to decide if we should go left to the walking trail or right into a six-foot arborvitae privacy hedge. We both dive right.

A branch pokes me in the eye as I huddle into a small alcove of bush next to Renner. It's kind of cozy, except I'm wheezing and dried shrubbery prickles my knees. The scent of damp wood and cedar elicits a violent sneeze.

"Shh!" Renner warns, shooting me a furious glare.

"Oh, like I did it on purpose," I whisper, brushing my forearm frantically at the tickle of something crawling across my arm. I don't even want to know what evil lurks in here.

Renner's arm grazes mine as he parts the branches to peek out. "The police cruiser is going by super slow," he whispers. "I think . . . I think it's Cole." He says *Cole* like he's his close drinking buddy, and I remember that Renner's dad is the chief of police. Or at least, he was, thirteen years ago.

"I forgot. You're above the law," I snap, while also letting out a sigh of relief. Renner's connections could come in handy.

"Nah, I'd still rather not get grounded." He sits, knees to his chest, as the cruiser does yet another slow drive-by.

"Grounded? Try *arrested*. We're adults, Renner. I wouldn't fare well in prison." I'm far too frail to make my own shiv and use it with any amount of gusto. This is the last thing I need.

"Ugh. Neither would I."

I shrug. "True. You'd be in for it. Your face kinda screams privilege," I say out of pure frustration.

"Well, in the end, you're the one who broke the window," he notes.

He has a point. But I can't let him have it. "You're the one who—who—"

"What? What else are you gonna blame on me now?"

I contemplate rattling off my list, which I have committed to memory for moments like this. But I don't have the energy.

A couple silent moments pass before he peeks through the greenery again. "I think they're gone."

I scramble to follow Renner out of the bush, looking both ways to ensure the police cruiser is gone before trotting back to our car.

We drive in silence for a few minutes before Renner finally clears his throat. "Want me to drop you off somewhere for the night?"

The coldness of his question catches me off guard. "I like how you assume I'll go somewhere else while you get the house. Besides, where am I gonna go?"

"Your mom's?"

"No." I'd contemplated staying with Mom, but from the looks of her texts (Are you sick? Do you need anything? It's normal to have cold feet! I'm sorry if mention of Dad upset you. Let's talk!), she's already worried about me after Ollie's. The last thing I need is her trying to counsel me out of what she thinks is some sort of quarter-life crisis.

"Nori's? Kassie's?"

Mention of Kassie's name feels like a knife twist to the heart. "Kassie and I aren't friends anymore," I say, turning my gaze to the passenger window. Renner is heading toward our house.

"Not shocked."

"Excuse me?"

He scoffs. "You really have no idea why you wouldn't be friends with Kassie anymore?"

"What's that supposed to mean?"

He rolls his eyes. "Never mind."

"Is it really that big a stretch to think Kassie would be friends with someone like me?"

No response, which somehow angers me even more.

I growl, unfastening my seat belt the moment we pull into the driveway, desperate to get Renner out of my sight. "You're unbelievable. Can you ever just keep your judgments to yourself?"

He juts his chin out, exiting the car. "That's rich, coming from you. All you ever do is judge people."

"That's not true."

"It is. And you'll never admit it. You refuse to listen to anyone else and see things from different points of view."

I steel my spine as I follow him into the house, slamming the front door behind us. "And you do? You fight me on everything. Every. Single. Thing. You've made student council a living hell."

He pinches his brow. "And you haven't made it hell for me too? I hoped it could be something we did together, and instead, you've made it World War III."

"Because you don't deserve to be president!" I bellow, shocking both of us, before stomping into the kitchen. It doesn't feel right to yell at him, but it's like the dam has finally burst from four years of pent-up anger toward him. I can't hold it in, as much as I want to. "You just breeze through life on your personality alone. King of Maplewood High. You even found a job that allows you to never grow up. Some of us don't get the luxury of playing with condoms all day, Renner!" My voice cracks with regret as soon as it all comes out.

I'm about to utter an apology when he says, "See? You just proved my point. Judgy. Do you even hear yourself?"

Sensing it's too late to put the genie back in the bottle, I revert to defense mode, my default around Renner. "I'm not in a good headspace. My life just imploded. I've involuntarily traveled through time. We're somehow getting married."

"I'm in the same situation as you, Char. You're not the only one stuck in this nightmare. Why would I ever choose to get engaged to you, of all people?" he practically hisses, though the softness of his brow doesn't match the anger in his voice.

"Believe me, the feeling is mutual."

"You're impossible to talk to." He turns on his heel and waltzes out of the kitchen.

I barely have time to let out a breath before he stomps back in like a petulant child.

"I'm still hungry," he says, pulling the fridge open. He lets out a frustrated groan at the state of it. "And we have no food. Great."

I shrug. "What am I supposed to do about that? I'm not your mother."

"I'm not asking you to make me anything."

"Good! Because I'm not!" I shout. Now it's my turn to march out of the kitchen. "You're sleeping in the guest room tonight."

"Gladly."

His blasé attitude doesn't sit well with me. "Go to hell, Renner," I call over my shoulder.

"Yeah, I'll save you a seat," he calls after me.

SEVENTEEN

This is officially the longest day of my life.

My body is drained. My eyes are sore. I need rest. But my mind won't stop racing through all the events of the day. From waking up to a naked Renner, to biking to Mom's work, to school, to the party, to running from the cops, to a brutal fight with Renner.

It doesn't help that Renner is downstairs loudly banging pots and pans. Whatever he's making, it smells delicious. Hearty. I realize I'm hungry for something substantial; I've barely eaten anything other than snacks at school and dip at Ollie's party. But I'd rather starve than go back downstairs and face him.

The fact is, I'm embarrassed. I owe him an apology for blowing up. I didn't intend to lose my temper. He didn't deserve it. He's in the same boat as me, technically. Not to mention, being angry at each other isn't going to help our situation.

A soft knock at the bedroom door interrupts my thoughts.

"Come in," I say, bracing myself.

Renner opens the door, juggling two heaping bowls of mac 'n' cheese sprinkled with what appears to be bread crumbs and pepper. There's steam billowing from the bowl. It reminds me of the mac-'n'-cheese-themed Valentine's Day card I found in my office.

"I wasn't sure if you'd want some," he says. His expression is relaxed, normal.

I eye the bowls like a starved hyena. "You just whipped this up?"

"Found a couple boxes in the back of the pantry. They might be expired. So eat at your own risk," he warns, handing me the bowl.

I take it gingerly, my annoyance fading. The ceramic is piping hot on my fingertips. Somehow, this makes me feel even worse. "Thank you."

When our eyes meet again, my heart lodges in my throat. I know I have to apologize, but the words won't leave my lips. Frankly, I'm just exhausted from the day, and from him. I hate how good he is in every situation, even one as ridiculous as this. I hate how amazing that kiss was. And I hate how he knows exactly how to push my buttons. And I'm afraid if I say anything else, he'll push yet another one.

I shove my feelings down and eagerly heap a forkful in my mouth, delighting in all its glory. Boxed mac 'n' cheese has never tasted so divine. I pause and eye him suspiciously; he hasn't taken a bite yet. "You haven't laced this, have you?"

"With what?" he asks innocently.

"Dunno. Rat poison. Bleach. Heavy drugs?"

"I searched the house high and low for poison, but looks like we're all out," he says, deadpan.

Poison or not, I'm too hungry to care. I take another giant forkful, contemplating whether I should tell him about the cheesy (pun intended) Valentine's Day card he gave me. "This is . . ."

He gives me his cocksure grin and watches me devour it. "Told you I can make a mean mac 'n' cheese."

"How do you even know I was going to compliment it? What if I was about to say it was disgusting?"

"You practically moaned when you took that first bite. I knew you liked it." The tips of his ears are pink.

My body erupts in prickles of heat. I chalk it up to my piping-hot meal, flannel pajamas, and thick duvet. "Well, it's good. Really good," I admit. If he did sneak in poison, at least I'll die satisfied.

"Consider it my peace offering."

"Peace offering?"

He nods. "I'm sorry about tonight. I lost my patience. I was just . . . really disappointed the school doors were locked and—"

"Me too. I appreciate the food. You didn't have to bring me any. I was being . . . extra."

"My dad always made my mom food when she was mad at him," he tells me. In all the chaos over Kassie, I forgot Renner's pain over seeing his mom with someone new. Our eyes lock in a moment of mutual understanding.

"Really?"

"Yup. Dad doesn't like to go to bed angry. Always tries, or at least tried, to make up with her before they went to sleep." His face falls. "Not that it did him any good, I guess . . ."

"I'm sorry," is all I can think to say.

"Kinda hard to be mad when they're in a better place now."

"Your feelings are still valid, Renner. This morning, when I found out my dad was having a baby—" I stop myself. Technically it wasn't *this morning*. "This is so weird. Anyway, I knew I should be happy for him. And I still felt . . . sad? I knew it was selfish. But I think it's still fair to let yourself have your feels for a little while. You only just found out."

"Thanks, Char." He pauses, lips twitching in a devious smile. "Hey, we just got through our first fight."

I level him with a look. "Our first fight? Try our millionth fight."

"True. But our first fight as a couple," he points out.

"Well, hopefully it'll be our last."

He turns toward the doorway. "Let's hope. I'll let you get some sleep. Night, fiancée."

"We're not a couple," I remind him. "We're trauma bonded."

He dips his chin in agreement. "Fair."

"Have a good sleep. We need to be well rested for tomorrow," I advise.

"What's tomorrow?"

"The day we go back to 2024," I say with faux confidence. "We're gonna work together and get back to our normal lives. Whatever it takes."

"Deal. Operation Back to Seventeen commences."

EIGHTEEN

So . . . are you, uh, gonna climb up?" Renner's baritone voice echoes around the gym.

We got here bright and early before any of the prom decorators arrived to do finishing touches, thanking our lucky stars the doors were unlocked.

"When I get to the top, I just . . . jump off?" I ask, white-knuckling the ladder, hands shaking.

"Yeah, exactly like last time. No big deal." He's trying his best to sound casual, like hurling one's self from the top of a ladder is a perfectly normal thing to do. But by the tightness of his jaw, I can tell he's nervous too.

We've propped the ladder against the same wall, in the same position, slightly to the right of the basketball net. Though it somehow looks higher than before. But I suppose from the view of someone who may be about to plunge to their death, the perspective changes.

Renner gestures to the ladder, stepping forward to stabilize it. I'm hesitant until his chest inadvertently grazes my back, which sets me off like a "Go" button.

When I reach the top, my stomach lurches. I train my eyes to the mats we set up around the ladder, just in case. Not that they'll do much to break my fall if this doesn't work.

If this doesn't work. I wince. The possibility is too depressing to comprehend. Mind you, we probably should have more than one viable plan for Operation Back to Seventeen. At least a measly backup plan. But we haven't quite gotten there yet.

Just as I psych myself up for the fall, Renner calls up, "You better hurry. Students are gonna start coming in soon."

"Please don't rush me," I snap, my full body shaking. "I'd like to see you voluntarily hurl yourself off the top of this ladder."

"Oh, I'm sure you would love to see that." He pauses, bottling his attitude. "And don't *hurl* yourself off. Just kind of, let yourself glide down gently."

"I don't know what you've been doing during science class, but gravity does not work that way."

He pokes me in the calf. "Hey, we agreed we aren't arguing anymore, remember? We need to work together to get out of this. Bickering isn't gonna help."

I hesitate. Bickering is simply our natural state. But he's right. We have no hope in hell of getting out of here if we spend the entire time fighting. "True." I hold my breath and stare down at him. It's now or never. The sooner I jump, the sooner I'll be back in my regular life, seventeen again, and *not* engaged to Renner.

One . . .

Two . . .

Three . . .

When I force my eyes open, I'm straddling Renner, legs splayed like a frog on either side of his body.

I blink a couple times, slowly taking in the surroundings. We're in the gym, on the dusty, narrow plank wood floor. Good news, we didn't hurtle ourselves into some other alternate dimension.

Bad news, when the wiry hair of Renner's beard tickles my forehead, I know I'm still thirty, C cups and all. Ugh.

At least I'm not in as much pain as I was when I woke up yesterday morning.

Apparently, I've uttered that thought out loud, because Renner lets out a derisive snort. "Yeah, I broke your fall with my body."

This alerts me to the fact that I'm on top of Renner, pressed into him like a panini. He grips both sides of my waist, gentler than I thought him capable. Our eyes snag for a second before he lets out a deep groan that jolts me with a fleeting spark of electricity. In my defense, this is just a normal biological reaction to having your entire body pressed into someone else's. These feelings are perfectly normal, right?

"You're still crushing me," he says with another low groan.

Our lingering eye contact is replaced with mutual *ick* before I roll off him. I make quick work to get back on my feet. "Let's try again."

Five ladder falls later, we're no closer to going back in time.

Laden with disappointment, and bruises, we find our way into the student council room down the hall. It feels more familiar than going to our offices. We've spent countless hours parked at the table, poring over lists, invoices, and logistics. It also happens to be where Renner and I have had some of our most dramatic arguments, like the homecoming-float debacle.

Renner flings himself onto the worn couch (the same lumpy orange couch we had in 2024), long legs dangling over the end. "Now what?"

"We brainstorm how to get out of here," I say, whipping out a spare notepad from the bookshelf, which contains MHS yearbooks dating back to the 1960s. "Let's separately brainstorm a list of ideas. Then we'll evaluate options and choose the best course of action."

He smirks. "How did I know you were gonna suggest a list?"

I rip off a piece of lined paper from the pad and toss it into his lap. "When in doubt, make a list."

"Do you keep lists for everything?"

"Absolutely everything. Including your hostile acts of aggression toward me."

His laughter echoes throughout the room. "Care to share what's on this list?"

"Stealing the presidency from me, for one."

"Okay, Donald Trump."

I clasp my chest. "Wow. I pride myself on my golden, non-orange skin tone, thank you very much."

He lets out another laugh. "Sorry. That was a terrible joke."

"Anyways, you did steal the presidency from me. You knew it was my dream. Everyone did. I'd been working for it every year leading up to twelfth grade. And you just swooped in without a platform and snatched it."

"Not everything is about you, Char." His mouth tugs up on one side.

"But I needed it. For college."

"I wanted it too. For scholarships."

My stomach dips. Mostly because I'd assumed he did it purely in jest. "Really? You're going to college on scholarship?"

"Yup." He nods. "My mom hasn't worked in years. My parents aren't the best at saving money. They didn't tell me I'd need to fund my own way until eleventh grade. And by September, it was too late to join any of the "smart" clubs, and I knew student council would be a shoo-in."

I lower my chin. Had I known Renner needed it on his résumé for college too, would I have taken the loss so badly? It's hard to say. But it does lessen my grudge, if only slightly. "Well, for the record, you were right. You were a shoo-in. Everyone loves you and you don't even have to try. You could walk up to someone and punch them in the gut and they'd still adore you. Do you know how annoying that is?"

"So you've told me." We have a weird moment of silence before he interrupts with a loud yawn and stretch. "All right. Let's make a list."

Brainstorming is one of my talents. It's where I excel in group projects. And yet, as I stare at the blank page, I can't help but watch Renner. He's slouched over, writing furiously in his chicken scratch, crossing things out, strumming his bearded chin. Meanwhile, I'm seemingly incapable of thinking about anything other than how his lips felt against mine yesterday.

I remember the way my breath caught against his mouth. The strum of his heartbeat against my chest. The way his low hum sizzled through me like a jolt of electricity.

Focus, Charlotte.

I can't let my mind go there. Of all the moving parts in my life with my parents, Mom's general chaos, the stress of senior year, having Renner as my rival has been my one constant. But this truth has suddenly flipped everything on its head.

Fifteen agonizing minutes tick by, and I have a total of three crappy bullet points to show for it. Renner, seeming to notice my lack of ideas, slides his two completely filled pages across the table for my viewing pleasure.

I pull the papers toward me. "Renner, you just listed a bunch of time-travel movies," I say, tone cut with disappointment. *Tomorrow War. Avengers: Endgame. The Adam Project. That movie with the ginger guy.*

He remains unruffled. "Hear me out. Maybe we should watch these movies for inspiration. Like, look at this one." He points to *Outlander*. "This is a TV show about a woman who accidentally goes back in time after touching some ancient magical stone in Scotland. My mom is obsessed with it. Even went on an *Outlander* tour in Scotland with my aunt a couple years ago. And guess what? Those stones exist. She took pictures with them."

"Magical stones? Really, Renner?" I flop myself back into the chair, aggrieved. "What are we supposed to do? Fly to Scotland in search of this magic stone?"

"Hey, this is called *brainstorming*. I brainstormed. More than you from the looks of it." He lifts his chin in the direction of my paper.

"Point taken. But the time travel in most of these movies is possible because of futuristic technology. We don't have a time machine. Or a magical stone."

He runs his finger along the arm of the couch. "Well, let's think about it. We got here by falling off a ladder. Obviously, falling off the ladder isn't working. But maybe it's something super simple like that."

"I don't know. Yesterday I tried falling off my bike, slapping myself. Everything short of hurling myself into oncoming traffic. Nothing worked."

He squints, resting his chin on his fist. "There has to be something. I listed some other ideas on the back." When he reaches to flip the page, our fingers brush ever so slightly, eliciting that tingling sensation again.

Am I really that desperate for affection? I stomp down the fireflies in my belly and continue looking at Renner's list.

"Bermuda Triangle?" I read aloud, barely holding back a whimper.

"Well, what are your ideas, then?" He reaches for my list. "Time machine, magical wardrobe, and police," he rattles off. "Really, Char?" When he says them out loud, they do seem pretty bad. Though the prospect of curling into a ball and remaining motionless in a dark wardrobe would be preferable to our strange reality.

I hang my head in my hands. "We need help. Outside help from an actual adult."

"We are adults."

"An adultier adult."

He looks at me like I've lost my mind. "We just ran from the cops last night, in case you forgot. You really want to walk into the police station and tell them we've come from the past?"

"Okay, when you say it like that, it sounds ridiculous."

"That's because it is. To the average person. Especially the police. We don't want to wind up committed in a hospital or something. We can't tell anyone, Char."

"There has to be someone out there who believes in time travel. A psychic maybe?"

His eyes light up. "Wait. I might know someone. My uncle Larry."

“He’s a psychic?” I try picturing him flipping tarot cards in front of a beaded curtain.

“No. Remember I told you he used to be a physics professor? He studied wormholes. Time travel.”

I bolt up. “We have to go see him right now.”

Renner seems to like this plan, following me out. “All right. Let’s go see Uncle Larry.”

NINETEEN

Renner wasn't exaggerating Uncle Larry's collection of Star Wars memorabilia. When we stepped onto his porch, there was a mat that read WELCOME YOU ARE accompanied by a picture of Yoda's face. Turns out, he has a second mat inside that says THE FORCE IS STRONG, WITHOUT SHOES.

The living room contains a life-size statue of a Stormtrooper next to a china cabinet filled with delicate action figures and a Death Star made of LEGO. The lamp on the side table even has a Darth Vader emblem spray-painted on the shade.

"Told you he's a nerd," Renner whispers as Uncle Larry leads us down a short corridor to his office. He was a little weirded out that we stopped in unannounced, especially given his Dungeons & Dragons meetup in an hour. But when Renner told him we needed his expert advice, he invited us in, so long as we "don't expect food."

The Star Wars theme extends to his office. There's a plaque containing a signed comic book and at least fifteen bobbleheads of the characters along the bookshelf housing what appear to be thick physics textbooks. He gestures for us to take a seat on the worn black love seat.

"So, what can I help you with?" His chair groans as he leans back. It's one of those hard-core chairs gamers use. From this angle, he looks nearly identical to Renner's dad, though slightly softer in the belly. I can see the family resemblance in the thick lashes, in the contemplative yet kind expression.

"We were curious about time travel," Renner tells him, shooting me a look. We already agreed that we aren't telling him the truth. Larry would immediately call his dad, who would call his mom, who would naturally freak out. This meeting is purely for information gathering.

Uncle Larry's thick, bushy brows part. "Time travel? Didn't expect that."

"You taught physics, right? We figured you might know a bit about it," I say.

"Time travel wasn't my exact field of study, but I know a thing or two, yes. What's your question?"

"Could you, um, maybe explain how it works? A quick 101? Time travel for dummies?" I squeak.

This elicits a rumble of laughter. "No one knows for sure. There are multiple theories. Time travel via speed, via light, gravity, suspended animation, wormholes . . ." My eyes glaze over as he starts to explain quantum mechanics, general relativity, and quantum gravity. Renner nods along, pretending to grasp each concept, though I know he has no clue what the hell Uncle Larry is saying.

I clear my throat at the first opportunity. "Hypothetically speaking, if a hypothetical person traveled into the future, could they hypothetically change an outcome?" I ask, thinking about Nori's question yesterday morning, about whether we'd been sent to the future to prevent something from happening.

"You're asking, hypothetically, whether that future would be predetermined no matter what, or if you could change it?"

"Yes. Hypothetically," I add.

He leans back in his chair, hands folded over his stomach, eyes tilted up as though the answer is on the ceiling. "You're talking about a reverse grandfather paradox."

"What's the grandfather paradox?" Renner asks.

"It's the theory that history can't be changed, even if one goes back in time to try to alter it." He can see we're both still confused, so he continues. "Take *Back to the Future*, for example. You've seen it, right?"

We both shake our heads. "Nope."

He shakes his head. "No wonder your generation is so . . . Anyway. In the movie, when Marty McFly goes back in time, he accidentally almost stops his parents from meeting, which would be disastrous because . . ."

"Because then he wouldn't be born?" Renner ventures.

"Exactly. But according to the grandfather paradox, Marty wouldn't have to worry because his parents would meet regardless, in a different way."

I blink. "But how? If he prevented them from meeting?"

"Think of it like a pool table. If you hit one of the balls, it knocks out a particular pattern. If you somehow interfered with the ball's journey, the theory states that somehow, the interaction with the other balls on the table would force the journey back on its original path."

"So what you're saying is, regardless of interference, the outcome remains the same?"

"Exactly." He leans forward and eyes us suspiciously. "Can I ask . . . why the sudden curiosity?"

We simultaneously shake our heads. Renner starts fidgeting and tapping his knee. "No reason. Nothing in particular—"

"We just watched a documentary on time travel and thought we'd come chat with an expert," I cut in. "Thank you for answering our questions. It's been really helpful."

His eyes move back and forth between us. "Just so you know, time travel shouldn't be fucked with. Ever. The consequences could be more severe than you can imagine," he warns, like a sci-fi movie character.

"But I thought you said destiny is predetermined?" Renner asks.

Uncle Larry points at him and nods. "I did. But I also said it's just a theory. Theories aren't facts."

~

Renner breaks the heavy silence as we drive home. "So if Uncle Larry's theory is correct, even if we do manage to go back to seventeen, we can't alter our path? We'd end up engaged regardless?"

My brain can't comprehend. I have free will. I must. Right? "It doesn't make sense. I mean, what if I purposely locked myself in a room for the rest of my life? Then I'd never have the chance to fall in love with you."

He gives me a side-eye. "You'd rather live in solitary confinement than marry me?"

I consider that. Solitary confinement would probably be hell, come to think of it. "I'll have to give that one some more thought."

A smile hovers on his lips as he studies the road ahead. "Hey, that's progress."

TWENTY

"Maybe my mom was right. Maybe adulthood is nothing but winging it and hoping for the best," I wonder aloud.

Case in point: we've spent the last hour googling how to make the perfect fluffy pancakes but not actually making any due to lack of ingredients. I know. We're supposed to do More Important Things with our Saturday afternoon—like time traveling. But we were starved by the time we returned from Uncle Larry's.

"It doesn't have to be," Renner says, sliding a plate of sliced apple and peanut butter in front of me. When I peer at it a little too long, he adds, "We need at least one nutrient today."

"I suppose that's fair," I say, plopping onto the stool, admiring how perfectly he sliced the apple. Even the skin is removed. "You don't eat skin?"

"Nope. Do you know how many hands touch it at the grocery store? This is how my mom does it," he says proudly, slathering his slice with a generous helping of peanut butter. He hands it to me.

"But this is exactly my point. Adulthood is boring so far. Who voluntarily eats apples without being forced by a parent?"

He shrugs. "Well, what do you suggest, Queen of Lists? Anything on your adult bucket list before we go back?" He nods at the pen and a crisp pad of paper. I note that the pad is personalized with *The Renners* in calligraphy across the top. Adult me is serious about stationery.

I flex my fingers, then pick up the pen, my list-making compulsions begging for release. "How big are we talking here? Because I have some dreams."

He smirks. "Anything."

I tighten my fingers around the pen, mind brimming with possibilities. "I want to go on a hot-air balloon ride over the Sahara."

He tilts his head in consideration. "Okay. Not sure we can afford that. But let's put it down as a maybe."

"Oh, I've always wanted to go to Borneo, Indonesia, to see the orangutans before they go extinct. We could take one of those riverboats! Or visit one of those baby-elephant sanctuaries in Thailand. Or drive a Formula One car."

"You like Formula One?" he asks through a bite of apple.

"Maybe. Why is that such a surprise?"

"It's just . . . I didn't know you were so adventurous."

I shrug, inwardly pleased. "There's a lot you don't know about me."

A tiny smile plays at the corners of his lips. "Anyway, Formula One is dangerous," he warns. "Let's put that in the maybe section too."

I swat his forearm. "Why are you pooh-poohing all my ideas? Aren't you the 'big-picture' guy?"

"I wasn't thinking literal bucket list or grandiose ideas. Just . . . realistic things we can do locally. Or at least in this country."

I shift on the stool, shocked and frankly a little turned on by Renner being the voice of reason. "What's realistic? Like skinny-dipping at the beach?"

He points at me, excitement renewed. "Exactly. Add that to the list."

Flames heat my cheeks as I write it down. I'm being bombarded with images of naked Renner.

"What realistic things do you want to do with our newfound freedom?" I ask.

He ponders for a minute, stroking his chin. "I've always wanted to be in a food fight. My mom would slay me if I ever got food on her furniture."

"Oh yeah?" I toss the last slice of apple at him and it bounces off his chest.

His jaw drops. "You just assaulted me with fruit."

"I did."

His gaze heats. "All right. I see how it is. You'll be sorry," he says, and turns to our nearly empty fridge. Before I can duck, he's squirted a stream of mustard in my face.

Through my shock, I manage to let out a bloodcurdling battle cry and dive over the island like a grenade has just gone off behind me. I retrieve the ketchup bottle from the refrigerator door and promptly squeeze it over his head.

Within minutes, we're collapsed on the floor, covered in every condiment in our fridge, including a can of expired whipped cream.

"That was epic," he says, chest heaving with laughter.

I relish the vibration of his voice; then something sticky drips into my eyeball. As I wipe it away with my fist, I spot the fridge door slathered in ketchup. It looks like oozing blood.

Our kitchen is a complete disaster. Like my life right now. And as exhilarating as food fights and elaborate vacation plans are, fun never got me anywhere.

"Now I get why adults are so against food fights. The cleanup." I let out a pained sigh. "Renner?"

"Yeah?"

"I've been thinking about something you said this morning. About movies with time travel."

"Right."

"In the movies, people are always going back in time to change things. But if Larry is right and we can't change things, what if we're just . . . meant to learn a lesson or something?"

"Interesting. What kind of lesson?"

I shrug. This is one of those abstract thoughts that sounded better in my head. "I don't know. Everything in our lives is different now, right? Your parents are divorced. Kassie and I aren't friends anymore.

We have no memories between then and now. What if we need to fill in all these gaps before we try to go back?" When I say it out loud, I'm not overly convinced of that path. But it feels better to do something, anything, than lie here and admit defeat.

He sits up. "That's not such a bad idea. I mean, worst case, if our future is set in stone, it'd be nice to know what happened the past thirteen years. Especially if we're stuck here."

"We won't be stuck here," I tell him, more to convince myself.

~

After spending the entire morning cleaning up condiments from the crevices in our kitchen, and our bodies, I hole up in my home office and set to work. Operation Fill in the Gaps.

Admittedly, I get a little distracted by the "wedding stuff" folder on my desktop. Adult me is seriously organized, with at least twenty separate files for things like "catering" and "dress inspo." There's even a folder with a seating plan. I double-click and do a quick scan, fascinated. It seems most of the guests are Renner's extended family. They take up two long tables at the front. My family table is relatively small, with Mom and my grandparents next to Alexandra and my two sisters. I expect Dad to be seated next to them, but he isn't.

My eyes strain as I scan the remainder of the tables for his name. Leave it to Dad to ditch out on his daughter's wedding. We must really be on bad terms if his new wife and kids are invited and not him. Then again, I'm not sure why I'm shocked. Dad's absence is expected. But not Kassie's. Remembering that sends me reeling again. I do another once-over of the chart. There's definitely no seat for Kassie.

It's time to find out why.

Social media stalking used to be our thing. Kassie and I would lie in my bed for hours on our phones, creeping our crushes' social media accounts four years deep. Admittedly, poring through Kassie's social media profiles like an FBI agent is a solid distraction from thinking about Dad and the fact that we're stuck here in 2037. We're still friends on most platforms, though a quick perusal confirms that we haven't interacted in years.

Kassie's lived an interesting life, compared to me. Not that I expected anything less. Right after high school, her feeds are filled with party photos. Glamorously posing behind a bar, modeling, and doing TikTok routines with gorgeous friends I don't recognize.

She lives in the city now, though she's done a lot of traveling too. Backpacking in South America and Europe. Her content has changed a bit since her travels. She's wearing less makeup, and her hair is naturally wavy—she never wore it that way before. It was always purposefully styled with a wand or flat iron. It seems she's now interested in a holistic lifestyle. She owns a yoga studio, something I never knew she was even vaguely interested in.

It feels like I'm creeping the profile of a complete stranger, not my best friend in the entire world. And it gets me no closer to my biggest question: *Why* aren't we friends anymore?

Finding the address for her yoga studio is easy enough. According to her online schedule, she's teaching a class today at four thirty. My fingers buzz, pleased with discovery. Maybe I should have been a spy instead of a school counselor. I'd be a good one. Maybe that's one plus side of being average. No one would ever suspect me.

As I research trains to the city, Renner tentatively pokes his head into my office. "Miss, I'd like to request an appointment."

I straighten my posture and feign professionalism. "You've come to the right place. I'm highly qualified."

I hear a soft chuckle as he settles into the chair across from my desk and stretches his long legs.

"What can I help you with today, Joshua?"

He coughs violently. "Did you really just call me by my proper birth name?"

When I nod, he proceeds to slide off the chair, hand over heart like the drama queen he is. "I'm floored. And a little touched."

I level him with an eyeroll. "Don't get used to it."

"Come on. Say it again," he pleads.

"No."

"Just once and I'll never ask again."

I shake my head. "Why?"

"I dunno. It's hot," he says with a shrug.

That catches me off guard. "Are you trying to flirt with me right now, Joshua?" I ask with a scrutinizing eye. Is it just me, or is this room suddenly ten degrees hotter?

"If I were flirting with you, you'd know it." He maintains strong eye contact, and I feel like the walls are contracting. Something pulses between us, like an elastic band being pulled tighter and tighter from either end.

"I'm immune to your charms, remember?" I twitch when those words slip out. Why did that feel like a lie?

Renner waves me off and reaches for the yellow stress ball near the base of my monitor, seemingly unbothered. "Yeah, yeah. So you keep telling me."

"I think I'm skipping prom-chaperone duty tonight," I tell him, desperate to rid the room of this weird tension. It might require some ceremonial sage burning.

He covers his mouth, scandalized. "You're skipping prom? What for?"

"I'm gonna go see Kassie. Right now."

Renner's flirty disposition quickly turns serious. "Really? Right now?"

"Yeah. She has a yoga studio in the city. If I catch the train in half an hour, I can make it to her class at four thirty."

He looks concerned. "Do you . . . need me to go with you?"

I contemplate the offer. Truthfully, having someone with me for moral support might be nice. But what if Kassie turns me away? Yells at me? I don't need anyone there to witness that. And if I'm being truthful,

I want to talk to her about Renner, which I can't do if he's tagging along. "No, it's okay. Besides, one of us has to chaperone."

He dips his head back and groans. "Ugh." I'd forgotten too until I received a calendar reminder (from myself) a couple minutes ago. My adult self is really on the ball. "But it's only noon. You'd be back on time, right?"

"Oh, come on. Mr. Former President surely has it covered," I tease, just to get a rise out of him.

He shakes his head, eyes wide with fear. "Nope. I absolutely do not. I need you."

That admission shouldn't make me smile so hard. But it does. And I don't like it one bit. "Okay, fine. I'll make sure I'm back on time."

TWENTY-ONE

I never thought I'd find myself hiding behind a potted monstera plant, creeping my best friend in her yoga studio. But here I am. Horribly out of place.

In my defense, I was casually seated in the lobby, eavesdropping on two yogis talking about balancing chakras and exercise mats made exclusively of hemp. Then Kassie came whirling around the corner in a blinding neon-pink workout getup.

She's in deep conversation with a sweaty dude with a skull-and-bones tattoo emblazoned on his thick bicep. I may have caught a glimpse of a scalp tattoo as well, but it's hard to tell from this angle.

Despite her typical flirty eyes, Kassie seems trapped in the conversation. I can tell by the way she's chewing at the corner of her lip and tightening her sleek ponytail.

While her mannerisms are generally the same, I notice some slight differences. What was once a button nose is now perfectly slender with the slightest turn at the end. Her round cheeks have slimmed as well. She's still lean and fit, though yoga has really toned her arms.

Her differences remind me of my own. I clasp my C-cup boobs, my first reminder that I was still trapped in this hellscape this morning.

My mind tornadoes as I watch Kassie. It's impossible to make sense of any of this. I think about what Nori said, about how maybe I should leave well enough alone. Is it desperate and creepy that I took a train all the way to the city to talk to her? Probably. And what if she hates me?

What if she banishes me from her studio in front of all these innocent, peaceful yogis?

As that terrifying thought flickers through my mind, I lose my balance and fall straight into the potted plant. I watch in horror as the plant topples forward, soil flying every which way across the gleaming oak floor.

Kassie's eyes snap to mine.

~

I'm still holding on to my C cups when Kassie says, "Char?" Her vibrant eyes bore into mine. They're still the same. The shade of those blue Jolly Ranchers we used to eat that stained our entire mouths. One time after we ate them, Kassie's crush texted her to hang out, and we spent a good fifteen minutes frantically trying to brush the blue from her teeth.

"I am so sorry about this!" I manage, clumsily pulling the plant upright. I don't know if I should hug her or keep my distance and awkwardly wave. So naturally, I do neither and drop to hands and knees and begin sweeping the dirt with my bare hands.

"Please don't clean. I'll get a broom." She dashes to the hallway closet, swiftly returning with a broom.

I'm still on my hands and knees when she finishes sweeping the soil. She sets the broom against the wall and extends her hand to help me up. When her hand touches mine, my eyes well.

"Oh no." Her eyes widen, and she quickly pulls me into a hug.

She still smells like sunshine and vanilla. She still feels familiar. Because she is. Just yesterday, Kassie was my best friend. I don't know how to act like a stranger. And I don't know how to reconcile all the time that's passed—well, allegedly.

"What's wrong?" she asks.

Everything in my body urges me to scream, *EVERYTHING!* But I can't summon a coherent response through my snotty sniffles. What comes out sounds like a dying rhinoceros. Mortified, I pull back, praying that I didn't snot all over her shoulder. "Ugh. I'm sorry for showing up at your work like a total freak."

Her eyes dim as they search my face. "I mean, I'm a little surprised, to be honest. Can I ask why you're here? Based on your . . . outfit, I'm gonna guess it's not for my beginner yoga class?"

Half of me is tempted to word vomit the entire strange story of my time travel. But if I were Kassie, I'd call the police and have me dragged out in cuffs. So I settle for, "I just missed you."

She tilts her head and winces, eyes dropping to my shoes before sweeping back to my face. "I missed you," she says simply. She's being genuine. She never looks anyone in the eye when she's lying. But despite the admittance, there's a distance between us I can't quite place. It's like a magnified version of that tiny crack in my heart I feel when she ditches me for Ollie. When she snubs my texts or isn't there for me like she should be.

"Why aren't we friends anymore?" I ask, though the reasons are starting to become clearer.

She goes quiet before forcing a smile. "Hey, I'm starving. Want to grab a smoothie from next door?" This kind of avoidance is typical Kassie. I can't say I'm shocked.

"Oh, um, sure."

We head to the shop next door. It's called Banana, with a bright-yellow sign in puffy, cloudlike font. The menu is complicated, full of various options to add almond butter, wheatgrass, matcha, all sorts of überhealthy ingredients to your concoction.

Kassie rattles off her order (dragon fruit pomegranate splash with two shots of wheatgrass, extra spinach, and a half scoop of plant-based protein powder). The freckle-faced employee turns to me, and I utter, "Um, something with strawberry?" out of panic.

Minutes later, we're sipping our smoothies in silence on the patio. Finally, we make stilted conversation about the weather like retirees. Is this how old people converse? Forced conversation about the hourly forecast? Kill me now. It's uncomfortable, but at least the June sunlight feels nice against my skin.

"You still chew your straw," Kassie points out, the corner of her mouth curving upward in a small smile.

I look down at my straw with a nervous chuckle. "Yeah, old habits."

Another long stretch of silence as she takes her ponytail out and fluffs her hair like she used to.

"How long have you had the studio?" I ask, slurping the remainder of my smoothie.

Her eyes trail two young girls skipping down the sidewalk ahead of their mom. "Um, about five years now?" She says it like a question, probably because she assumes I already know the answer. I'm not the type of person who asks questions for fun.

"Sorry again for showing up at your work, by the way. I didn't know where you lived and—"

"I'm still in my place on Crystal Street," she says.

Again, another detail I don't know. Have I stayed at her place? Have we had sleepovers? Have we had horror movie marathons where we can't fall asleep unless all the lights are on? Have we talked all night surrounded by junk food? Have we made up stupid dance routines to oldies playlists? How long has it been since I've been there?

As if she can read my mind, she says. "So you and J. T. Can we talk about how adorable your engagement was? When I saw it on online, I actually squealed in my Uber." She must be referring to the photos I have on my phone of Renner proposing on some tropical beach. There were rose petals, because of course there were.

I squeeze my eyes shut, in denial that my best friend would find out about my engagement on social media. "Did you really find out we were engaged on social media?"

She looks confused. "Are you okay?"

"I, uh . . . I hit my head. A stupid accident, really. My memory has been fuzzy lately," I say. Technically, it's the truth. I've only omitted one small detail—transcending time. "I guess it just struck me that you weren't at my bachelorette last night." My eyes dropped to my engagement ring, glimmering in the sunlight. "You were supposed to be my maid of honor. We promised we'd be each other's maids of honor."

She stares down at her now-empty smoothie cup. The straw scrapes against the plastic lid as she moves it up and down with an impish smile. "I know. We practically made each other do a blood oath. And I made you promise you'd never make me wear a yellow or beige dress."

"Are you engaged? Or married?" I blurt, desperate for crumbs about her life. I feel pathetic asking, especially seeing as Kassie looks so blissful in her life without me.

She wastes zero time responding. "Oh hell no. Settling down is not for me."

My slack jaw gives away my shock. Since we were nine years old, I've walked a step behind her and her various boyfriends on narrow sidewalks, through the hallways. Kassie in a relationship was simply the norm. In fact, I can barely remember a time when she was single. This Kassie feels like a whole new person I don't know. And I tell her so. "But you've always been in a relationship. The day we met, you proudly told me you already had a boyfriend—a kid who lived across the street."

"Oh my god. Timothy Smith. Guess what? I saw him working at a booth selling cell phone cases a couple years back," she blurts with a laugh. "Anyway, that's exactly why I've been single for a while. Even in college I kept getting myself into these all-consuming relationships. I just got lost in them. I promised myself a couple years ago that I'd start dating more casually. And I haven't gone back since. I'm too busy building my business. And I love the freedom to just do my own thing, have my own schedule. I have my friends, my dog. I don't feel like I need someone else to complete my life, you know?"

I can't help but well with pride over the person she's become. I think she could take over the world if she really wanted to. "I'm proud of you. Though who would have thought it would be me engaged and you happily single?"

"Well, either way, I'm glad you're happy. With J. T. Last time I saw him, he seemed so . . . dedicated to you."

"When was the last time you saw him?"

She bites her lip, perplexed. "Um . . . that would have been . . . last year at your dad's funeral."

TWENTY-TWO

"My dad's funeral?" I repeat.

"I mean, we didn't really talk," she says, shrugging. "You hugged me . . . but you were pretty busy running around, making sure everything was okay. Being your usual organized self."

I repeat the words to myself. *Dad's funeral.*

Dad is dead. Dead.

I'm too numb to move. To do anything but sit here, white-knuckling my smoothie until my fingertips dent the cup. It doesn't feel real. How can it? Dad is dead, I don't know what happened, and I can't ask Kassie without her thinking I've lost my mind.

She gives me a pained expression. "I'm sorry. I know it's probably still really hard."

"I wasn't close with him anyway." The words don't feel good coming out, but it's the truth. Especially since I've lost the last thirteen years.

"I know. But you loved him."

As I fight to keep the tears at bay, my mind pivots to our phone call at the party rental store. Pacing around the hot parking lot as Dad invited me to spend the summer with him and his pregnant girlfriend out of nowhere. I think about how mad I was that he didn't show up to our party last night. How mad I was when I saw he wasn't on the wedding seating chart. About all the times he wasn't there when he should have been. And now I have nowhere to target that anger. Because Dad is dead.

So instead, I just sob. Uncontrollably.

Kassie kneels next to me, wrapping her arms around me tight. She doesn't say anything. She just lets me cry. It's like all the pent-up anger has boiled up inside me, and now it's overflowing like lava, splattering in salty tears off my knees. And while I know my anger and disappointment are valid, those feelings now feel unfair. Unjust. I guess it's hard to be mad at a dead guy.

"I'm sorry," I mutter, blowing my nose into a napkin. "I'm a total mess right now."

"Oh my god. Don't be sorry."

"I know comforting some grieving rando on the sidewalk isn't exactly how you saw your day going."

"You're not a rando, Char." She leans forward and places her hand on my leg, which I can't stop bouncing out of anxiety. Yet another thing about my thirty-year-old self that hasn't changed. "I'm always here for you if you really need me. Okay?"

"Promise?"

She extends her pinkie, and for a fraction of a second, I see nine-year-old Kassie with a purple streak in her hair the summer we met. "Promise."

> Christopher "Chris" Wu passed away suddenly on March 19, 2036, at 56 years of age. He was a loving and devoted husband, father, son, coworker, and friend.
>
> He was born to Michael and Lisa on September 20, 1979. After graduating college, Christopher chased his dreams by attending Columbia Business School, which paved the way for a successful career in finance.
>
> Christopher leaves behind three children, Charlotte (29), Marianne (11), and Lily (8), and a loving wife, Alexandra.

I read Dad's obituary at least fifty times on the train ride home, and spent the rest of the time stalking Alexandra's social media. Sure enough, there are a few photos of Dad, Alexandra, and my sisters. They're posing for a photo among fall foliage and they look like a quintessential family from a catalog. You'd never guess he had another daughter.

The older girl, Marianne, closely resembles Dad, while the younger one looks more like Alexandra. I keep scrolling through photos, expecting to feel anger and resentment toward them, but I don't.

I conduct a quick scan of my older texts from Alexandra, stumbling upon one from six months ago.

Alexandra: Hi Charlotte. Sorry to bother you, but I wanted to let you know that I was going through your father's old stuff and found a couple boxes I thought you might want. I know he'd want you to have them. You're more than welcome to come by anytime to go through some of it. I know the girls would really like to see you.

I'm overwhelmed with the need to speak to her. I need to find out what happened—like, did Dad and I talk? Do I have any relationship with Alexandra or my sisters? But part of me is scared. Scared to see how perfect his new life was. And what if I don't like the truth about our relationship?

The easy solution would be to ask Nori, the only person who won't think I'm a lunatic. But I never confided in Nori about stuff with my dad before. It's not that I don't trust her, or that she's not sympathetic. Quite the opposite. She's one of the most trustworthy, empathetic humans on the planet. It's the fact that her family is perfect. Her parents have a storybook romance; they met in Korea when her dad was on exchange.

Every time I've brought Dad up, she reacts with an idealistic sense of optimism. She's convinced all I need to do is talk to him more. That I just need to tell him that missing my graduation hurt. She's convinced that a dash of honesty will magically heal our relationship.

The only person who truly understood my brand of angst was Kassie. Yet another thing that's changed.

As I watch the city skyline disappear, replaced with industrial warehouses and trees, I realize I still don't know what actually happened between Kassie and me. Did we naturally drift apart like Nori said? Or did we have some sort of disagreement? Does it even matter at this point?

Truthfully, we've been at odds since we started high school. When she joined the cheer squad, I joined Model UN. Whenever I wanted to stay in with snacks and a movie, she was itching to party. I had to beg her to join student council with me freshman year. And sometimes I think she only stayed because she knew I wanted her to. Our love of scary movies was the only tangible we really had in common.

Still, I was drawn to Kassie's energy, her light. She was vivacious, fun, spontaneous, everything I wasn't, and still am not. I guess I've always wanted a piece of it, hoping her radiance would rub off on me. She also got me through some of the worst times of my life. Like my parents' divorce. And the best. Maybe I needed Kassie. But if I'm being honest, I'm not sure I need her by the end of senior year. And maybe that's why I didn't notice her absence right away at Ollie's party. Because I haven't needed her for a long time.

I check my phone as the train nears Maplewood. Renner has texted a couple times.

Pain in my ass ♥: Hey, you on the way back yet?

Pain in my ass ♥: I had to leave for school without you. Let me know when you're on your way. 🙂

Nori: Ollie is having a bonfire tonight. You and Renner should come after prom.

~

Biking in a dress and heels isn't exactly ideal. I may or may not have inadvertently flashed my goods to an old man on a motorized scooter. But since Renner already left, I had little alternative.

I found an off-the-shoulder little black dress in the bowels of my closet. I texted a picture to Nori, who said I looked like a tired middle-aged woman on a once-a-month date with her husband to keep things "fresh." Precisely the look I was going for. Very teacher appropriate. Besides, it was either this or my wedding dress—a simple, yet elegant lace A-line with a drop sleeve—still in a fancy plastic garment bag.

I contemplated ditching prom after finding out about Dad, but I couldn't leave Renner in the lurch. And if anything can take my mind off devastating news, it's prom.

The beat of a fast, bass-heavy song vibrates under my feet as I approach the gymnasium. A man in a navy suit is casually leaning on the doorframe, chatting up a table of formally dressed students taking tickets at the door. It stops me in my tracks. See, I have an Achilles' heel. Guys who lean on things (preferably pensively, with muscly forearms exposed). I can't exactly explain why, but there's something about that pose that gives me the flutters.

This mystery man's relaxed, überconfident stance reminds me of a dashingly handsome A-list celebrity on a red carpet. Who is this relaxed, confident man, and what is he doing in the likes of Maplewood? It's only when he turns his head that I realize: it's Renner.

He's smiling that wide Mr. Congeniality grin that makes me want to scream into my pillow. He looks like the Bachelor in front of the mansion, eagerly awaiting a limo of women vying for his affection. This isn't ninth grade Renner, who attempted to eat a Kinder chocolate egg whole like a pelican on a dare. Or the Renner who rode a bike off Ollie's roof into the lake for a TikTok.

I curse the fact that Adult Renner looks this dapper in a suit. Either that, or I've caught some severe virus on the train and am venturing into delusion.

"Hey, beautiful," he says smoothly, eyes literally sparkling. I'm waiting for him to laugh and yell, *Just kidding!* But he doesn't.

The students next to him *aww* in unison, staring up at us with wistful doe eyes. "You guys are so perfect," says a girl in tortoiseshell glasses.

"I want a marriage like that one day," the other girl says to her friend.

Renner's ears turn pink. He's watching me, silently encouraging me to play along. We are supposed to be getting married, after all.

I force a smile and pull him in for a brief hug. All for show, of course.

"I was beginning to think you were leaving me to the wolves tonight," he whispers in my ear as we head into the nearly empty gym. Prom only officially started five minutes ago.

The room is entirely transformed. The lush purple drapery, glittery streamers, and balloons make it feel like we're really in New Orleans. Mardi Gras feathers and beads drape the tables, along with fancy masquerade masks of varying colors and designs.

I tilt my head. "Oh, trust me, I considered it."

"I know you did." He playfully nudges me in the ribs and gives me a rueful smile.

Maybe it's the suit, but looking at Renner is making me nervous. "So what exactly is the job of a chaperone?" Tasks are the best distraction.

"According to her"—he points to Hedgehog Lady, who's waving from the other side of the gym—"we're on watch for students who are drunk or sneaking in booze. Oh, and apparently making sure no one's crashing without a ticket."

I can't help but giggle at Renner. He's so earnest. "Glad to see you're taking your duties seriously."

"So how was the city?" he asks.

"The city was . . . interesting."

His brow shifts and I can tell he wants to prod. Instead, he nudges me with his elbow. "Ah. Did you do a little adult indulging while you were there?"

I contemplate telling him about Dad right then and there. But the last thing I want to do is ruin prom with death news. "Oh yeah. I went wild," I say sarcastically.

"You went to see strippers, I bet."

I choke back a laugh. "That's what any responsible person would do the moment they reach adulthood."

"It's only logical."

"How did things go with you?" I ask. Before I left, he mentioned he was going to go to his mom's for dinner.

"Good. My mom made lasagna, so I can't really complain," he says good-naturedly. "Met her boyfriend, Jared. Honestly, he's a cool dude. Apparently, he and I go for beers every Thursday. And he helps me coach the junior track team."

I feel much lighter knowing he's feeling better. Before I can tell him that, Hedgehog Lady sidles up next to us. "Charlotte, thank god you're here. None of the other chaperones will listen to me." She points to a white-haired man in the corner, head down, arms folded over his chest, napping right next to the DJ booth. His face is familiar. It's Mr. Kingsley, our career-planning teacher. Just a little older.

"All he's done is drink all the strawberry punch and sleep," Hedgehog Lady says. "And the parent chaperones are just gossiping and eating all the snacks."

I crack my knuckles, ready for the challenge. Delegating is my superpower. I was born for this. "I've got this. Don't worry."

"Need help?" Renner asks, taking my hand as I head to the small kitchen attached to the back of the gym.

A tingle spreads down my spine at his touch, and I take a minute to make sure I've heard him correctly. This is a first. He's never offered to help me with any student council tasks. Like when I was struggling to carry two full buckets of soapy water at the car wash fundraiser and he snidely told me to *keep up the good work* while he flirted with Anya Holton.

"I'm good. Thanks," I say, dropping his hand.

It doesn't take much to set the chaperones straight. When I intrude on the mom gang in the back room, they stand at attention, steeling their spines as though I'm some drill sergeant. Waking Mr. Kingsley from his slumber proves to be a task. After shaking him, Renner tries poking him with a measuring stick. He remains conscious for ten minutes before falling asleep again.

Students flood the gym in packs over the next hour. By nine, the entire dance floor is crammed. Turns out, kids from the future have brought back grinding. I keep accidentally making eye contact with students, bent over, gyrating against each other's junk.

Twerking isn't the only relic that's been resurrected. Frills and ruffle dresses are back too. They remind me of Mom's old prom pictures. Gotta love cyclical fashion.

Renner and I hold down the fort like nightclub bouncers. We've confiscated multiple flasks of vodka hidden in toilet tanks. Renner thinks we should let "kids be kids" and go easy on them, but the last thing we need is students leaving wasted on our watch.

"Caught these ones trying to drink it behind the bleachers," I say, handing Hedgehog Lady the tenth flask of the night.

"You're a boss. Putting this straight in the collection." By *collection* she means the stash teachers are going to hoard in their desks for emergency prep periods. "Hey, you and J. T. have been on the ball all night. Go have some fun," she says, giving me a light shove.

I stumble backward into someone.

When I teeter around, Renner grabs me by the waist. "You're good," he says. His breath feathers my ear.

"Sorry. Hedgehog Lady pushed me," I explain, cheeks heating with our proximity. Before I can gather the wherewithal to move away, a familiar tune fills the air. It's "(I've Had) The Time of My Life" from *Dirty Dancing*. One of Mom's favorite movies.

Hedgehog Lady makes a funny motion with her hands, pretending to waltz with the air.

"Looks like she wants us to dance," I say, uneasy.

Renner tightens his grip on my waist. "It would be illegal not to. This is a banger."

"You've seen *Dirty Dancing*?"

"Who hasn't?"

"Just didn't know you were familiar with '80s romance movies."

He lifts a shoulder. "It may be ancient but it's a classic. You should do the run and jump," he urges. "I'll catch you."

I wince at the thought. "No. I don't trust you. And I haven't had good luck with falling lately." I imagine my face hitting the floor and waking up fifty years in the future, wrinkled like a prune.

He pouts. "Come on. I won't drop you."

I stay put, feet on the ground. "Nope."

"Fine. I'll just sing it," he says.

"Please don't sing it."

"Oh, come on. I know all the lyrics." He does not. In fact, he butchers them. It's quintessential Renner, going for gold with zero forethought. But strangely, it doesn't make me as angry as that day in his van.

He spins me awkwardly, my arm tangling with his. "So how did things with Kassie go?"

"I showed up at her superfancy yoga studio and knocked over a plant. Made a massive mess," I admit, letting myself feel the music as I spin back into his chest.

I feel the vibration of his laugh against my cheek. "Was she mad?"

"No, actually. We went next door, had a smoothie, and I asked why we weren't friends anymore."

He nods like he understands, smoothing his palm down the small of my back. "And?"

I shrug when he spins me around again. Adult Renner isn't too bad of a dancer. "I didn't get a clear answer, but I don't think it was anything dramatic. She seemed super happy for us." I work down the lump in my throat, still not ready to talk about Dad.

"Really? I expected something more dramatic."

"I know. I mean, whatever happened, it kind of feels like we just gave up on almost ten years of friendship." My stomach twinges saying it.

We sway around for a couple moments before he speaks again. "Can I be honest about something?"

"When aren't you honest?"

"I always thought you deserved better than Kassie," he says.

This surprises me, mostly because I've never heard him talk badly about Kassie. In fact, I assumed the opposite. That he'd encourage her not to be friends with me. I blink at him. "Really? Why?"

"You were an amazing friend to her." I watch the green strobe light dance across his face as he finds the words. "You were always there for her. Always stood up for her, helped her pass high school. Come on, you know it's true," he says when I shake my head. "You did all her homework for her. She cheated off you all the time."

"Okay, in her defense, she was a good friend to me too," I point out. Aside from the fact that she never let me take photos on my good side. Or her inability to text me back in a reasonable time period. Or her inability to keep even the tiniest secret. "She's always honest with me. Gives great advice. And sure, she always put Ollie first. But can I really blame her? He was her boyfriend and—"

"You deserve better friends," he cuts in. This hits me in the gut. No one has ever said anything like that to me before. "Even if you are insufferable," he adds with a laugh, pulling me closer. I actually like it. I want to be closer to him.

"As insufferable as you?"

"Not quite. But at least we can be insufferable together."

I giggle into his chest, allowing myself to sag against him as the song comes to an end. When I dare to lift my face up, our eyes lock. It isn't the intense staring contest we often find ourselves in. There are no daggers in his eyes. It's something else, a softness I can't quite pinpoint.

My body buzzes, and the sensation intensifies when he pulls my hips flush against his. My gaze drops to his mouth, and I can almost imagine myself popping onto my toes and brushing my lips against his. I wonder if he'd taste sweet, like the fruity punch we've been drinking all night.

He dips his chin, dropping his lips closer and closer until we're exchanging short bursts of breath. But the moment my lips graze his, the song changes and the mood evaporates into dust and nothingness as the pack of students fills the dance floor again.

We stumble aside, the moment broken.

TWENTY-THREE

My ears are ringing by the time prom wraps up at eleven. We only had one projectile vomiter, which our fellow chaperones deem a huge win.

"Nori texted me. She said Ollie's is a little boring," I tell Renner as we climb into the car. When he gives me a funny look, I'm quick to add, "Not that I don't want to go over. I really want to go. I'm not ready to go home yet. Are you?"

Great. Now I'm babbling. This is new. I've never felt nervous or tongue-tied around Renner before. But after our almost-kiss on the dance floor, it's like we've been tethered by an elastic band. And that band is now tight, wrought with tension. I wonder if he feels it too. Either way, I'm too much of an awkward potato to be alone with him much longer. Plus, I need a distraction from today.

Renner studies me. "You okay, Char?"

"Why wouldn't I be?"

"You seem a little . . . off. More off than usual. And that's saying a lot," he adds teasingly.

"My dad died," I say suddenly.

Renner does a double take, jaw falling open. "What?"

"Today when I saw Kassie . . . she told me the last time she saw us was at his funeral. Last year."

He shakes his head in disbelief. "Fuck. Really?"

I nod.

"That explains why . . ." He runs his hand over his beard. "My mom said something about how cute it was that your mom is walking you down the aisle. I didn't even think—" He pauses, frantic. "Are you okay? You know what? We should just go home."

"No."

"Char, you just found out your dad died. Why didn't you tell me sooner? You shouldn't have had to put on a happy face at prom—"

"No. Really, it's fine. I mean . . . I cried in public over it. I don't really have anything left," I say honestly, grimacing at the memory of Kassie comforting me on the sidewalk. "If anything, I feel worse for my sisters. They knew him better than I did. I haven't talked to him—really talked to him—in forever."

"It doesn't make it any less difficult."

"Maybe I'm just in shock. Maybe there's a part of me that still feels like this isn't real, you know? Like we'll magically go back to seventeen and forget all this ever happened."

He contemplates, eyes trained out the windshield. "Maybe . . ."

"I killed the mood, didn't I?"

"No! Not at all."

I give him a look.

"I mean, okay. You totally did. Your dad dying is kind of . . ." He waves his hand, summoning the words.

"Tragic? Rock-bottom depressing?" I offer.

"To say the least."

"Can we just . . . not talk about it tonight?" I ask, turning away from the pity in his eyes. The last thing I need is him treating me like I'm breakable.

"Sure thing. We could even . . . have fun . . . if you want to?" he offers, earnestly.

"I want to," I say eagerly, clamping my eyes shut when the words come out. Should I really be out having fun after finding out my dad died? Probably not. But my brain still isn't ready to process it.

"All right." He purses his lips as he makes an effortless, one-handed turn toward Ollie's neighborhood. He's taken his suit jacket off, revealing a dress shirt pushed up to the elbows. His ropy forearms flex with the slightest turn of the wheel. "Brace yourself."

"For what?"

"For the funnest night of your life," he tells me confidently, reminding me he's still seventeen years old inside, despite the fact that he now looks like a Greek god chiseled from stone.

"And what do you consider fun?"

"Dunno. Car hide-and-seek?"

"Car hide-and-seek," I repeat. The last time we played, Renner and I got in a huge argument. Kassie and I were in her car, and Renner and Pete were in his van, racing to find Ollie and Andie's hiding spot. Renner claims he won because he was first to reach the car, even though Kassie and I entered the parking lot first.

"What? Beats heading home to drink Sleepytime tea," he teases.

I give him a funny look. "Hey, don't knock Sleepytime tea. That's the good stuff. And do you really think thirty-year-olds will want to play car hide-and-seek at eleven at night?"

~

Thirty-year-olds do, indeed, want to play car hide-and-seek. Then again, I'm fairly certain most people would follow Renner into a multilevel marketing scheme if they could.

Renner is fired up, drumming the steering wheel and tapping his knee impatiently as we wait for Ollie and Nori to text their first clue. He decides to stop at the Wendy's drive-thru in the meantime.

"Want anything?" he asks as we pull up to the illuminated menu.

"Just fries, please."

"What can I get you?" barks a scratchy, deep voice over the intercom. Whoever it is sounds like they could use a bubble bath, a meditation tape, and a good night's rest.

Renner shoots me a funny smile. "Hey, how you doing tonight?"

"Um . . . okay," the voice responds, taken aback.

"Good. Nice night, huh? I'm sure you're looking forward to the end of your shift."

"Yeah, actually. I get off in an hour." The voice is smoother now.

"Cool. Well, I hope you have a great night. Before your shift ends, I'd like to order a medium chocolate Frosty and a large fry, please."

"Sure thing. Drive up to the second window."

The person on the intercom turns out to be a woman in her forties. She looks like she needs her chakras balanced by Kassie. Still, she manages to put a small smile on her face as Renner pays for our order.

"I gave you a large Frosty instead," she tells Renner, handing it over with a small, grease-stained brown bag.

"Hey, thanks, Stacy," he says, eyeing her name tag. "You have yourself a good night."

"How do you do that?" I ask, shooting Renner a pointed look as he dumps the hot bag in my lap.

"Do what?"

I wave my hand vaguely in his direction as I stuff my hand in the bag. "Whatever magic you do with people."

He pulls into a parking space ahead. "You mean like being a decent human?"

I chew off the end of the first fry. "Yeah. How do you do it? You made that woman's night."

"Customer service sucks. I'm sure she'd rather be at home with her family, if she has one. If I have the luxury of going home, why not try to raise her spirits?" He asks like it's a no-brainer. Something everyone should just do.

My heart twinges as I consider. I've seen Renner's magic at work all of high school. He's often used his charm on teachers so he could get away with doing the bare minimum in class. I always harbored jealousy because I assumed it was purely for personal gain. But maybe I was wrong.

My breath hitches when he reaches over the console and digs his hand into my fries. "Hey, get your own fries."

"You have to share with your doting fiancé," he teases. I watch as his ice-cream-dipped fry disappears behind his lips. I turn away as heat gathers between my legs. I work at an ice cream store, and soft-serve never looks this enticing.

Before that thought burrows too far into my mind, my phone vibrates.

Nori: Hint—Pete Takedown.

I angle it so Renner can read.

"The ball field," we shout in unison. This is an easy one. In tenth grade, Pete was famously tackled there by a police officer after an elaborate prank. He stuffed ripped-out pages of a corner store porn magazine into all the mailboxes along the street. The incident ended up on the cover of the local paper. It was all anyone could talk about for weeks.

Renner speeds through Maplewood's old, empty streets, while I shout directions in his ear and pass him fries. With each turn, I'm besieged with flashbacks of that morning in his van picking up prom decor. Only this time, being with Renner doesn't feel like punishment.

Apparently, we're a great navigational team. We arrive just seconds before Lainey and Pete.

Renner gives me an enthusiastic high five. "Good job, navigator." He flashes me an adorable wink, and I promptly stuff a handful of fries in my mouth as the heat prickles down my back. I crank the AC and notice that my mouth is set in the slightest smile. Logically, it feels wrong to smile hours after finding out Dad is dead. Things have never been worse, and yet, I'm happy. I don't want to be anywhere else, with anyone else. It's strange how these two things can exist in parallel.

"All right, your turn to hide," Nori says, pointing to our car.

"It's on." Ollie points dramatically to Lainey and Pete's vehicle. "Make it a tough one," he shouts toward us from his car.

Renner and I drive down Main Street, brainstorming possible hiding spots.

"I feel like it has to be somewhere new. To throw them off," I suggest.

He strokes his chin in contemplation. "How about Walnut Creek? Me and the guys used to fish there sometimes. They might actually catch on depending on the clue. And there's a lot of tree coverage to hide the car. Fry me." He leans over as I slip a fry between his lips.

I take in a breath and shift my gaze to the window. "That works. What's our hint?"

Renner shrugs, eyes fixed on the dark road ahead. "Dunno. You're the brains of this operation."

I drum my fingers on my thigh. "How about *good fats*? Since nuts and fish are full of fat?"

Renner raises his brow. "That's . . . abstract. You really think they'll guess that?"

"Okay, fine. Something simpler . . . How about *nuts about fishing*?"

"I like it."

It's pitch black when we pull into the Walnut Creek parking lot. A thick, spooky expanse of dense woods closes in on either side. Renner pulls into a little private clearing with a partial view of the water.

He kills the ignition and reaches into my lap for another fry, lingering as he tries to locate one at the bottom of the near-empty container. I wonder what it would be like if his hand shifted to my thigh. I let the visual consume me for all of two seconds before tossing the traitorous fantasy out the window into the cool night breeze.

I cross and uncross my limbs, distracted by his charming smile, and I have no idea where to avert my gaze. I frown at him. "Please don't smile at me like that."

His smile broadens, and I feel like he can read my mind despite his innocent little shrug. "What's wrong with smiling? You don't like smiling?"

I shield my eyes. "You sound like Buddy the Elf."

He places a hand over his chest. "That's the nicest thing you've ever said to me."

"And your teeth are distracting," is all I can think to say.

"My teeth?"

I fold up the greasy fry bag and roll it into a ball, setting it on the ground at my feet. "They're very white."

He closes his mouth, but his grin lingers. "Sorry. I'll abandon my strict oral hygiene routine if it'll make you feel better."

"It will make me feel better."

He smiles. "Fine."

"Fine," I say, intent on getting the last word.

We stare at the dock for a while. It's quiet, save for the shift of fabric as Renner settles and resettles in his seat, unable to sit still. Since we parked, he's moved the window up and down at least three times.

"Guess our clue wasn't that easy," he finally says.

"No. It was super obvious. But it's only been, like, ten minutes. Give them some time. If they don't get here in fifteen, we'll fire off another hint."

"I'm gonna stretch my legs," he says, getting out of the car and strolling toward the dock. He sits on the edge and stares into the smooth blackness of the creek.

I could use some fresh air too. The uncalled-for fantasies are clouding my head. I follow him into the cool night, onto the swaying dock. I don't speak as I sit next to him. Our thighs are just barely touching, though I can still feel the heat from his body.

It smells a little like swamp, but the croak of nature soothes whatever strange energy has been flowing between us.

"Can I ask you a question?" Renner finally asks.

"Sure, at your own peril." I straighten my shoulders, bracing myself for a dumb joke or insult.

"On a scale of one to ten, how much do you want to push me in the creek?" he asks.

I take in a breath, pretending to be offended. "About a solid six. Drowning is way too basic, though. And it's a relatively quick death—"

My breath hitches when I realize what I've just said. Renner freezes too, awaiting my reaction. "Oof. I went there and brought up death already."

"Yes, yes you did."

We watch each other for a few breaths before simultaneously bursting out in laughter. Strangely, laughing my ass off feels much more relieving than crying.

"Why must I be so morbid?" I manage, gripping the dock for support with one hand, and clutching my now-sore stomach with the other.

"Hey, there's something to be said for dark humor. Speaking of, glad to know you'd draw out my suffering as long as you could."

"Yeah. Casual torture seems like a good starting point for you. But I'm trying to work on being a team player, so I'm open to suggestions," I note.

"Whatever you do, just don't do that one where you make me listen to some annoying song over and over for seventy-two hours."

"Look, it's the only way to force you to learn the proper lyrics. I think 'Baby Shark' is sure to push you over the edge."

He snorts. "Sheesh. You really hate me." In the moonlight, I see a slight crease in his forehead.

Our eyes snag and my shoulders drop. "I don't hate you, Renner." And it's the truth. Regardless of how much he's impeded my bucket list, I've never truly hated him.

"Well, you severely dislike me. Every time I walk into a room, you get this look on your face like you're using every last bit of strength not to end my life."

I cover my eyes with my hands. "Are you saying I have a murderous face?"

"Yes. Yes, you do." He pretends to inch away from me.

"You've been known to drive me to homicidal rage."

"See? Exactly my point."

I shrug. "For the record, this is just my face. I don't mean to make you fear for your life. But to answer your question, I guess it all started when you stood me up at homecoming for another girl."

He tilts his head. "Wait. What? I never stood you up for another girl."

"I beg to differ."

"But I didn't. I had a family situation," he explains, brows knit.

"Then why would Kassie tell me you were seeing Tessa from Fairfax?"

"I don't even know a Tessa."

I blink, eyeing him suspiciously. "Then why would Kassie lie to me?"

"I don't know," he says, frowning. There's a flash of anger in his eyes. "But it was a complete lie. Maybe she was trying to get back at me for turning her down."

"You turned her down? When?"

"After we first met. I wasn't interested in her that way, and I told her straight up the next day. This was right before school started. Before she even met Ollie."

I nod. I still remember Kassie, clear as day, telling me she wasn't interested in him after their make-out session. "But she always tells me everything," I say, catching myself midsentence. "I mean . . . at least she used to."

Renner runs a hand through his hair. He has a horrified expression, as though someone's just punted a baby across a field of AstroTurf. "I'm telling you the truth, Char. I turned her down. Not the other way around. And I never stood you up for someone else."

I'm stunned into silence, trying to come up with a logical explanation. When I think back, she and Ollie started flirting immediately during that welcome assembly. Maybe she was doing it to make Renner jealous. But believing Renner over Kassie feels unnatural. Then again, this whole situation is unnatural.

"To be fair, I could only go off what Kassie told me," I say, raising my shoulders in defense.

"You really hated me all this time because Kassie lied and told you I was into someone else? Wild. All this time we could have—"

I hold my hand up to stop him from continuing. "All right, slow your roll. I'll have you know I had other reasons."

"Like what?"

I realize that all my other reasons seem ridiculously petty, and I look away. "I don't know, Renner. I guess it was also all the little things along the way. Mostly because you're annoyingly likable."

He gives me an adorable, knowing look. "Oh, come on. People like you too."

"Not in the same way. I have to work so hard to make people like me."

"Honestly, I do try. Harder than you think."

I think about the Wendy's cashier. The exchange just seemed so natural for him. "Are you saying your charm isn't some generational family witch curse?"

He laughs. "Sadly, no. Actually, I have a phobia of people not liking me. Like, Mrs. Webber, the school librarian, hated my guts in ninth grade after I messed up her bookshelves. And it took me years of groveling, giving her compliments, and bringing her those magazines to make her like me."

"Why go to all that effort? If people don't like you, it's on them."

"Dunno. I've always been that way. Ever since my sister . . ." His voice trails.

I hang my head. When Kassie first met Renner, she told me how his little sister passed away when we were ten. She'd gotten hit by a car playing outside. It's kind of an unspoken thing that no one brings up. To be honest, I'd almost forgotten. "I'm so sorry, Renner. What was her name?"

"Susie," he says affectionately. "She had the cutest laugh. The biggest smile. It's been seven years and sometimes it feels like yesterday. I can still hear my mom screaming in the middle of the street, holding her." He pauses. "Well, I guess it's been more like twenty years if we're thirty."

I grit my teeth, trying to find the appropriate words. But there are none.

He continues. "That's why I couldn't do the prom errands the other day. It was the anniversary of her death and my parents usually do something in her memory and—"

"You don't have to explain."

"No, I feel like I have to. It's actually the reason I didn't show up to homecoming. My mom was having a really bad night. She knew I was supposed to go to the dance but I just couldn't leave her."

I let that settle for a few moments. All this time, I assumed he'd ditched me because he didn't want me as his date. "Knowing that would have changed everything." I think he knows it too.

"Yeah. Well, you didn't want to know. And to be fair, I don't think I was ready to talk about it at that time."

"I don't blame you at all."

He runs a hand across the back of his neck. "No. You should. I handled it . . . terribly."

I shrug. "You handled it like a fourteen-year-old boy. I mean, losing your little sister . . . I can't even imagine how hard that must have been."

"The hardest part is thinking about what she could have been. She enjoyed life, laughed constantly at every little thing. I guess I feel obligated to fill that void. Like making my parents laugh, like she did, is the only way to make them happy again."

His admission makes my heart hurt. It's like the last piece of the Renner puzzle sliding into place. After four years of not understanding this person, of assuming he had everything easy, I finally get him. His larger-than-life personality makes sense now. And it makes me like him even more. "Renner . . ."

"I still remember, a couple months after the funeral, my parents were just zombies. Going through the motions of the day. I made some dimwit joke and they laughed. Like, really laughed. For the first time since she died. Since then, I've just felt like it's my job to keep them happy. Though *happy* isn't the right word. They were functioning, mostly." The pain in his eyes is like nothing I've ever seen before. It's like he's dropped his walls entirely, for me. As sad as the circumstances are, I feel grateful that he's sharing this with me. "When I saw my mom happy that first morning, and then later at Ollie's, it threw me. Because I didn't know she could be like that again."

"She really did look happy."

"I don't know how much of it has to do with Jared. But if he's any part of it, I can't be mad at that. I guess I just feel shitty that I couldn't make her happy myself."

"Don't say that. You do make her happy. And even if you didn't, you can't make everyone you meet like you. Well—I mean, maybe *you* can. But you shouldn't have to."

He shrugs. "It's just this weird compulsion. I can't stop. Like, even after Susie died, my parents made me see a therapist. And I even tried to impress her by telling her how great I was doing all the time. And today, I bought vegetables at the grocery store just to impress people."

"Who?"

"I don't know . . . random shoppers. The cashier. I have no idea how to even prepare vegetables." His modesty threatens to melt me into a puddle on the spot.

"Vegetables? You really are a people pleaser."

"It's exhausting being me," he says with a smirk.

"Did it bug you, that I . . . wasn't your biggest fan?" I ask, careful not to use the word *hate*.

His simmering eyes meet mine. "More than you know."

"Then why did you try so hard to make me hate you? You could have told me why you needed the presidency . . . Maybe I wouldn't have—"

"Char, you already had your mind made up about me no matter what I did. I guess I'd rather get negative attention from you than none at all."

"But why? That's so . . . foolish."

He turns to face me. "You really have no idea, do you?" he asks, voice dropping with a distinct edge. It's husky and sexy in a way that makes me both want to curl into a ball and reach for him.

"About what?"

He opens his mouth to respond just as a blinding headlight floods my vision. Ollie's Jeep.

I pull back, half-blinded by the light, pulse thrumming under my skin. I'd entirely forgotten we were still playing a game. The existence of anyone else momentarily forgotten. "They finally found us," I say, standing abruptly.

"Yeah. Perfect timing," he mutters behind me. I can't tell if he's being sarcastic. And I'm too scared to ask.

~

We only play one more round before Ollie admits he's tired and needs to be horizontal.

"Looks like Operation Back to Seventeen was a bust," Renner says on the way home.

"Don't remind me."

He bites the inside of his cheek. "Guess we should actually tell people the wedding is off, huh? My mom is not gonna be happy."

"Yeah, mine either," I say. "But let's hope it doesn't come to that. We'll get out of here." My ribs tighten at the thought of canceling. That's strange. Why does the thought of canceling make me want to cry? The grief must be making me extra emotional.

His eyes roam my face and hands, then my lap, before reverting to the road. "On the bright side, we did find out some crucial information. You got some closure with Kassie and I got to talk to my mom. Is there anything else you still want to find out? Maybe we can revisit our brainstorming list," he adds.

"There is still something . . . ," I start, nervously biting the inside of my cheek.

"What's that?"

"I think I want to visit my dad's wife." Talking about Renner's sister piqued my interest. His sister was taken away from him far too soon.

And it seems like I don't even make an effort to see mine, both of whom are alive and well. That doesn't sit right.

He's quiet for a moment. "Want me to come with?"

My heart warms at his offer. "Yeah. I do."

"Then I'll be there."

His words have a soothing effect. And when he reaches over the console to give my hand a squeeze, the knot in my stomach uncoils, just a little bit.

We may be stuck in this strange, strange reality, but for the first time in my life, it feels good to rely on someone. Even if it's Joshua Taylor Renner.

TWENTY-FOUR

When Dad told me about the lake house in Fairfax, I pictured an ultramodern boxy structure similar to his high-rise in the city, all cement and floor-to-ceiling windows. I certainly didn't picture this lived-in, farmhouse-style home.

One look at the disheveled Barbie in the rosebush and the overturned child's pink bicycle in the middle of the pebbled path, and it's clear a family lives here. There's a tug in my stomach when I spot the pastel chalk hearts and hopscotch. These were drawn by my little sisters.

Renner senses my hesitation when we reach the door and nudges my hand gently. I don't know what to make of this strange shift between us. Last night at prom and again at Walnut Creek, I could have sworn he wanted to kiss me. And I secretly wanted him to. But the moment we returned home, both of us tensed up and retreated to our respective bedrooms (him in the spare room, me in the main bedroom) for the night without a word.

I can't help but wonder if his kindness toward me is just an extension of his people-pleasing. Trying to make me feel better, because he's an absurdly good person.

"Are you gonna ring the doorbell?" he asks.

"Don't rush me," I whisper, just as the door swings open before I even have the chance to knock.

A dark-haired girl with a ponytail and a cute purple outfit greets us. When our eyes meet, she shrieks and flings herself into my arms. "Charlotte! Charlotte's here!"

Based on her enthusiasm, I'd wager she knows me. The fact that we have some sort of relationship makes me feel marginally better, and I return her hug.

"Lily, who's there?" a distinctly older voice calls. A woman hustles down the wooden staircase in a pair of track pants and a stained white T-shirt. It's Alexandra. The nonglamorous version with thick, chocolate-brown hair cascading down her back. Even without makeup and fancy clothes, she's naturally stunning, with dark brows that somehow convey everything she's thinking. Right now, she looks shocked. "Charlotte?"

"Hi," I squeak.

~

I find myself squished in between my sisters on a beige couch with too many throw pillows. Lily, the younger of the two, doesn't want to leave my side. Before I can properly greet Alexandra or Marianne, she's pulled me to her bedroom to show off the dress she's going to wear to my wedding.

Marianne is less bubbly, but no less eager to see me. I think she's the more inquisitive of the two, slightly suspicious of people in general. Not unlike myself. She's also enthralled with Renner, who she's been staring at like melting ice cream since we arrived.

As Marianne bombards me with questions about whether I've seen *Molly and Polly*, a new Disney movie that she's obsessed with, it strikes me that they don't treat me like a stranger. They treat me like their big sister.

Alexandra brings us to the family room, with a sweeping view of the lake. If I'd known the lake house had views like this, maybe I'd reconsider spending my summer here.

"I hope you're not too offended by the pigsty that is my house. Cleaning has fallen to the wayside with this nasty flu," Alexandra says, cheeks pink with embarrassment as she sets two glasses of lemonade on the edge of the coffee table.

Usually, when people apologize for a messy home, there's no mess at all. Mom likes to say people just want the opportunity to humblebrag about how clean it actually is. But Alexandra isn't exaggerating. While beautiful, the house is admittedly a mess, with pieces of construction paper, glitter glue, and toys littering the table. It's the opposite of how I imagined her, and it makes me like her, just a little.

"We should be the ones apologizing for dropping in unannounced," I note.

She tilts her head. "The girls really missed you. Both of you."

"How long has it been?" I ask, clumsily trying to discern how close we are.

She hesitates, her eyes dropping to her lap before responding, "Since the funeral, I think."

My throat tightens as I digest her words. It's been almost a year since I've seen them? That doesn't sit well. "I'm sorry. Things have just been busy and—" I stop myself. "It's not an excuse. I want to come see you guys more."

"It's okay. I know you've been busy," she says, graciously letting me off the hook.

"I realized I never responded to your message about picking up some of Dad's things. I know you probably don't have it anymore but—"

She stands, brushing the wrinkles from her track pants. "I do. Follow me. It's all in his office."

Renner stays with the girls while I follow her down the hallway. As I step around a pile of laundry, I catch a collage of family photos in mismatched frames and pause. My breath hitches when I spot my high school graduation and seventh grade photos next to pictures of

Lily and Marianne. There's even a photo of Renner and me in front of a Christmas tree in a gold embossed frame.

Alexandra doubles back and gazes at the photos beside me. "Your dad liked to keep photos of you around. So the girls would know who you are." That's the last thing I expected. I've always assumed Dad saw me as inconvenient baggage from his past life.

"He did?" I whisper under my breath as I follow her into Dad's office.

It smells like him. Of mahogany and fresh printer paper. Alexandra hasn't cleared much out. Work papers and files are still piled atop the desk, seemingly undisturbed. Alexandra lets out a slow breath when she passes through the doorway, as though entering the room deflates something inside her. I feel even sadder for her than for myself. She's stuck in this house with reminders of him everywhere.

She pulls down a box from the closet and sets it on the desk. "I know it's a lot to go through. No pressure if you don't want to take all of it. I know you have a lot on your plate this week with the wedding and all."

At the top of the box is a stack of paper-clipped drawings I made for him when I was a child, with *To Dad, From Charlotte* written on every single one in perfectly straight handwriting. I was always obsessed with making my letters perfect. Below is a binder with printouts of all my report cards, from grade school until the end of high school.

"He kept all of this?" I manage.

"Of course he did. I think you were his favorite topic," she says with a soft chuckle.

My first instinct is to deny that. How could I be his favorite topic when we didn't even speak?

Alexandra places her hand on my wrist, expression sincere. "He never wasted an opportunity to brag about how smart you were to all our friends. How his daughter had a 4.0 GPA in college. How she became a school counselor and changed kids' lives. Every time I turned around, he was scrolling your social media."

My eyes well. "I didn't know that." How did I not know that? Why wouldn't he tell me?

Alexandra looks toward the contents of the box. "I know he wasn't the best with communication. But he was so incredibly proud of you."

~

Renner and I stay for the rest of the day, laughing with Alexandra and the girls. They're a riot, especially Lily. The way she squeezes her eyes shut and tosses her whole body back when she finds something amusing is so reminiscent of Dad, it makes my chest ache.

I'm an admittedly awkward potato. I don't know exactly what I should say, or even know, about the past thirteen years. Of course, Renner handles the situation like a champ. I don't know why I'm surprised by how good he is with Lily and Marianne. He doesn't even hesitate when Lily asks if she can put butterfly clips in his hair.

It feels good to be here with them. All of them. It's familiar somehow, and frankly long overdue. Because they're pieces of Dad I never had. And even though I can't claim to know Dad well, it feels like this is something he would have wanted.

"Thank you for coming with me. It meant a lot that you were here today," I tell Renner when we get in the car. The sun is going down now, painting the sky a hue that reminds me of cotton candy.

"I'll always be here for you, Char," he tells me.

We drive in silence for a couple more minutes before I turn to him. "I don't want to go home yet."

"Who says we have to?" He gives me that wink. The wink only he can pull off. "We're adults now. We don't have a curfew, remember?"

"Well, it is late."

"All right, now you sound like an old lady."

"I told you. I'm a proud geriatric."

"Char," he says, leveling me with his look. "We can do whatever we want."

TWENTY-FIVE

Ninety percent of stress can be avoided with planning and forethought. That's my mantra.

I've never entered a situation without a plan. I used to lie awake at night, spinning with hypotheticals about how I could mitigate risk in my life. *Maybe if I study another hour, I can ace that exam. Maybe if I go over my list for the student council bake sale one more time, we can avoid hiccups.*

So I'm very much a fish out of water at a roadside thrift store called Dead People's Stuff.

It caught Renner's eye on Fairfax's main street en route home from the lake house. Its bright-blue paint stands out among the red-bricked historical buildings. There's also a life-size cutout of Chucky, the creepy redheaded serial killer doll, in the window.

"So what are we looking for?" I ask Renner. While it isn't a large space, they've managed to pack clothing and miscellaneous items in every nook and cranny. Everywhere you look there's something odd and obscure. Like the beaded dream catcher dangling from a shelf of assorted snow globes.

Renner tosses an arm around my shoulder as we stroll under the watchful eye of the raven-haired, purple-lipsticked owner. "Our objective, if you choose to accept, is to find each other the most ridiculous outfit possible for our wedding-that-won't-actually-happen."

"Oh, I was born for this." I squint around the chaotic store, already plotting.

My eyes pivot to a black-and-white cow-print vest. It actually feels like real cowhide. Horrified, I stuff it back on the rack.

Renner gives me a look. "Not my color?"

"Not enough drama for you," I conclude, turning on my heel. Usually, I have a methodical way of shopping. I scour every rack from the right side of the store to the left. But today, I'm content to let my heart guide me wherever it wants to go.

Renner can see from my expression that I've taken our mission very seriously, so we part ways in our search.

Then I see it. The perfect over-the-top-ridiculous Renner outfit for our wedding-that-will-not-be. The top is a plain white triple-XL tee with a picture of an adorable golden retriever puppy in a basket. Below the puppy is the phrase *You think you know fear? You think you've felt actual pain?* For his bottom, I select red leather (bumless) pants, which I suppose makes them more like chaps, two sizes too small, paired with a turquoise gemstone belt. Then I find fuzzy brown slippers shaped like bear paws and a thick gold-plated chain with a statement medallion that reads *Classy* and *Sassy* to round out the full look.

Renner selects a long-sleeved rainbow leopard unitard that smells suspiciously of cough drops and reckless decisions with a floor-length trench coat that I'm certain was generously donated by a playground flasher. My accessories include a pair of infant-size oval sunglasses with microscopic red lenses and black chunky platforms with plastic fish in the heels. (He says I'm sure to bring platforms back in style.)

"All right, we'll take them," Renner tells the poor cashier, who has to scan the items on our bodies.

On the way out, I catch a glimmer of silver in my peripheral vision that stops me in place. Renner crashes into me, gripping my elbow for support.

"Are you seeing what I'm seeing?" I ask.

He follows my upward gaze and swallows. "I think so . . ."

There, on a shelf overflowing with bits and bobs, is a steel cylindrical object. The engraved letters across the front are partially covered by a massive wide-brimmed periwinkle hat covered in wild flower appliqués. Renner removes the hat, revealing the dirt-encrusted engraving: *Time Capsule—Graduating Class of 2024*.

"That can't be our time capsule, can it?" I ask as Renner pulls it off the shelf. When his fingers make contact, he jolts slightly, pulling his hand back.

"Ouch. It just shocked me."

I run my finger over the smooth edges, and a tiny jolt rolls through my fingertips. "That happened last time. In the storage room."

He nods, studying it for a beat before grabbing for it again, forearm muscles flexing under its weight. "But how did our time capsule end up in some random store in Fairfax?"

"No idea," I say, shaking the capsule, ear pressed against it. "Do you think our letters are in there?" I ask, resting my arm on the shelf behind me, a smidge dizzy all of a sudden.

"We're thirty now, right? I assume we already opened it." Sure enough, when he opens the latch, it's empty. "Guess we'll never know what we wrote."

"That's okay with me," I say, helping him place it back on the shelf. Maybe it's the privilege of knowing far more than I wanted to know about my future self, but I know enough at this point. I'm more than happy leaving some things a mystery.

We walk onto the bustling sidewalk hiccuping with laughter. I don't usually like to stand out. In fact, I've spent my entire life desperately trying to fit in. Being dressed like a loon in public would typically send me into hysterics, but it doesn't, even though we're being gawked at.

People are even moving a little to the side to give us a wide berth. Renner has a huge grin, and I can tell he's living for this. Each glare or gasp provides extra pep to his bumless-leather-pant swagger. (Don't worry, he has boxers underneath.)

"We're from the past. Time travel," he happily tells an elderly woman with bulging eyes. She shoots us a stern look and walks a little faster in the opposite direction.

Renner continues on this course, telling everyone who makes eye contact that "we're from the past." I can't stop giggling. I'm not one to talk to random strangers, but with Renner, I'm starting to feel brave. By the time we reach the intersection, I whisper, "We're time travelers," to a cherub-faced baby. (His dad has earbuds in, but everyone has to start somewhere.)

High on adrenaline, we skip hand in hand over an air vent and into a magenta-colored store that reminds me of a carnival fun house meets *Willy Wonka & the Chocolate Factory*. The store exclusively sells candy, even vintage candy, with rainbow lollipops the size of dinner plates. There's a giant wall of clear plastic boxes filled with candy, scoops, and tiny rainbow-striped bags to fill. It's a child's dream come true. Renner and I go wild, filling our bags to the brim.

The clerk, a bushy-haired guy with a goatee, stares us down as we set fifty-five dollars' worth of candy on the checkout counter.

Giddy at the prospect of sugar, we stumble into a lush green park and flop into the thick grass, a cushion for our sore bodies. We're on a slope overlooking a flat area where a group of teens are playing night Frisbee.

"Oh god. It feels good to lie down." Renner groans, reaching into his bag for a gummy worm. "Is this thirty? Being too tired to get through the day?"

"If this is thirty, I'm scared to know what fifty feels like," I say, tearing open the bag of Skittles.

"Why are you touching all the Skittles, you little freak?" He eyes me sideways, attempting to snatch the bag. I pull it out of reach, and he's too lazy to fight for it.

"Everyone knows the green ones are disgusting."

He holds his palm out. "You're a wasteful monster, Wu. Give me the green ones. Just don't touch them all."

"Scared of my germs?"

"I'm scared of everyone's germs. Like your hair in the Skittles." He points toward a rogue strand of hair in the bag.

I grimace. "Ew. Sorry. My mom says I shed like a dog."

"Yeah, I saw the bathroom sink this morning."

"Welcome to married life," I tell him, pulling my hair back into a ponytail. "If we're stuck here, you'll have to snake the drain of my hair too."

He studies me, eyes softening under the yellow glow of the lamppost above. "Why don't you wear your hair like that more often?"

I hesitate. "Do you really want to know?"

He dips his chin and nods.

"Ninth grade. When Ollie's mom rented out that go-karting place for us. You told me my head was, and I quote, 'humungous,' and that no helmet would fit me."

Renner's eyes cut to me, horrified. "Are you serious?"

"Yup. Haven't worn my hair up since."

"Char, I didn't mean your head was humongous *literally*. I meant it's big because you're a know-it-all."

My cheeks heat. Frankly, I feel a little foolish I took it that way. "Oh. I'm a tool."

"No, no. I never should have said that. It was dumb of me. But hey, listen." When I turn away in embarrassment, he cups my chin and turns my face back toward him. "Your head is a perfectly normal size."

"Gee, thanks," I say, hiding my face.

"Perfectly proportioned," he adds. "You know, the first time I saw you, I—I remember feeling out of breath, like I'd just run drills in the gym or something, even though I was just sitting there. You're beautiful. Big brain and all." My entire body heats at his words, and my whole face flushes.

"You're one to talk," I say, deflecting so he won't notice I've turned into a human tomato. "I actually wrote about your face in my diary once. I think it was like, a five-page entry," I confess.

"Let me guess, you wrote an essay on how horrible my face is?"

"It was more of a feverish, unhinged rant about how beautiful your face was. How I didn't think you deserved it. And how I thought you should have been born with a huge upper-lip mole, or a weak chin at the very least," I admit through a snort.

"I come from a very long line of strong chins, unfortunately for you."

When he nudges my shoulder affectionately, I think about tomorrow and how we'll inevitably have to find a way back. It's the last thing I want to think about right now.

It's completely dark now, and the white lights strung around the trees twinkle like stardust all around us. It's magical, somehow.

Until the sky opens up and it begins to pour.

TWENTY-SIX

Damn. It's raining." He takes his hoodie off, using it as a makeshift umbrella for us.

"It's okay. It's not raining . . . *that* hard." A moment later, a crack of thunder booms in the distance, unleashing a torrential downpour.

"Not that hard, huh?" Renner asks as silver sheets cascade, cocooning us in our little world. It's as if someone has taken a knife and split the sky down the middle.

I don't know if it's the quick escalation or the fact that his triple-XL T-shirt is now plastered to his chest and completely see-through, but I start to laugh. Gut-clenching, knee-slapping laughter. Renner loses it too.

Two days ago, I couldn't stomach being in the same room as him. And now we're laughing in the pouring rain. It's like someone's wrapped me in a heated blanket when I didn't know I was cold.

He extends his hand through the rain. "Come on. Let's find some shelter."

I could easily stress about being drenched, or potential pneumonia. But all those thoughts disappear when our fingers lace together. Side by side, we run straight into the rain, fearless, as though we're running into war. On the same team.

We run about a block before ducking into a rain-slicked alley and finding the overhang of a restaurant.

"Come here," he says gently, eyes like beacons.

I inch my way onto the step and huddle with Renner like we're in a tiny cave. He pulls me close, flush against him. Though the cold rain still manages to pelt us, I've never felt so solid, so sure of myself. So sure that I belong here, in this moment.

I rest my palms against his wet chest and sigh. "Why do you have to be so . . ."

"Handsome? Intelligent? Spectacular?"

I give him a soft, wet flick in the chest. "I just feel like an ass."

He pulls back, studying me. "For what?"

"For everything," I admit, stomach tangled with emotion. "I can't help but wonder how different things could have been if we'd just been . . . friends. This whole time."

"Is that all you'd have wanted?" he whispers, resting his forehead against mine. "To just be friends?"

I contemplate as the blood rushes to my ears, pulsing everywhere, thrumming just beneath the surface of my skin. No. That statement doesn't capture what I really want right now. Not in the slightest. Because, beyond all logic, I think I like Renner. A lot. And I hate it. "No. That's not all. This wasn't the plan," I murmur.

"What? Falling in love with me?" he asks, unable to hold back that Renner smile.

I playfully punch him in the chest. "Shut up. I am not in love with you."

"Yet," he adds with no shortage of confidence. "And to be fair, catapulting into the future wasn't really in my plan either, so we're even."

I laugh into his chest. "Seriously, though. It's weird."

"Things don't always have to happen exactly as you plan them," he points out.

"They do," I counter.

"Why?"

I lift my shoulders. "I guess the unknown scares me. I mean . . . I don't know if you've noticed, but my mom is a mess. She's a hoot, don't get me wrong. But after my dad left, if I wasn't on top of my own schedule, things just weren't done. I guess it got me in the habit of compulsively planning things."

"I get that. But I also think . . . if you're compulsively planning for everything, what are you missing out on?" he asks, running the pads of his fingers down my spine, sending a rush of heat to every limb.

"Easier said than done. If I could relax and find peace every time someone told me to, I'd be the Dalai Lama."

He gestures around. Though it's hard to see anything through the silver sheets of rain. "Okay. But look where we are. We're stuck in this strange . . . strange world. We don't know if it's real, or if it's a dream, or some weird alternate universe. But we're here. And we're never going to get this moment again, are we?"

"No. We're not."

My brain feels fuzzy, like there's static electricity when he pulls back to look at me. It's not a normal moment of prolonged eye contact. He's really looking at me. Like he's found my soul.

If this is a dream, it sure as hell feels more real than any other moment of my life. Every brush of his thumb against my skin. His soft, searching gaze, catching in the moonlight. The way he slides his warm hand into my hair, massaging the nape of my neck, lighting a spark inside that's been dormant, shoved down by the order of my mind.

My entire world is off kilter. It feels like I have no control over anything. Usually, just the thought of losing control is enough to send me into a spiral. Yet, in this moment, I feel a strange, weightless peace. It's as though all my stress washed away with the rain. And Renner's embrace.

Now that the spark is lit, I'm not sure even dousing it in this downpour would put it out. So I lean in and catch his lips with mine, finishing that kiss.

~

How did I waste the last four years not kissing Renner?

Hindsight is a serious bitch, because he kisses with his entire damn body. Kassie always told me he was a good kisser, but she vastly undersold his skill. Our kiss at the engagement party has nothing on this one. This is a mind-altering, time-bending, unicorn-glitter-magic-level kiss that threatens to change my entire worldview from here on out.

Despite being drenched in cold rain, our bodies are scorching, pressed tight. In this moment, there's nothing that could pull us apart. Our rain-soaked lips slide against each other in short bursts, breath colliding. As his tongue slides a little deeper against mine, my hands skim up and down the plane of his back and over his shoulders, grasping at the wet fabric of his shirt.

His lips are so soft, coaxing my mouth open with hungry intensity. We fall into a rhythm, tilting, sighing into each other until I'm gasping for breath. One of his hands is tangled in my hair while the other fans across my waist, pulling me closer.

"Char," he mumbles in between kisses.

"Mm-hmm?" I study his face for what feels like the first time.

"This is the best day of my life." He says it with such conviction, I nearly melt into him. "I know that sounds weird because I don't know if any of this is even real, but I—"

"It's the best day of my life too," I cut in. And I mean it. For the first time, I don't know that I'd choose to go back to seventeen if given the chance. I want to hold on to this moment for a little while longer, if I can.

He gives me that signature, wistful Renner smile. I take a mental photo, logging this moment in my mind.

The rain lets up and I can finally see that the alley leads to a square of restaurants and patios. The shops boast overflowing flowerpots and vines that snake from the windows, down the sides of the buildings. It reminds me of a woodland fairy tale. It has a European vibe—at least, based on the movies.

There's a big, old-fashioned clock in the middle of the square. Music from the nearby pub blares through the patio speaker. It's a familiar tune.

The *Dirty Dancing* song. The same song we danced to at prom.

We stop in our tracks. Renner smiles and extends his hand, pulling me into the center of the bustling square. "Come here. Dance with me."

"We're in public," I whisper as he places his hands around my waist, swaying to the music as a mom with a stroller angrily swerves to avoid us. "And no one else is dancing."

"I hate to break it to you, but look at the way we're dressed. I think we're past caring what anyone else thinks," he says, dipping me back dramatically.

"I still kind of care," I admit, though I let him keep spinning me around.

"I know you do. You always have."

"Is that a bad thing?" I ask, hypnotized by his smile.

He shrugs. "No. But you shouldn't let it stop you from living in the moment. Now come on, do the jump."

"What jump?"

"The *Dirty Dancing* jump." He bends his knees, ever so slightly, impaired by his impossibly tight pants.

I look around at all the people around us, rushing to get to their destinations before the rain starts again. A few curious folks have stopped to take in the show, whispering among themselves. I hear one of them say, "They must be new buskers."

"Come on. You can trust me," Renner says, holding his arms out, steady.

Trust. That's the one thing I've never had with Renner. But after the past few days, I think he might be the person I trust most.

So I do it. I run into him and he seamlessly lifts me above his head. I hold my arms out and it feels like I'm flying, weightless, filled with air. From up here, I feel powerful, strong, like I can do anything.

He holds me for a moment before his arms start to shake. "Um, Char?"

"Yeah?"

"I—I think my pants just split down the front."

I laugh and crane my neck to see for myself, and my body shifts more dramatically than I meant it to, straight out of Renner's arms.

Within a blink, I'm hurtling face forward into the concrete.

TWENTY-SEVEN

There's a familiar dull ache behind my eyes. Something hard jams into my forehead, and my breath hitches, as if a boa constrictor has coiled itself around my chest.

My eyes snap open, body rigid and on high alert. I'm disoriented, like when you're blindfolded in those pin-the-tail games and someone spins you around and around.

That's how I feel as I take in a few facts:

1) I'm lying facedown.
2) My nose is squashed into a dusty wood plank floor. The gymnasium floor.
3) We're no longer in a random alley in Fairfax. I am no longer in Renner's arms.

How did we end up here? Did I have a concussion after Renner dropped me?

I rake my hand through my hair, expecting my fingers to snag on knotted, rain-drenched strands. But it's dry and otherwise smooth.

Speaking of Renner . . . I can smell his clean, lemony scent all around me, as though I've bathed in it. And that's when a low groan vibrates against my chest.

Renner's chin pokes my chest wall, right between my boobs.

"Yup. That's gonna hurt tomorrow," he croaks.

I'm unable to respond, mostly because I'm disoriented. Every muscle and joint in my body aches. I make a mental note to schedule a chiropractor appointment. That seems like an adult thing to do.

Renner gently sets his hands on either side of my waist and rolls me off him. And that's when I get a good look at his face.

He's clean shaven.

Boyishly familiar.

Gone are that broad jawline, the facial hair, the added crinkle lines around his eyes.

I scan the gym, my eye catching a glimpse of the tacky cardboard seaweed affixed to the wall.

We're seventeen again.

We're back.

And so are the blisters on my feet.

~

I feel like I've fallen from a balcony twenty stories up. Everything hurts.

I gather the strength to pull myself into a seated position, and Renner snaps his fingers in my face abruptly. "Char? Are you hurt? You look like total shit."

His words are like an ice bath. It's like being cast into darkness after relishing in the sunlight. Gone are the softness and affection in his eyes.

I shake my head. Before what? The future? The Renner staring at me like I'm a freak of nature is not the Renner who confessed his feelings for me. He's not the Renner I made out with in the rain. Which means . . . it wasn't based in any sort of reality, alternate or otherwise. Because if it were an alternate reality, surely he experienced it too?

Could it have been a dream? Perhaps.

But that doesn't compute. Usually, after a vivid dream, the thrashing heartbeat fades once you regain consciousness. But my heartbeat shows no signs of slowing.

"Hello?" Renner waves his hand annoyingly close to my face.

I recoil before he pokes my eye out. "Yeah. I'm great. Never better," I say sarcastically, batting his limp, outstretched hand away to pull myself up.

Renner remains kneeled over me, stupid seventeen-year-old face backlit by the fluorescent gym light like a tacky, yet annoyingly handsome, angel. A supercut of memories floats through my mind. Walking into the school with him. Being surrounded by friends and family at our bachelor/bachelorette party. Ripping through town playing car hide-and-seek. His chest against mine as we danced to "(I've Had) The Time of My Life" while chaperoning prom. Clutching my stomach with laughter in the thrift store dressing room. The sweet taste of candy on his lips. The feeling of his chin on my head as we hid from the rain.

I'm half tempted to pull his face to mine and see if Real Teen Renner kisses like Adult Renner before logic takes over again. This is the real Renner, after all. The one who insults me whenever possible. The one who delights in all my failings. And the one who lives to make my life a living hell. How could I possibly conjure up anything different?

"I'm . . . I'm gonna go get the nurse," he says, standing.

"N-No," I stammer. "I said I'm fine."

He gives me an *as if* look. "You're not. You can barely get up."

It's natural instinct to prove him wrong. And I try to, at least. I start pulling myself up, but he presses my shoulders down, anchoring me in place. "Jesus, will you just listen to me for once in your life and stay there? You could have a concussion." His tone takes me aback. It's strict, but has an edge of warmth. Not unlike how he addressed his students in phys ed class. When we were thirty.

"Okay. Fine."

About ten minutes later, he returns with Nurse Ryerson. It's a running joke that anyone attracted to women will make an excuse to see Nurse Ryerson. She's admittedly hot for forty.

She performs a quick assessment and badgers us about safety.

"How in the world did you manage to fall off the ladder?" she asks, almost as if it's my fault.

Renner's eyes flicker to mine, daring me to blame it on him. Before he can conjure up some lie to get me in trouble, I steel my spine.

"I fell trying to take a roll of streamers from Renner. He was holding it too far away on purpose, and I guess my weight tipped the ladder off balance," I tell her.

Renner grimaces. "Are you really accusing me of making you fall on purpose? How was I supposed to know that ladder wasn't stable?"

"Well, you two better get your story straight. I'll need to write an incident report for Principal Proulx. And Charlotte, I'm calling your mom to pick you up. You'll need to go to the ER as a precaution."

~

The ER is the stuff of nightmares. Waiting rooms are always anarchy, full of people on their worst days, germs floating about. It's extra stressful for Mom, given our shoddy health insurance.

Luckily, all my scans come back clear. The doctor says I likely have a minor concussion, so I should take the rest of the day to rest, with limited screen time. Mom cackled the entire drive home, my phone in her clutches.

I'll admit, a whole day of forced rest with no electronics is actually more peaceful than I would have imagined. It also gives me time alone with my thoughts.

Only, the moment my head hits the pillow, I sleep straight into Thursday morning.

TWENTY-EIGHT

Two days until prom

Renner has outright ignored my entire existence all morning. It's the norm for him to grind my gears, but snubbing me like I'm a ghost has never been one of his tactics.

Exhibit A: He didn't even bother to race me to our lockers before first period. In fact, he just stood aside, eyes locked to his phone. He let me grab my books without a hassle.

Exhibit B: During homeroom, everyone crowded into the student council lounge to retrieve the new yearbooks. Almost the entire senior class has signed mine, except Renner. There was a lingering moment when our eyes snagged. We could have passed each other our yearbooks, but we didn't.

Exhibit C: He's barely spoken two words in our career-planning class. Even Mr. Kingsley called him out for being uncharacteristically quiet.

I should be working on my time capsule letter to myself, but instead, I stare out the window, brainstorming a list of potential reasons for his behavior. Maybe his ego is hurt after I told him I'd never marry him in the event of a zombie apocalypse before falling off the ladder. Nah, not likely. He views my insults as badges of honor. At least, I think he does. Maybe he's been body snatched by an alien and replaced with a silent version of himself.

I consider what Adult Renner told me—yesterday was the anniversary of his sister's death. Maybe that's the reason for his sullen mood. A quick Google search of her name pulls up an old obituary from the *Maplewood Monitor*. Date of death is exactly seven years ago yesterday—exactly as Adult Renner said. I consider the possibility that it wasn't just a dream. But what's more likely? Subconsciously remembering the anniversary of his little sister's death? Or him slipping into some strange wormhole with me?

Besides, if we had time traveled, he would have mentioned it the moment we woke up in the gym. He's a blabbermouth. I know this from four years of him purposely revealing the ends of movies and TV series. I still haven't forgiven him for spoiling the *Euphoria* season two finale. It's simply not in his nature to withhold information, especially information of this magnitude.

Still, as I stare at Renner's profile two desks up, I find myself appraising him with a strange affection I never had before. It's a feeling I can't quite place. It's like I'm looking at an ex-boyfriend or something, probably because I can't tamp down the memories, especially from the rain. I had such strong feelings for him. And yet, it wasn't a surprise feeling. It was a feeling that crept up on me slowly, so naturally that it felt like coming home.

When I look at him now, I'm not immediately filled with anger and annoyance. I see the kindhearted, stupidly charming Adult Renner. The one who's desperate to make people like him. Who makes me late-night mac 'n' cheese after a gigantic fight.

Maybe I'm just tired. Cranky. Disoriented. I am concussed, after all. Maybe I need to go back to the ER. Surely I'll feel back to normal once I'm fully recovered.

~

At lunch, I find out why Kassie and Ollie didn't show up to help decorate the gym yesterday.

Kassie stomps into the cafeteria in sweatpants and a baggy T-shirt, hair in its natural wave. It's similar to Adult Yoga Kassie's natural hair. Her mouth is set in a stoic line when she sits across from me, gripping her lunch tray. I'm tempted to inquire about her hair when she slams her reusable straw into her water bottle.

"What's wrong? Allergic to the goat?" I ask. Yes, there is a goat at MHS today. You know you've done senior prank week right when there's livestock in the halls, eating people's homework.

Our class is really committing to prank week. Aside from the goat, we've TP'd the gym, poured bubbles in the vents, and set off confetti bombs in the lockers.

"It's nothing," she grumbles.

By the way she says *nothing* and slams her elbows on the table, I know it is, in fact, something. And while I hate that she's upset, part of me is also just thankful we're still best friends.

"Ollie is just being . . . annoying," she finally says.

She and Ollie never fight, especially in public. They're that sickeningly-in-love couple who feeds each other in the cafeteria.

It's an effort not to gasp. I can't help but connect the future, where Kassie and Ollie are history, to the sour face she's making right now as she says his name. My stomach pretzels into a knot, and I place my hand over hers and squeeze. "How is he being annoying?"

"We've been fighting all week. It started Tuesday night," she says with a frown.

Tuesday feels like forever ago. But I force my mind back to that day—the day of the tampon explosion. The day Mom tried to convince me to call Dad. I texted Kassie to vent and she didn't respond. Now I understand why.

She shoves a forkful of beet salad into her mouth and chews vigorously, like she needs sustenance to fuel her explanation. "Every time I bring up apartment hunting in Chicago, he gets pissy. I think he resents the idea of living with me next year instead of being in the dorms. Who wants to live in a 130-square-foot room when you can live with your hot girlfriend in a fabulous downtown apartment?"

Kassie has always had a weird thing against dorm life, especially since Nori and I found out we're going to be dormmates. She's always turning her nose up at the prospect of common bathrooms and shower shoes. But I suspect it's less that she hates the idea and more that she's missing out, not going to college.

I tilt my head in consideration. "Agreed. He should be more excited to get a place with you."

"That's what I thought. But he's being so weird about the whole thing lately. He's heading to the college next weekend to meet with the coach, and he doesn't even want me to come with him. I don't know what to do. I feel like he . . . sees me as some cling-on? I don't chase guys, Char. They chase me." Her blue eyes well with tears.

Normally, I'd be tempted to take the opportunity to commiserate with Kassie about Ollie. Anything to make me feel closer to her. But after experiencing kind and generous Adult Ollie, bad-mouthing him feels wrong. "Ollie wants you there," I assure her, unable to stop envisioning Adult Yoga Kassie, sipping her smoothie, telling me she's over long-term relationships and that she's living her best single life.

"He doesn't. He made that pretty clear."

"Maybe he wants it to be a family thing?" I ask meekly. "I dunno, Kass. Maybe tell him it hurts your feelings that he's being so *meh* about your future together. And that you're feeling a bit left out."

She considers this as she moves the salad around her plate. "Maybe. He's at practice now."

"Yeah. Don't creep outside the locker room again. I'd wait until you're feeling more chill. Like, maybe after school."

Her eyes light up and she squares her shoulders, her confidence locked and loaded. "True. He kinda deserves the silent treatment for the afternoon anyway. It'll keep him on his toes." She pats my hand across the table. "You always know what to say. I'd be lost without you, honestly."

"Same. Who else would work so tirelessly to find me a prom date?" I tease, trying to distract myself from telling her about my ladder fall. It probably isn't the right time. Though let's be real, it'll never be an appropriate time to share that one.

Kassie's smile turns serious. "For real, though. You're always there when I need it. I've been shit. Nori and Renner did all the decorating last night."

Her statement catches me off guard. "I thought Renner was busy?" It was the anniversary of his sister's death, after all.

She shrugs. "With you down for the count, we needed an extra hand. He volunteered."

I nod. Nori told me this morning that Kassie didn't lift a finger. Not that they needed her help.

"I want to be a better friend," she continues, gathering her hair over one shoulder. "How can I improve?"

I don't know why, but my first instinct is to crack a joke. "Well, you can stop airbrushing yourself in group pictures. Leaving the rest of us with yellow smiles and oily foreheads is messed up."

She snorts. "Noted. It is a toxic habit of mine. But what else can I do?"

"It's fine, Kass. You can make it up at the Senior Sleepover tonight. There's lots of setup to do."

"Yes. Totally. It's gonna be a girls' night like old times. I'll even bring the mini Reese's Cups and Funyuns," she adds, wiggling her brows up and down suggestively.

I cringe at the thought of her stinking up my sleeping bag with the smell of onion crisps. "You can leave the Funyuns at home."

"Shut up. They're God's gift to humankind." She rolls her eyes and pulls her phone from her back pocket. "Anyway, I made a new list of prom date contenders during stats class. Thoughts?"

I smile and nod as she presents her case for each guy on the list. This is the Kassie I became best friends with years ago. And even though things have been a little rocky lately, I'll be damned if I let us drift apart.

TWENTY-NINE

When I get home, Mom is rooting through our kitchen drawer of takeout menus, nails encrusted with soil from gardening yesterday.

"Want to order from Smith's tonight? I'm craving their mac and cheese."

I'm bombarded with images of Adult Renner standing in the doorway of our house, two steaming bowls in hand, and my heart aches. I shake myself. I need to get a grip. Stat.

"Um, I don't know about mac and cheese. What about Chinese? From Kozy Korner. You like their wontons," I say, flinging my still-ripped schoolbag on the bench.

She shrugs. "Okay. Sure. Hey, how is your noggin feeling today?"

"Hard as usual," I say, pretending to knock my skull.

"Sounds about right."

"I did think about what you said yesterday morning," I say, collapsing onto the couch, legs dangling over the armrest. The mention of food reminds me of how Renner took me to the drive-thru after I told him about Dad.

"What did I say yesterday?" she asks, half-distracted as she riffles through the drawer.

My heart twinges at the thought of Dad. He was gone. Leaving Alexandra and two technically-unborn-sisters behind. "About calling Dad."

Truth be told, I'm still mad at Dad and the way he's handled things. But now I understand how it feels to no longer have the chance to speak with him, even if I wanted to. So turning down the opportunity now, especially since he extended an olive branch, doesn't sit right.

Her brows rise with surprise. "Oh, really? Okay. Great. He'll be happy to hear from you."

"I'll call him. Maybe when I get home from the sleepover."

"Oh right. The Senior Sleepover is tonight!" She does an embarrassing shimmy. "I remember my Senior Sleepover. Georgia and I made a pact to lose our virginities—"

I toss a throw pillow at her and pretend to gag. "Ew. Mom!"

"You're such a prude, Charlotte," she says, tossing the pillow back. It bounces off my knee and lands on the floor.

Mom has read one too many books on how to talk to kids about sex. Instead of having "the talk" like most parents, she tries to relate to me by using real-life examples, like when she told me all about losing her V-card in the back of a rusted Sunfire, Titanic-style. She's under the impression (delusion) that the more open she is, the more I'll tell her about my nonexistent sex life.

"Anyway, I didn't actually lose it at the sleepover. Turns out the boys and girls had to stay on opposite sides of the gym," she says, seemingly still disappointed.

"We're separated too. If all goes smoothly, at least. Though who knows. Renner was supposed to arrange the chaperones." I lurch. "That reminds me. I never confirmed them."

She gives me a warning look. "You're going to get a hernia if you keep this up. It's Senior Week. These are the best days of your life. Have some fun for once."

I think about Adult Renner. He told me to stop stressing and just enjoy life. "Easier said than done."

She gives me a knowing look. Before she can say anything else, my phone pings.

It's an email. From Cynthia Zellars from the Katrina Zellars Foundation.

My stomach flips.

I brace myself for what I already know. My official denial. I turn my face to avoid Mom's inquisition. I'll fall apart if she sees my disappointment. So while she's distracted ordering dinner, I race to my room, close the door, and dive onto my bed.

Heart racing, I take in a deep breath and open the email.

> To: Charlotte Wu <charlottewu@xmail.com>
> From: Cynthia Zellars <zellarsc@zellarsfoundation.com>
> Subject: Scholarship
>
> Dear Charlotte,
>
> I am pleased to inform you that you are the recipient of the Katrina Zellars Foundation scholarship in the amount of $20,000 USD.

In a blurry haze, I finish reading the rest of the email. And then I reread it, and read it again. Ten times.

Is this a joke? After that abysmal interview, how was I selected for the scholarship? Surely they had many more qualified applicants who didn't ramble off topic about human rights matters.

Striking a huge goal like this off the bucket list feels beyond satisfying. I squeal into the mattress, ecstatic, already rethinking my budget for next year.

My body buzzes with frantic energy. I head back to the living room to tell Mom, but she's hunched over her writing desk, tapping away on her keyboard. Sometimes she gets random bursts of inspiration. I've learned not to disrupt her in these moments.

I pull up my texts and contemplate telling Kassie and Nori ASAP. But my finger hovers over Renner's name. And I remember his behavior at school and the anniversary of his sister's death yesterday. I can't imagine how difficult it must be for him and for his parents. Frankly, it sucked seeing him all sullen and withdrawn. So I click his name. Before I can think too hard, I send a message.

Charlotte: Hi

He responds almost immediately.

Satan 😈: Hey

Charlotte: How are you?

Satan 😈: This feels like a trap. You never ask how I am.

My lips tug upward into a small smile. His cheeky response feels like putting on my favorite sweatpants. They're not the nicest pair, probably a little tattered. But they're comfortable. They're what you know. His text reassures me that I can forget all about the alternate universe. Life can continue on as it was. Our rivalry. My friendship with Kassie. Everything.

Charlotte: I have some news. I got the scholarship.

Satan 😈: See!??? I knew you were overthinking it!

Charlotte: No. It was truly an awful interview. Cynthia hated me.

Satan 😈: Nah. No one hates you.

I stare at that text, unsure where to go from here.

Charlotte: Well . . . you do.

Satan 😈: When have I ever told you I hated you? I don't hate anyone.

Charlotte: You hate me . . . just a tiny bit.

Satan 😈: You can be very difficult.

Charlotte: It's part of my charm.

Satan 😈: I'd say. And let's be clear. You're the one who would rather die than marry me in an apocalypse.

Charlotte: Is it too late to change my mind?

Satan 😈: Really?

Charlotte: I mean . . . if it's life or death, I can't be too picky.

Satan 😈: Lol well thanks. You're a real sweetheart.

Charlotte: I meant to ask, did you take care of the chaperones for tonight?

Satan 😈: Lmao I was waiting for you to ask about that. It's done.

THIRTY

"Do you think bangs would screw up my face?" Nori asks when I slide into her mom's Volvo, tossing my sleeping bag in the back seat. She's giving me a ride to the Senior Sleepover since Mom had a breakthrough on her book tonight.

"What did you say?"

"Bangs. Do you think they'd look good on me?" She fiddles with her hair, pulling a thick section over her forehead to mimic blunt bangs. "Sometimes I think my forehead is too rectangular for them. Maybe I should just cut it real short, like one of those spiky pixie cuts. Thoughts?"

A coldness expands in my core as she reverses out of my driveway. I make a concerted effort to right my face, mind reeling back to Adult Nori. *Tell my younger self not to get bangs,* she'd requested. "Where did that come from?"

She eyes me with suspicion. "Is it really that random? Why are you looking at me like I've sprouted an extra boob?"

"No . . . It's just . . ."

"You're super pale. Is it your concussion?"

I shift toward her, sucking in a deep breath. "Okay, Nori. I'm about to tell you something bizarre. Something that's going to make you think I've lost my mind." I've been itching to tell her since I woke up in the gym yesterday morning. But this is the first time we've actually been alone.

She pulls her focus from the road and shoots me the stink eye. "Weirder than having three boobs?"

"Quite possibly. At least, on a similar level."

"Okay. I need to pull over for this one," she says. We're in front of Old Lady Brown's house with the creepy doll in the window. The giant oak tree is still standing, very much alive.

I tell her about falling off that ladder, about waking up next to Renner, about being thirty. How we were getting married the following week.

A moment passes as she takes it all in, slowly nodding. I can't read her expression. It's hard to say whether she's about to burst out laughing, suggest I see a doctor again, or launch into a black site–style interrogation. Finally, she drums her fingers together and narrows her gaze. "So you're saying I had blue hair?"

"Nori!" I give her a light smack on the shoulder. "That's your one takeaway?!"

She checks herself out in the mirror, running a hand through her hair. "Sorry! It's just—I sound *badass*, aside from the fact that I moved back to Maplewood. That's kinda disappointing."

"To be fair, you were badass."

"So you think this was all in your head?"

"What else could it be?"

She drums her fingers on the steering wheel. "What if it was like, one of those psychic premonitions of the future? Or—ohmigosh! You know the third *Spiderman* movie? With the multiverse? What if it was something like that? Wait, actually, I watched a documentary on the theory behind parallel universes. This is proof. Your brain should be studied. For science!"

I shoot her a skeptical look. "Do you really think any of that stuff is true?"

She shrugs, chewing the inside of her cheek in contemplation. "I believe there's a lot in this world we can't explain."

"I don't know. It was probably just a very vivid dream."

She hums, grabbing a gummy bear from the bag stuffed in the cup holder. It reminds me of when Renner and I bought candy the night we kissed in the rain. "But now that you mention it, J. T. was acting weird last night when we were decorating for prom," she notes.

"Weird how?"

"He was super quiet. Didn't really seem up for chatting, which was fine, because I had my true crime podcast. But obviously J. T. not talking isn't normal."

"Did you know it was the anniversary of his little sister's death yesterday?"

Nori lowers her head. "Oh no. I forgot about that. That would explain it." We sit in silence for a few moments before she speaks again. "But can we please discuss the fact that you saw J. T.'s adult penis. How big are we talking? On a scale of pen-cap micro to forearm ginormous? Tell me everything," she asks, fascinated.

I shake my head as she pulls the Volvo back onto the road. "First, there is no human penis in the world the size of a forearm. At least I hope not. Unless it's the forearm of a baby or a very tiny person." I shake the image out of my head. "Anyway, the point is, I kind of . . . liked it?"

She chokes. "His penis? Or him?"

I shrug. "Both?"

"I . . . yeah. That's some weird shit. I kinda figured you'd have castrated him. But that's growth. I'm proud of you."

I can tell my face is turning red, so I cover it with my hands. "Never, ever bring this up ever again. You will go to your grave with this information," I warn.

"You know I'm a vault."

"Good, because I'm not telling anyone else about this. Not even Kassie. She'll just tell Renner, possibly in front of everyone. Keeping secrets isn't exactly her forte."

"You should tell J. T.," she decides, waving at him as we pull up into the parking lot.

He's in one of his smedium T-shirts again, forearms on display, though less veiny than they were peeking out of his dress shirt as an adult. He gives me a salute and a half smile, which is new. Then again, since I texted about my scholarship news, we've been going back and forth, mostly about the Senior Sleepover logistics. But still.

I snort. "He's the last person I'm telling."

"Why, though? It's possible he experienced the same thing."

"Nori, be serious. I can't just casually ask him if he slipped into the future and was about to marry me. That's way too much ammo. He'll make fun of me for eternity."

She unfastens her seat belt, sneaking one last glance at Renner through the window. "We have one week of high school left. You're not ever going to see him again. What's the worst he can do?"

THIRTY-ONE

I decide not to tell Renner a thing. I'm still not convinced it was anything but a deranged figment of my overactive imagination. And frankly, peace of mind isn't worth my reputation. Besides, the Senior Sleepover is far too hectic to broach the topic.

Who knew having all four hundred seniors stuffed into the B gym would be complete and utter chaos? Well, I guess I should have known. Maybe this is why it was such a challenge to find chaperones.

Kassie and Ollie are nowhere to be seen, yet again. Renner texted Ollie, but he hasn't responded. This leaves me, Nori, Renner, and some of the more helpful teachers to set up the photo booth, the movie projector, all the games and snacks, and order the pizzas.

We have to barricade the outside of the gym with stacked chairs and leftover Halloween caution tape from the drama club's haunted house in October. No one is permitted to leave the gym, unless it's to use the restroom. Of course, not half an hour into the night, a group of band kids already managed to hot-box the bathroom.

After completing most of our tasks, Nori and I finally get to relax and find a quiet corner to set up our sleeping bags.

"We need to make a space for Kassie," I say, moving slightly closer to Nori to make room.

Nori gives me a look. "Um, I dunno if that's necessary." She points over my shoulder, and that's when I see her.

Kassie is here, on the far side of the gym. She looks effortlessly cool in a pair of pink mirrored aviators and a distressed denim jacket. Her blonde hair is tied back with a retro headband, and her sleeping bag is tucked under her arm. She's laughing with Andie and some of the girls from cheer squad, and I see them make room in the middle of their pack for her sleeping bag.

"Isn't she supposed to hang with us?" Nori asks.

"Yup." Kassie eagerly plunks down and tosses Andie a candy bar. Something stirs in my gut and it's not shock, despite our conversation at lunch about hanging out tonight. Kassie said it would be like old times, Funyuns and all.

Everyone gets up when the pizzas arrive. Kassie waltzes right up to Nori and me and grabs a box for the squad. She's casual, friendly, as though she has no idea she's ditched our plans.

Nori darts me a side-eye, annoyed on my behalf.

Eventually, Renner and Ollie help us in the pizza assembly line. Nori gives out plates, I'm on napkins, Ollie opens the pizza boxes, and Renner doles out soda and water. Once we finally get into a groove, Kassie comes sauntering back, distracting Ollie with a dramatic hug. Clearly, they've made up and then some. I'm guessing she can see that I'm stressed because she says, "Hey, what can I do?"

"Nothing, everything's already taken care of," I respond bluntly, handing Reggie Wilson a napkin. Technically, Kassie could be on garbage duty, or running the empty boxes to recycling. But the four of us already have a good system going, and frankly, I don't need her pity help.

"I'm sorry I got here late," Kassie says. "But everything is all good now."

"All good with what? Did you make up with Ollie?" I ask, unable to hide the bitter undercurrent in my tone.

She flinches, uncomfortable that I've mentioned their fight. I regret it when Ollie shoots her a betrayed look.

This is uncomfortable. Send help.

She twists her glossed lips. "Why do I feel like you're shooting me daggers? Are you mad at me or something?"

It's tempting to yell, *Yes, I'm mad at you!* This is certainly not how I imagined our girls' night. I've been looking forward to spending time with Kassie, the way we used to, before we leave high school. We're supposed to do all the Senior Week activities together. But I can't explain all this to her in front of the entire senior class.

"It's fine, Kassie," I snap, turning my attention to the next person in line.

"It's not fine," Renner cuts in, his voice terse and sharp. He sets down a new box of pizza and shoots her a look.

"Dude, what's your problem?" Ollie eyes him suspiciously. In his defense, I'm not sure I've ever heard Renner use this tone.

Renner huffs. "Char and I got to the gym yesterday morning at 6:00 a.m. to set up for prom. We also got here an hour and a half ago. And you haven't even lifted a finger. As a member of the student council, it would be nice if you showed up to do your job."

A hush falls, everyone stunned at Renner's serious tone.

Kassie blinks, taken aback. "Chill, J. T. I'm here now, offering to help. Char literally just said there's nothing for me to do. Why are you freaking out?"

I expect Renner to smile and apologize, but he doesn't back down. "Because you always do this. You always leave all the heavy lifting to Char and then swoop in at the end and take credit for things."

Her jaw falls open. She hitches her shoulders, arms crossed, well aware that everyone in line is overhearing the argument. "Maybe I would do more if Char didn't boss everyone around. You said it yourself, J. T., she's not a team player."

Nori gasps.

"Someone has to organize all the logistics, Kass. I can't take care of everything. I have to delegate things," I shoot back.

But she doesn't back down. "I signed up to be on student council as a *member*. We all did. We're supposed to be a team. And you treat everyone like some minion, ordering us around, expecting us to do everything your way. It's like no one else is allowed to have an opinion."

That's it. I'm done. I slap the napkin bundle on the table and turn to her. "This isn't just about student council. We were supposed to spend the night like old times, and you've spent the entire time with the cheer squad."

"You're really that mad that I'm spending the night with the cheer girls? Seriously?"

"It's not just tonight. You're not reliable. You ditch me. All. The. Time. For Ollie, ninety-nine percent of the time. We're going to be in different cities in two months and we haven't done a single Senior Week activity together—like we were supposed to. You're going to live with Ollie next year. Why do you need to spend every waking moment together?"

She blinks, shaking her head in disgust. "Char, you just don't get what it's like to have a boyfriend."

"Maybe not. But I know what it's like to be a good friend. I can't say the same for you." I regret my words the moment they come out. In front of the entire student body. Everyone's eyes are on me, and it's dead silent. I feel a wave of nausea mounting. I think I'm gonna pass out. I spin on my heels and do the only logical thing. Flee.

~

It's dark in the stairwell. Cooler, much cooler than the stuffy gym. I place my hands on my knees and bend over, letting my breath pass slowly, in through my nose and out through my mouth. When I finally manage to get my heart rate back in check, the stairwell door creaks open behind me.

I expect to see Kassie or Nori. But no, it's Renner. My face is inches from his neck.

"You scared me. I thought you were someone else," I say, my cheeks reddening when I meet his eye. I stiffen and look away to conceal my face—which I'm sure says it all.

One time I had a hard-core dream about making out with Clay. And the next day in Model UN, I could barely look in his direction without wanting to keel over and die. This feels infinitely worse.

"That was . . . a lot," he says. "You good?"

"Yeah. I'm just . . . tired. Senior Week is stressful." I still don't feel like my body has caught up from the exhaustion of yesterday.

"Want to get some air?" He tilts his head up toward the stairwell.

"It's off bounds. We're not supposed to leave the gym," I remind him.

"We already have, technically. Come on. Live a little," he says, tugging my pinkie finger.

I let him guide me, grateful for the opportunity to delay facing Kassie and everyone else who witnessed my epic meltdown. "Where are we going?"

"Somewhere you've definitely never been."

I'm not sure how that's possible. After four years on the student council, I've seen nearly every nook and cranny of this school. We reach the next floor and he leads me through a darkened hallway near the English department, then through a door I always thought was a janitorial closet. It opens to a narrow set of cement stairs.

"What is this?" I ask.

"You'll see."

Turns out, the super-secret stairs lead to a super-super-super-secret rooftop. It boasts a sweeping view of the parking lot and part of the football field. I stare out at the field wistfully, reminiscing about all those brisk fall evenings Kassie and I spent watching Ollie's games from the bleachers. She always made me paint my face in school colors, though her paint would magically stay on all night while mine would smudge in a matter of minutes.

"How did you know about this? I had no idea you could get up here," I say, rubbing the gooseflesh that's emerged on my bare arms.

"That's what happens when you live dangerously," he teases. "Some of the guys on the football team used to come up here to work out when the weight room was too full. Run drills and stuff. Everyone liked it because the coach didn't come to check on us much here. I used to hate it, though." He peers over the edge, gripping the wall for support.

A bubble of laughter rises in my throat. I'm not used to vulnerable Renner. "Still haven't conquered your fear of heights, huh?"

"Not quite."

"Remember when you had to be rescued from the zip line on Ollie's birthday?" I clutch my chest at the memory. Renner climbed the very first tree, froze, and needed the skinny instructor to rappel him down. He was first in line, so everyone saw.

"Yes. Thanks for the reminder." He nudges me and sits on the gravel.

I plunk down next to him, pulling my knees to my chest.

"So . . . that was interesting back there," he says.

"Everyone heard, didn't they?"

The corner of his mouth slants upward, ever so slightly. "I mean, not everyone. Only about seventy percent of the seniors."

I turn to him. "Look, before you say anything, I know what I said to Kassie was wrong. It was mean. I'm going to apologize to her."

"No. You were right. You may need to work on your delivery . . . but what you said was true. She isn't a good friend to you, Char." He says it with such conviction. It reminds me of when Adult Renner said exactly the same thing about her.

"She tries to be. She really does," I pledge, pushing the fine gravel back and forth. "Like, I don't think she means to fail me so much. It's not malicious. And maybe my expectations are too high?"

He waves me off. "Remember that time in ninth grade when you planned her birthday party and she came for like an hour and then ditched you to go to Ollie's?"

I definitely remember that. It was when they first started dating. She and Ollie were already attached at the hip, and I remember selfishly hoping it would only be temporary, until she moved on to another guy she was less obsessed with. But she never did. In fact, their infatuation only grew. Don't get me wrong, I've always loved Ollie. But it's hard not to feel a twinge of bitterness toward him. He's the reason our friendship changed.

I wince at the memory. "I went all out for that party. I biked everywhere to find the right streamers. I taped them around my house. Spent the whole night blowing up balloons. I even got her a cake from the bakery downtown she likes."

"Have you ever just told her how you feel?"

"I have a couple times. But it doesn't really fix things, so I've kind of given up and accepted this is how things are. And she was probably right about me back there—maybe I do kind of take control and order everyone around."

He seems disappointed in that answer. "For what it's worth, I don't agree. You do a lot. You're always covering for everyone. Including me. All year you've saved my ass. You've basically run the council single-handedly. I've never actually thanked you."

My breath hitches. Real Renner has never acknowledged the work I've done, let alone thanked me with genuine appreciation. "I don't know what to say. I appreciate it," I say, tepidly.

"Good." He gives me a playful nudge.

I close my eyes, basking in the warmth of the setting sun against my face. I feel so at peace, which is a small miracle after what just happened in the gym. "How are you feeling? I know yesterday was rough."

His body tenses. "It was hard. My mom was in a bad place. Didn't get out of bed to spend time with my dad and me."

"I'm so sorry."

He shrugs. "I tried to cheer her up, but nothing made a difference."

I think about when he told me about his mom at Walnut Creek. "It's not on you to make her happy again, Renner. That's way too big of a burden. You can't be the sun to all people without eventually burning out."

I see him nod in my peripheral vision. "How about you? Have you spoken to your dad since the other day?"

"He wants to have brunch. Before prom." I decided to call him before Nori picked me up. He seemed happy to hear from me. Strangely, he wasn't distracted. He asked a couple pointed questions about Senior Week and who my prom date was. I had to confess I was going solo. Part of me suspects Mom briefed him on what was going on with me beforehand. Before I could bring up the lake house, he said he wanted to come to town and take me out for brunch. Just the two of us.

"How do you feel about that?"

"Scared? Nervous? It's been so much easier not talking to him all these years. Because then I wouldn't be disappointed. Now it feels so strained. Knowing he's talking to me because he's engaged and having a baby. But then the other part of me feels so guilty for not talking to him. Like, I want a relationship with my future sister—or brother," I correct. "But it's hard to imagine having one with him. Am I making any sense?"

"Yeah. You are. And you don't need to feel guilty at all. He left you. He's the one who missed out. And that's on him to fix."

"I guess."

He stares ahead for a few breaths. "If you want . . . I can go with you?"

I squint in confusion. "Go with me? To meet my dad?"

"I mean, not like . . . to brunch. That would be awkward. Unless you wanted me to," he adds, voice trembling in almost a nervous lilt. "But I could drive you and just wait outside?"

"Really? You'd do that?" I'm reminded of how willing Adult Renner was to accompany me to see Alexandra and the girls. How comforting his presence was when I was a bundle of nerves the entire drive there.

"Of course."

I narrow my gaze in suspicion. "Why are you suddenly being nice to me?"

"I could ask you the same question. You haven't bit my head off in twenty-four hours." He pulls his phone out theatrically to confirm the time. As he slips his phone back, his leg brushes against mine.

I want to tell him the real reason. But I don't. Because I don't want to ruin whatever this is. "Do you ever wonder what things would have been like if . . ." I let my words drift, head heavy with familiarity. Because we've had this conversation before.

"All the time," he says simply, like he knew what I was going to say.

"I guess it's too late now," is all I can think to say. Senior Week is almost over. And then all of this will be over. We'll be off on our separate paths. Life as we know it is going to change forever.

"Is it too late?" he asks simply.

I look over, eyes meeting his. I study his gorgeous eyes, the dense line of his lashes. His breath ghosts my cheek and I close my eyes, reveling in this feeling. My body buzzes with warmth and brightness that could rival the now blood-orange sky.

The moment hangs between us, stretching, threatening to snap as his nose grazes the tip of mine. His breathing is ragged, hollow, mixing with my own. And then he kisses me.

THIRTY-TWO

The real J. T. Renner kisses with his whole damn body too.

He's hungry, catching my lips hard and pressing firmly. And it feels good, like a long-awaited release.

Maybe I'm no longer able to distinguish between dream and reality. But I kiss him back without inhibition. Because this doesn't feel like the first time. It's an indescribably familiar feeling, like déjà vu on steroids.

He traces my jaw, threading his hands into my hair and angling my head just so as his tongue slides against mine. I lean in, bringing myself closer to his body. I can feel the heat radiating off him.

"You have no idea how long I've wanted to do this," he pants as I drag my fingers down his back, admiring each muscly ridge along the way.

I peer at him and contemplate requesting specifics. How many months, weeks, days, hours, seconds, exactly? I'm a woman of detail and precision, after all. But bringing arithmetic into this seems like a surefire way to kill the vibe and sabotage the hottest moment of my entire life. So I keep kissing him. And kissing him. Absorbing every bit of him as if making up for lost time.

I don't know how much time has passed. It feels like hours, but simultaneously only seconds. Either way, it isn't nearly as much time as I'd like. Somehow, we end up horizontal, with him on top of me.

By the time he pulls back and we sit upright, my lips are swollen and numb. He gives me that heart-stopping smile before wrapping his arms around my waist. A deep breath escapes me as I nestle my forehead against the cove of his neck and relish his lemony scent. This feels safe. Real.

For the past two days, I've desperately tried to untangle and separate dream vs. reality. But here, with him, the two collide and fuse together, rendering them indistinguishable.

I think about what he said when we were sitting in the park watching the sun go down, about how I need to live life to the fullest. Take chances. Stop dwelling and worrying. Normal me hasn't asked anyone to prom for fear of being turned down. Normal me would rather just stress and despair over being dateless than take the chance. But I don't want to live that way. I want to take more chances, do more that makes me happy. I can't think of anything that would make me happier than going to prom with Renner. My mortal enemy.

"Renner. This is gonna sound random . . . ," I start.

He smirks. "Uh-oh."

"Do you maybe, um . . . want to go to prom with me?" I ask. It comes out more like *doyouwannagotopromwithme*. It's also much louder than intended. I've practically yelled it in his face and I don't even care.

Maybe I'm experiencing endorphin overload. Maybe Renner's kiss is making me delusional. But I expect him to smile and shout *Yes* from the rooftop (literally). Instead, my words hit dead air like a foghorn. He blinks like I've just splashed him in the face with ice water.

And that's when the door creaks open.

"There you are! I've been looking everywhere for you." It's Andie.

Renner jumps back like I'm a disease.

Andie's expression flickers with suspicion. "What are you guys doing up here?"

Redness heats Renner's cheeks as he drags a hand over the back of his neck, almost like he's guilty of something. "Nothing. Just talking about . . ."

"Prom," I blurt, crumbling under Andie's stare.

Her face lights up and she gives Renner an expectant look. "Okay, that reminds me. We need to talk about your tie. I don't know if it's the lighting, but the picture you sent me doesn't go with the color of my dress."

My stomach sinks like a bag of bricks tossed into the frothy ocean. Renner and Andie are going to prom together?

Renner's eyes dodge mine and immediately dart to his shoes. "Uh, does that really matter? Orange ties aren't really easy to find—"

"It matters. The pictures will be forever."

"So . . . you guys are going to prom together?" I ask.

Renner's eyes remain glued to his feet, blatantly avoiding me. "Yeah."

My vision blurs. Sweat practically rains down my forehead. I turn away and say something to the effect of, "Oh. Um, cool." This must be what it feels like to have an out-of-body experience. And I thought time travel felt strange.

This is the point where I question every decision I've ever made that led me here. I'm positively mortified. What I wouldn't give to defect to a remote jungle. I've watched enough Discovery Channel. I'd have a decent shot in the wilderness, trading twigs and berries with forest animals. I didn't think anything could be worse than dropping my tampons in front of Clay Diaz. But asking Renner to prom takes the cake. What was I thinking?

"I'm sorry," he says, though the words don't settle. Like water on leather.

I can't stand the way he's looking at me, expression full of anguish and something that closely resembles pity. I need to get off this roof. Stat.

"Char, wait—" Renner calls when I beeline it for the stairwell door.

Before he can finish, I'm gone.

THIRTY-THREE

I'll admit, there's a lot in this world that brings me displeasure. But running is somewhere at the top of that list.

There's that spiking pain in my calves and shins that doesn't go away for days. The fact that my lungs feel like they're caving in on me. That I'm slower than a turtle so time feels like it stretches for eternity.

And trust me, I've tried to love it like everyone else (liars). Really, I have. When Kassie and Nori joined the cross-country team in ninth grade, I tried my hand at it too. Five minutes into a practice run around the block, I nearly keeled over on a random person's lawn.

But tonight, I run.

I've sprinted at least ten blocks in my white Keds. Sure, I feel the burn. But the shin splints are nothing compared to the searing pain inside. After seventeen years, I've finally discovered the secret to running. Anger and turmoil.

Flashbacks of meeting Kassie for the first time catapult through my mind. We're nine, laughing at the park, seeing how high we can go on the swings. Then we're thirteen, feeling very adult at the mall with our Pinkberry frozen yogurt, unsupervised for the first time. We're sixteen, driving around and around Maplewood, singing at the top of our lungs. Maybe the glue that held us together all these years is drying and crumbling. Part of me knows it's true. I just don't want to admit it.

I'm huffing and puffing as I tear down the road, only shifting over toward the ditch when headlights flood my vision.

I squint into the light as the car approaches, coming to a near full stop behind me. It's only when my eyes adjust that I recognize the vehicle. Kassie's white Prius.

She honks once, probably because I'm staring straight into her headlights, stunned. What the heck is Kassie doing here on the side of the road? She should be at the sleepover.

I head over to the passenger window and look in. Her expression is a little forlorn and skittish, like she's bracing for me to ream her out. I don't say anything, mostly because I'm still completely out of breath. And also, because I'm staring at her like she's a mirage. She leans over and opens the door for me.

Silently, I slide into the passenger seat. She tosses a full bag of puffy Cheetos into my lap, a peace offering, before pulling back onto the road.

For the next two hours, we drive aimlessly through the side streets of Maplewood, scream-singing Olivia Rodrigo and Taylor Swift until our fingers are permanently orange and caked with Cheeto dust. It occurs to me as we head back toward my house that we haven't had an actual conversation, aside from a brief rant about how she thinks turtlenecks are sexier than they get credit for.

While I can't get on board with turtlenecks, I can't help but laugh. It's moments like this with Kassie that I've missed. Moments where we don't have to say anything to each other. Moments where we're not worrying about our impending futures or the next big school event. When all we care about is having fun. Living in the now.

Logically, I know I've let her off the hook too easily. Nori likes to remind me that this is our cycle. Kassie lets me down on the regular, then apologizes elaborately with some rom-com–style gesture. Like the time she ditched out last minute on spending the weekend in the city with Mom and me. She showed up the night I got back and threw snowballs at my window. And there are all those times that she's called out of the blue and picked me up for an adventure in the middle of the night. Of course, it's always on her terms.

The situation deserved to be talked out properly. But after everything that's happened, I'm craving the familiarity and comfort of being with my best friend—even if it doesn't feel right.

It's also hard to stay mad at Kassie for long. She's like a big-eyed puppy who chewed your passport into smithereens days before your international vacation, but you still can't help but forgive her. She may be selfish. Incapable of considering how her actions affect other people. But I know deep down she has a big heart. She cares about me and our friendship.

Besides, being unwilling to forgive would mean holding my anger inside, letting it fester, and potentially fulfilling the future prophecy. While my patience with our friendship is waning, I could use Kassie's wisdom right now. Especially after what happened with Renner earlier tonight.

I'm angry at Renner, but I can't help but think about what Adult Renner said in that alleyway. How I need to have more moments like this where I'm not stressing. Where I'm just living in the now.

I extend my hand out the window, feeling the wind against my palm. The faint smell of KFC from a couple streets over. The navy sky. I take it all in, cementing it in my memory. I just wish this weren't so fleeting.

I don't want to stress about Senior Week events, or prom, or being valedictorian, or everything that comes with packing up my life in Maplewood. And I definitely don't want to think about my journey into the future.

"So what happened with J. T.?" she finally asks as we pull back into the school parking lot.

I blink, like I've been caught in some sort of twisted lie.

"I know you guys went to the roof. He seemed upset when he came back into the gym. Told me you'd left and that I should go after you," she explains.

"He told you to come after me?" I repeat.

She nods.

Would Kassie have left the sleepover if Renner hadn't asked her to? I shove that thought aside and focus on the current situation. Based on her casual, curious tone, I know Renner didn't tell her we kissed. If he had, she'd be unable to keep her cool. And she certainly wouldn't have been able to resist confronting me for so long.

I sigh, mourning the comfortable silence. I can't *not* tell her. But I also can't tell her about the chain of events that led to kissing Renner. First, she's not Nori. She'd think I'm a total weirdo. And second, she has a big mouth.

She waits as I gather my thoughts.

"A bunch of things," I say vaguely, choosing my words carefully. I want to sidestep the truth without blatantly lying.

She shoots me a knowing look, drumming her nails on the console between us. "Ugh. I know I'm beating a dead horse here, but you've really gotta stop letting him ruin everything for you. First prom, now the sleepover—"

If only it were as simple as kiboshing my prom theme idea or something equally petty. If only a complete delusion hadn't created such a longing, and a void, a feeling that was never there before.

"It wasn't like our normal fights," I say. "We kissed," I admit, because it's the only thing that will partially make her understand.

Her eyes widen like pancakes. "Wait, what? You kissed J. T.? J. T. Renner?" she whispers, enunciating *kissed* slowly, like she's speaking a foreign language. I hide my face in my hands before she whacks me on the shoulder. "Tell. Me. Everything! Right now!"

"I don't even know how it happened," I blurt. It's a partial lie. I know where the feelings come from and I know why I kissed him. The question is, Why the hell did he kiss me?

She flicks me in the arm, something she does when she doesn't find my responses adequate.

"Renner came into the stairwell to check on me after our . . . fight." I look away. Kassie and I still haven't addressed it. Strangely, this is easier to talk about. "Somehow, we ended up on the rooftop for some air. And it just happened," I say with a shrug.

She blinks, not buying it. "You didn't just go from being on a rooftop with someone you hate to making out. I know you. You'd rather have pushed him off the edge than let his lips touch yours."

I snort, cheeks burning. "He used his magical Renner charm, I guess. I was stressed over setting things up, spiraling . . . thinking you hated me," I add cautiously.

She gives me a knowing look. "I obviously didn't hate you. But go on."

"Anyway, he was being weirdly sweet. Uncharacteristically understanding."

"Char, J. T.'s a nice guy. He's always been this person, if you'd have just let him."

My lips tighten at the memory of what happened after the kiss. Does a nice person really tell someone they have feelings for them when they're already going to prom with someone else? Doubtful. And to be honest, that's the version of Renner that's more palatable. The one that feels more comfortable, because it's all I've known. Until recently, at least.

"Well, he's not," I tell her. "It was just another one of his stupid mind games."

"Mind games? Why would you think that?"

"Because I asked him to prom," I admit.

She lurches forward, pressing the inside of her wrist to my forehead to check my temperature. "Are you ill?"

"I asked myself that same question," I say.

"He's going to prom with Andie," she says matter-of-factly.

I cringe. This is not one of those realities that gets easier to swallow the more I hear about it. In fact, it's the opposite. "He told me. After we practically dry humped on the roof," I explain, my tone laced with bitterness.

"Dry humped?" She descends into maniacal laughter, slapping the steering wheel, and inadvertently punching the horn. And while none

of this is remotely funny, I can't help but join in, giggling alongside her until we're both slouched in our seats, clutching our stomachs.

"Please tell me that counts as an ab workout," I say.

Once we've recovered, she looks at me and sits up again, hair a total mess. "Nope. We're not avoiding. I can't believe you *dry humped* J. T.!"

"First, please stop saying *dry hump*. That's a disgusting term."

"You said it first!"

"And you're one to talk. I can't believe you never told me he was going to prom with Andie," I counter.

Her mouth twists with a hint of defensiveness. "But why would I? It's not like he was on my list of contenders for you. Lest we forget, you demanded to be as far away from him in the limo as possible. And now you're mad that he's going with Andie? What's going on with you?"

That is the question, isn't it? She's not wrong. *Mad* isn't the right way to describe how I'm feeling. "Because he obviously just kissed me to . . . I don't know . . . embarrass me? I'm shocked he didn't brag about it to everyone." It's the only plausible explanation I can think of.

She shakes her head. "I don't think that's true. He didn't say anything about kissing you." She smiles at me knowingly, eyes glinting. "You have to admit, J. T.'s a good kisser, though, huh?"

THIRTY-FOUR

One day until prom

It's perfect weather for Senior Beach Day. It's hot enough to require multiple dips in the lake to cool off, but not so hot that every step in the sand feels like trudging through Satan's lair. The sky is pure blue and cloudless, except for a few cotton candy wisps.

I take full credit for this, given I scoured fifty years' worth of historical weather reports, pinpointing the day during Senior Week with the least history of rain. I've also been monitoring the long-range forecast for weeks, fully prepared to shift to our backup day if need be.

Everyone's here, swimming in the lake or suntanning on beach blankets with music. And there's no shortage of activities, from beach volleyball to football, spikeball, and Frisbee.

I'm intent on enjoying this day, despite being forced to third-wheel on my own extra-large beach blanket with Kassie and Ollie. And yes, it is as painfully awkward as it sounds, especially when they start making out next to me. Every lip smack and slurp sends a shiver down my spine, and not in a good way. I think Nori's also offended because she lifts her sunglasses and fires silent laser beams at them.

My attempt to avoid Renner has proven successful for the past two hours, as well as last night when Kassie and I returned to the sleepover. He's been playing in a spikeball tournament while I creepily watch but pretend to be sleeping (bless sunglasses). Unfortunately, the spikeball crew returns right as I'm fixing myself a sandwich from the cooler.

Renner parks himself on the towel a couple feet in front of me and doesn't even bother to spare me a glance. Though I'm not surprised. What is there to say? Aside from bragging about making me look like a total nimrod? Even he's not that vicious, at least in front of other people.

"Rough loss, J. T. Sucks to suck," Ollie calls to him playfully, drawing his gaze in my direction.

Our eyes snag for a second until he's distracted by Andie. Because of course. She's frolicking near the water, long dark hair slicked back, beads of moisture shimmering on her perfectly ripped *Sports Illustrated* bod. There's no mistaking Renner's eye, fixed on her as she runs through the sand, like she's auditioning for a *Baywatch* reboot.

I grumble under my breath when she flops beside him, ample cleavage spilling over her bikini. I am sincerely jealous of her cleavage and wish I had my own. Now. Not at thirty.

"Hey, you. Can you help? I don't want tan lines with my prom dress tomorrow." Andie tosses a bottle of sunscreen into Renner's lap and points to her back.

My jaw tightens. Renner jumps without hesitation, squirting a pile of lotion into his palm. Andie even asks him to untie her bikini top. I am trapped in a nightmare.

To avoid them, I'm forced to glare directly into the sun. I shouldn't be upset. Renner isn't mine. I have exactly zero claim to him. Not that I'd want to anyway. Because he's a turd. And yet, I can't shake this intense jealousy at the sight of Renner's hands all over Andie's back. The same hands that were all over me on the roof. The same hands that were all over me when we were thirty.

Unable to stomach their lotion massage, I take off down the beach, bypassing a crew of kids guzzling extra-large thermoses.

It doesn't take long before I pick up the scent of hot dogs a ways down the beach. It's the barbecue station, manned by Principal Proulx, who's sweating profusely through his dandelion-yellow T-shirt. My stomach grumbles as I take my place in line.

The line moves painfully slow, mostly because Principal Proulx is flirting with Nurse Ryerson, and she's responsible for the condiment table.

Just when I move close in line, a familiar voice sounds behind me. "Hey, man. Mind if I cut in front of you? I just need to talk to Char real quick."

I spin around. It's Renner.

He's somehow managed to charm Tommy Dixon, a goth dude wearing a thick black hoodie at the beach. He doesn't typically speak to anyone if he can help it, except Renner, apparently. I watch in awe as Renner compliments one of his paintings displayed in the hallway at school. Tommy seems flattered and explains that it's an abstract representation of his mortality before eagerly waving him ahead.

Renner flashes me his megawatt smile, as though everything is peachy keen. "Hey."

"You can't just cut in line," I whisper.

"Tommy's cool with it," he says, looking back. Tommy winks at Renner and gives me an army salute. (Tommy has never acknowledged my existence before.) Renner turns back around, eyes narrowed. "I need to talk to you."

I let out a groan. I already know how this will go. He's going to explain he was already taking Andie to prom before we kissed. He's going to deny kissing me with nefarious intent. I'm not going to believe him. The end.

I move up in line, arms crossed. "I don't think there's anything left to say."

He follows a step behind me. "Seriously, Char? You just stormed off the roof last night. You didn't give me a chance to explain," he says, not bothering to lower his voice.

"Why do you have to talk so loud?" I ask, irritated that the entire line is now privy to our business. "And you don't need to explain. Why don't you go continue lotioning your girlfriend and leave me—"

Before I have the chance to finish, my gaze is pulled to a familiar face. It's Clay. He's heading toward the barbecue line, tattered flip-flops in hand. His hair is blowing in the breeze as he squints into the sun. He's tall, lean, one of those guys with natural abs, unlike Renner, who works for his chiseled gym bod and flaunts it at any opportunity.

Clay gives me Cole Sprouse vibes, the type who's into poetry and anything ironic and offbeat.

When he sees me looking his way, he waves and saunters straight toward me.

I will the sand beneath me to turn to quicksand. There's nothing more awkward than coming face-to-face with someone who blatantly ignored your DM.

"Hey, Canada," he says with effortless cool. "I've been wanting to talk to you."

I blink into the sunlight, mute, my usual self around him until Renner pokes me to move up in line. He's eyeing Clay suspiciously.

"You—you have?" I manage.

Clay smiles. "Why do you look so surprised?"

"I messaged you the other day. You didn't respond." I immediately regret speaking. Silence is best. Silence is safe.

He knits his forehead in confusion. "What? You did?" He pulls his phone from his pocket.

"On Instagram," I clarify.

His mouth forms into an O shape. "I deleted Instagram from my phone during exam week and forgot to download it again. I'm so sorry. I would have answered otherwise."

He looks genuinely apologetic. A sense of relief washes over me, and I wipe the bead of sweat that's about to drip into my eyeball. This whole time I thought he was purposely ignoring me.

"Oh. No worries. I didn't, um . . . care too much," I say.

He gives me a funny smile. "Oh, well, okay then."

"No. No. I did care," I say quickly. "I wanted you to message me back."

He breaks into a blinding smile and I start to lose myself, but I snap back at the sight of Renner frowning at me in the periphery.

"It's your turn to order, Char," Renner says. All the meat on the grill is nearly scorched. Principal Proulx is still paying far more attention to Nurse Ryerson.

"Oh, right." Frazzled, I accidentally order two hamburgers instead of two hot dogs. I also manage to squirt the entire contents of the mustard container all over my chest.

When the conversation lulls, Clay turns on his heel to go. I squeeze my eyes shut. This can't be how this afternoon goes. If Renner is going to fall madly in love with Andie, I need to move on. I think about Kassie's advice—to be bold. Take charge. So I go for it.

"Hey, Clay?" I call after him. "Are you going to prom tomorrow night?"

He turns back and points to his chest, as if to say, *Who? Me?* "Wasn't planning on it. I'm not really much of a dancer," he admits.

"Ah. You didn't come to the sleepover either. High school traditions aren't your thing?" I ask, trying to keep my voice steady.

"They would be . . . if I had someone to go with," he says shyly.

A lump lodges in my throat. "Well . . . I'm planning to go."

"Yeah?"

"Yup. Do you . . . do you want to maybe go with me? If you don't already have other, better plans." Good lord. I'm awful at this. I need to go home and lie down.

"Sounds like fun. DM me the details," he says. "I'll make sure to download Instagram again." He flashes the signature Clay Diaz smile before turning away.

A squeal escapes me and I practically dent my paper plate with my fingertips. I just asked Clay Diaz to prom. Clay. Diaz. The guy I've been hopelessly and pathetically pining over for the past four years. In what world did I drum up the lady balls to do that?

By the time I remember that Renner was behind me in line, he's gone.

THIRTY-FIVE

I find Renner back with our group, sharing grapes and flirting with Andie, of course.

Kassie takes a break from sucking face with Ollie to acknowledge my return and I plop down next to them. "What's up with you?"

"IjustaskedClayDiaztoprom," I word vomit, wiping the sweat off my forehead.

She blinks. "What?"

"I just asked Clay to prom," I repeat, handing her my extra hamburger.

Nori sits up and swipes it before Kassie has the chance, and shoves her sunglasses on top of her head. "What? What did he say?"

"He said *yes*."

Kassie screeches, which catches everyone's attention, including Renner's. "You're going to prom with *Clay*."

"Clay!" I blurt in a poor attempt to match Kassie's enthusiasm. Strange that she's more excited than I am?

Everyone congratulates me, except Renner. In fact, he's turned back to Andie, far too enamored to care. Not that I want him to.

~

The rest of the afternoon is filled with excited chatter about the details of prom the next night. How we're doing our hair, what time we're showing up at Ollie's for photos, who's responsible for what tasks.

"You and Clay are gonna look way too adorable in couple photos," Kassie tells me. "Did you ask him to match your dress?"

I scan the beach for Clay. But there's no more sign of him, or any of his friends. "We didn't have time to talk about that. But I'm gonna send him all the details. Tonight."

Kassie rests her head on my shoulder. "Look at you being bold and going after what you want. I'm so proud."

I nod, thinking about how I asked two guys to prom in the span of twenty-four hours. I have no idea where I found the strength to do that. But it feels good, despite being turned down by Renner. Then again, I like to believe everything happens for a reason. Had Renner not turned me down, I wouldn't have had the courage to ask Clay.

This is all I've wanted for years. I've dreamed of the moment when Clay Diaz would take interest in me. And now, he's agreed to be my date for prom. I should be doing cartwheels along the beach.

And yet, I can't seem to summon the excitement I should be feeling.

THIRTY-SIX

Prom day

I expected to wake up on prom morning and spring out of bed all peppy and buzzing. Everything is exactly as it should be. Kassie and I made up. Renner and I are full-on rivals, enemies, foes, nemeses again.

But instead, all I feel when Mom opens my curtains is *blah*. I just want to hide under the covers. Not because I feel depressed or anything, but because I want it all to slow down. I've spent endless hours thinking about Senior Week all year, but it's crept up faster than I can keep up with, like brick painting, yearbook signing, and now prom. It seems unfair that it all feels so anticlimactic.

"Did you just hiss at me?" Mom asks.

I shield my eyes like a vampire and dive underneath the covers, where it's safe. "Maybe."

She gives me a gentle shake over the blanket. "Come on. Get excited. It's prom night! You've been waiting for this since you were a little girl."

I croak a weak "Yayyyyy," but it comes out like a wounded animal. How else can I explain my lack of excitement? I feel total apathy every time I envision myself taking pictures at Ollie's, walking into the crowded gym.

"And you're going with Clay Emmanuel Diaz. The hottest guy at MHS."

I lift the blanket and shoot her an icy look. "I don't even want to know how you know Clay's middle name."

"I creeped him on my burner Instagram account," she admits proudly, as though having a covert IG account to keep track of your kid and their friends is totally normal. I shiver when she tugs the blankets off me, exposing my skin to the cool air. "Come on, get up. I'm not letting you sleep away the best days of your life."

I cast a skeptical glance. "Are these really the best days of my life?"

"That's the thing about the best days of your life. You don't know they're the best until they're already gone," she tells me, eyes brimming with nostalgia.

That's a truly depressing thought. If that's true, what does it mean for someone like me who lives for crushing goals and milestones? Will I ever experience the true joy of achieving them in the moment? Or will the best part always be remembering those times after they've already passed?

For a moment, I think Mom is going to bust out her high school yearbook again before she stands. "It's ten thirty, by the way. Don't forget you have brunch with Dad in an hour," she reminds me.

Brunch with Dad. Maybe that has something to do with my mood. With all that's gone on the past few days, I haven't had a ton of time to think about it. But it's been in the back of my mind. Maybe once this brunch is over, my excitement will surface.

~

The diner's aesthetic is what Nori calls grunge-retro. Only, it doesn't seem deliberate. The space hasn't been renovated in decades. The black-and-white-tiled floors are cracked and scuffed. There's one crater toward the back of the diner that everyone knows to avoid. The torn, sun-stained booths are a mint-ish color. It's a hot debate whether they were originally blue or green. (I'm team green.)

There's a jukebox in the corner that only works if you kick it at exactly the right angle and with just the right amount of force.

While the ambiance isn't exactly ideal, it's got the best diner food in Maplewood, which is why people put up with the space. The same family has owned it since it first opened, and their recipes have been passed down from generation to generation. Even the gigantic plastic menus haven't changed since I was in a booster seat.

I expected to arrive first. Dad is perpetually late. But when I walk in, taking in the scent of deep-fried goodness, I see him hunched over at the window table, perusing the menu. Our table. He always requested it because he knew I liked to look out the window and play the car game. The one where we'd lay claim to alternating cars that went by. He'd always let me cheat and claim the pretty cars.

From the entryway, he looks thinner. His thick black hair is now a little sparse around the crown of his head. It reminds me that almost a year has passed since we've been face-to-face. He doesn't really know me, and maybe I don't really know him. I think about Renner's offer to come with me. I really could use one of his pep talks right now, even if he is a nitwit.

But Renner's not here, so I take a step forward, and then another, until I reach the booth.

"Hi, Dad," I say, tepidly sliding into the booth across from him.

His eyes widen and he opens his mouth, like my appearance is some sort of shock. "You made it," he says, in the awkward way an old dude would greet his business associate. "Hope you don't mind. I ordered the grilled cheese for you. I know you used to love them."

He's not wrong. I do love the diner's double-decker grilled cheeses.

"Oh, uh, thank you. How was your drive from the city?" I ask, studying his face. Mom always said I get my looks from Dad. We share numerous features, dark eyes, thick brows, heart-shaped lips, and the same crooked smile.

"Long," he says with a chuckle. "Summer traffic is picking up."

"Ah. Any vacations planned?"

"I mentioned that we are moving into Alexandra's parents' lake house. So we'll probably just take things easy—" He pauses, because he knows what I'm thinking. My heart twinges, hurt for younger me who would have given anything to have a summer vacation with Dad. I try to push that thought away, reminding myself that I have a busy summer ahead before college.

"Sounds fun," I say, distracted by the waitress dropping off our orders. His order is the same too, a club sandwich held together by a toothpick with colored foil. He used to let me have them.

"Enough about me. I hear you've been busy. How were your exams?" he asks, removing the toothpick. His jaw cracks a little when he takes a bite, as it always does.

I shrug, still not feeling up to eating, even though I'm hungry. "Good. Really good, actually. I aced them all, I think."

He smiles proudly. "Of course you did. Oh, your mom sent along an invite to your graduation ceremony. Alexandra would like to come with me if you can spare an extra invite." He catches my reaction and hesitates. "If that's okay with you, that is."

I remember how it felt to cross the stage at my middle school graduation, searching every darkened row for his face in the audience. And how crushing it was to shake the principal's hand and pose for a photo with Mom as my sole guest.

I clear my throat. "If you can make it, sure. If you can't, that's fine too. I'd rather you not cancel last minute."

"No, we'll be there," he promises. "Alexandra really wants to meet you."

My lips twitch. "That's why you're coming to my grad? So Alexandra can meet me?"

"No. I wouldn't miss your graduation for the world. It's a huge deal. But," he adds, "of course I want you to get to know Alexandra, especially with the baby coming. That's why I want you to spend some time with us this summer." He lights up when he talks about Alexandra and the baby. It actually makes me kind of happy. Happy for my future sibling. The sparkle in his eyes seems so genuine, and everything in my heart wants to believe him.

"I'm sorry for how I reacted on the phone," I say, lowering my head. "It took me by surprise. It's not like we've been in regular contact."

He lowers his chin. "I know. And that's on me. I'm sorry I haven't been around as much as I should have."

"What made you come to this conclusion?" I ask.

"The baby," he says without a beat. "Going through it with Alexandra made me realize how much time I've lost with you. I know you'll probably never forgive me and I don't blame you—"

"It's okay," I cut in when his eyes well with tears. I don't think I've ever seen Dad cry in my life.

"No. I let my work take over my life. I let my relationship with your mom sour ours. And by the time I realized it, I thought it was too late. That you already didn't want me in your life."

The words pierce my heart, especially since I felt the complete opposite. "I did. More than anything. I've wanted your approval my entire life, and I never felt like I had it."

"You've always had my approval. I've always been immensely proud of everything you do."

"Really?" I ask, voice barely above a whisper. I think about the box that Alexandra gave me at the lake house. She'd said the same thing. Real or not, I was starting to think Dad actually did care about me.

"I just assumed you knew that," he says. For some reason, I always thought adults made decisions with purpose. That they knew what they were doing all the time. But maybe adults are just like teens, bumbling around aimlessly, unsure if they've gotten it right.

"I definitely didn't."

He looks hurt, but he accepts it. "I'll be better about telling you from here on out. Okay?" He extends his hand to me.

I accept his promise and return his handshake. The feeling of Dad's hand around mine fills me with a sense of relief. For the first time, I feel inclined to let go of my anger and move forward. Maybe it's not too late to have a relationship with him. Maybe this is just the beginning.

THIRTY-SEVEN

In tenth grade, I made a list of my dreams for senior prom. First on that list was Clay Diaz picking me up with a corsage, admiring my beauty. I wanted to take those cheesy couple photos at Ollie's in front of his mom's rose garden, which I'd frame and display on my bedside table until the end of time. I wanted to Boomerang a cheers with champagne flutes in the back of the limo with Kassie. Also cheesy? Totally. But rom-coms have deluded my expectations, okay?

I've dreamed about this night ever since Kassie and I watched *The Kissing Booth* at a sixth-grade sleepover. We consulted Google immediately, ogling sequined gowns, making collages filled with celebrities we'd love to go with, curating the perfect romantic slow-dance playlists, and gushing about the day it would finally be our turn to go to prom.

And now, here it is. The best day of a teenager's life, after years of anticipating, commiserating, and meticulously planning.

Things aren't going exactly as planned. My hairdresser, Alice, butchered my updo. She went buck-wild curling the hair framing my face into tiny old-lady ringlets. It's not that I have anything against curls. But this is far from the loose, old-Hollywood glam waves I presented in my album of inspiration photos.

"I have to do them tight because your hair is so pin-straight and coarse. It'll fall throughout the day, trust," she kept insisting as I watched the horror in the mirror.

It's been two hours since I left the salon and it has yet to fall. In fact, I kind of resemble a hobbit. This does not bode well for my trust issues. Even Mom had to stifle a snort when she picked me up.

Unfortunately, my appointment ran late so I don't have time to fix it. I have exactly forty-five minutes to do my makeup and get dressed before Clay picks me up.

I'm naked in the bathtub frantically shaving a patch of hair on my upper thigh when Clay shows up. He's a good half hour earlier than I instructed last night via text.

As I hastily rinse the shaving cream off my legs, Mom answers the front door. I hear her squeal in delight. Footsteps pad into the living room and she says, "The famous Clay Diaz. Charlotte has told me so much about you!" Kill me now.

I struggle to zip my dress without assistance as Mom fawns over Clay in the living room, asking about Model UN, where he's going to college next year, and what he hopes to do with his life. Then she tells him he's the spitting image of one of the characters in the book she's writing. I'm shocked he doesn't flee.

By the time I muster the strength to emerge from my room, Clay is sitting stiff backed on my couch, gripping the armrest. He's wearing a black suit with a pinstriped gray tie. There's something different about his hair. Gel, perhaps? It's combed back like an old-school gangster. All he's missing is a fedora.

"Hi," I say. I spot my dirty llama-print socks strewn over the cushion next to him. Cool. Cool. Cool.

"Hey, Charlotte," he says with a half smile, eyes darting to my hair, and then back to Mom behind me. He looks flat-out nervous, very different from his usual chill self.

"S-sorry I'm late." My face is hot from rushing around and blow-drying my chest to get a water stain out of my silk dress. "You look . . . nice."

He smiles. "Thanks. My mom insisted I wear a suit."

I laugh, disturbed. What would he wear to prom other than a suit? There's an awkward beat of silence as I wait for him to return the compliment, but he doesn't. Maybe my hair really is that bad. Instead, he extends a hand toward me, clutching a clear plastic box containing a pale-pink corsage. The corsage is beautiful, with a little bracelet attached made of tiny pearl-like beads.

I open the box and put it on my wrist, admiring it from all angles. "It's gorgeous. Thanks, Clay."

Mom claps her hands together, stands abruptly, and pats herself down like a TSA agent. She does this when she's looking for her phone, which is usually either lost between the couch cushions or in the cup holder of the car. This time, it's on top of the microwave. "Can I take some photos of you two in the front yard before you leave?"

We head outside and snap a couple unflattering photos before Mom lets us go.

"Kinda shy, eh?" she whispers as Clay heads to his Jeep. I can tell she's really thinking, *Hmm, not too sure about him.* I give her a warning look and her expression softens. "Don't be nervous. Just have fun! And don't forget to be safe tonight." She gives me a suggestive wink. My mom has turned into Amy Poehler in *Mean Girls*.

"Bye, Mom," I say before hopping into Clay's Jeep. "Sorry about her, by the way."

"It's cool. She's nice." He seems unbothered, eyes trained on the road ahead.

I really should have planned some talking points ahead of time, because right now, my mind is blank. Why is it that I can't summon a single word in Clay's presence? It's like he has some weird hold on me that renders me unable to speak English.

In fact, the only words we exchange the entire drive are the directions I give to Ollie's.

When we arrive at Ollie's, a whoosh of relief escapes me. Maybe things will be better once we're around everyone else. Being alone in a vehicle with someone you don't know all that well is awkward, after all.

~

The low pitch of Renner's laugh carries across Ollie's sprawling waterfront yard. I squeeze my eyes shut as I adjust my dress at the end of the long gravel driveway.

Just ignore him like you always have. Don't let him ruin yet another monumental high school event.

Unfortunately, Renner is the first person I see as Clay and I enter the yard.

His charcoal suit is perfectly tailored, fitting nicely along his broad shoulders. The warm summer breeze pushes his hair slightly askew, like a SoCal surfer dude. But it's his dazzling smile that makes my stomach roll.

His eyes quite literally crinkle at the edges. I imagine them bursting with cartoon hearts as he admires Andie, who's striking pose after pose for the professional photographer. A ping of envy hits me as I take in Andie's long, flowing, bright-orange two-piece that accentuates her fit body, making her runway-ready legs appear even longer. While most of the girls have opted for curled updos, she has a sleek, pin-straight ponytail, softened with newly trimmed curtain bangs that fall on either side of her face. She's a vision, even next to Kassie, who looks like an ice queen in a silver-blue, crystal-adorned gown, half updo, and lush stick-on lashes. And I'm a stubby toad compared to them both.

I guess I've always been a little jealous of Andie, even before this whole Renner debacle. While Kassie has always been my best friend, she's never made that distinction between me and her other friends. Whenever we're in photos together, she always calls us both "besties." And in birthday posts, she calls me "one of" her favorite people. She's political, I'll give her that.

After Clay ditches me to play beer pong with the guys, I take refuge in Ollie's kitchen, helping his dad prepare appetizers. His dad is a sweet, soft-spoken man who takes every opportunity to lament about how music "just isn't the same these days."

He's chattering away about how the Red Hot Chili Peppers should be required listening in American high schools when Nori summons me outside to take group photos. Despite her gorgeous gown, the first thing I notice are her bangs. They hang just above her brows, slightly uneven on the left.

"You. Look. Hot," Nori whispers, arm linked with mine as we head toward the photo area.

"I look straight from the Shire. But you look amazing. And you . . . you cut your bangs," I say, reaching to adjust a strand before the photographer snaps an unflattering pic.

"I know. I didn't want to. But then I felt like I shouldn't mess around with fate, you know?" While I've explained to her multiple times that my "time travel" was just my overactive imagination, she's still convinced it was some strange cosmic event.

"So you cut them anyways?"

"I had no choice. Haven't you seen those time-travel movies? If you try to screw with the outcome, you always wind up drastically screwing up your life," she says through a smile. "You said I seemed happy in the future, so the last thing I need to do is not cut my bangs and end up destitute on the streets or something."

I consider explaining Uncle Larry's reverse grandfather paradox to her, but that's a lot to digest as we take prom photos. So I just nod. "Fair enough."

Group photos are a whole new brand of chaos. There are variations of pairings, poses, full group photos, girls' shots, guys' shots, et cetera. An argument even breaks out over who gets to be in the center of the group shots and who gets stuck on the end. (Spoiler alert, I voluntarily go to the end to avoid controversy.) And when it's our turn for couples' photos, the photographer decides Clay and I need a lesson on "natural smiling."

When we pile into the limo, Clay sits with the guys in the back. Kassie and Andie are taking selfies near the front. The only open seat is smack dab in the middle. Right next to Renner. Of course.

He stiffens when I plop next to him, eager to rest my poor feet. "Feet still hurt?"

"How'd you guess?" I groan.

Renner digs into his pocket and pulls out a handful of Band-Aids as the limo pulls out of Ollie's driveway. "Need one?"

I give him a wary look, half-mad at myself for not packing extras. "Why do you have a pocket full of Band-Aids?"

"Am I not allowed to carry first-aid supplies?"

I don't bother to answer as I gratefully pluck two from his hands. "Thanks."

"How was brunch with your dad?"

His question takes me off guard. I didn't think he'd remember.

"So . . . ," he starts when I don't respond. "You're here with Clay."

"Obviously. Why do you care?" I ask, placing a Band-Aid over a newly formed blister next to the strap of my heel.

He shrugs, readjusting in his seat. "I don't. I just—I wanted to make sure you were having a good time together. I know tonight is important for you."

"We're having a blast, thank you," I say deadpan, although I'm not so sure about Clay. He seems wholly uncomfortable with this whole prom thing.

Renner follows my gaze to Clay, who's sought solace with the guys, seemingly forgetting I exist. "Are you, though? Because you've got your mad face on."

"My mad face?"

He nods.

"A natural by-product of being near you, yes," I say, too tired to come up with anything wittier.

"All right. Whatever you say," he says, though his tone tells me he doesn't buy it.

"Instead of pestering me, why don't you go dote on Andie? Your actual prom date?"

His eyes widen. "Come on. You can't be mad that I agreed to take Andie days before anything happened between us."

My instinct is to deny, deny. "I'm not mad about that, Renner," I say, though I'm pretty sure my face is a dead giveaway. "But good on you for always thinking everything is about you. And for the record, nothing happened between us."

"You really think that kiss was nothing?" he whispers. He's right, of course. It was everything. But my pride won't let me admit it.

I shake my head. "Nope. Nothing. Nada. Zilch."

"Okay, if you say so." We sit in awkward, stilted silence. Renner finally deflates, exasperated. "You never even gave me a chance to explain. You just ran out—"

I hold my hand out to stop him. "Why are you doing this? You know I like Clay. Why can't you just let me be happy for once instead of always trying to ruin everything?" It comes out louder than intended, catching Andie's and Kassie's attention in the front of the limo.

I can see the pity in his face. The downturn of his lips. The sad, dopey eyes. Before he can respond, Andie plops herself smack between us, half on my lap and half on Renner's.

I take this as my cue to move and snag her previous spot next to Kassie.

"Everything good with you and J. T.?" she asks pointedly, fluffing her hair in her compact mirror.

I flash her a fake smile, willing Renner to disappear into a cloud of dust. "When are things ever good between us?"

"Don't let him get to you," she warns.

"Oh, I won't," I declare.

J. T. Renner may have ruined freshman homecoming, but he won't ruin my prom.

THIRTY-EIGHT

Clay ditches me the moment we enter prom. I don't blame him, given I'm in full-blown student council mode, ensuring everything and everyone is where they're supposed to be. Admittedly, it's not the fairy-tale night I envisioned with him.

Though I saw the gym earlier today, it's an entirely different experience at night, with the lights down, the candles lit, and everyone dressed up. It's an underwater oasis. The uplighting really does wonders for the ambiance, casting blue and pink rays that appear to be moving, like water. Even the DJ's strobe lights make the seaweed look like it's swaying in the water. It may even be nicer than the Mardi Gras prom from the future. Maybe Renner was right about the theme, after all.

At most dances, it takes a while for the dance floor to fill. But it's already packed by the time we arrive. Everyone is circled around Patrick Stone, MHS's resident break-dancer, who's currently spinning on his head.

I'm in hot pursuit of a missing centerpiece when Nori pulls me onto the dance floor. She's always fun to dance with, mostly because she embodies the phrase "dance like no one's watching."

By the third song, Kassie and Andie join us. Despite my weird feelings toward Andie, I soak in the moment. After four years, this is the last time we'll all be together like this. There won't be another high school dance.

A melancholy slow song fills the air, an abrupt shift. The lights dim and everyone rushes off to find their dates. I catch myself smiling, watching Nori and Tayshia laugh maniacally at something as they twirl each other. Meanwhile, Ollie is whispering sweet nothings into Kassie's ear. My heart flutters, seeing my friends so happy. What it must be like to find love like that in high school.

I scan the dance floor filled with closely entwined couples and catch Clay in my peripheral vision. He's hanging out near the bleachers in what appears to be animated conversation with his friend. The last thing I want to do is force him to dance with me when he's already shown zero interest in dancing—and also as my prom date.

"Hey, having fun?" Clay asks as I approach.

I shrug. "I'd probably have more fun if my date was dancing with me." I try to say it casually.

"All right. Let's go," he says, monotone.

I place my hands on his shoulders. His fall to my waist, and we dance like preteens allowing space for the Holy Spirit for the last half of the song, before a fast one begins. I can't help comparing dancing with Real Clay to Adult Renner. But it's just not the same.

"So, um, thanks for being my date," I tell him, relieved when the song ends and I can pull away.

He scratches his head. "For sure. Though I kinda think you probably would have preferred to go with someone else."

"What?" I say, jaw slackening in denial.

He laughs over the music, raising a brow knowingly. "J. T."

"Renner? No. Why would you say that?"

"Dunno. Call it intuition, I guess? Looked like you had a pretty tense conversation in the limo. And you both couldn't stop staring at each other at Ollie's."

I blink, mortified. "I definitely wasn't staring at Renner."

"It's okay, Char. Really. I'm not mad." He gives me a look as if to say, *The jig is up. It's cool.*

Unable to admit it, I press my hands over my face. "I'm sorry, Clay. I don't know what to say. I've had a crush on you for literally ever and—" I don't know where my courage comes from. Maybe it's the fact that I probably won't see him again after we leave high school. And maybe it's because I'm starting to realize that maybe, just maybe, the awkwardness I feel around him isn't solely about nerves like I've always thought. Maybe it's because we simply don't have a spark between us.

"Yeah. I kind of got that impression. I've always wondered why you didn't just talk to me."

I hide my face. "I'm sorry. I just always felt awkward, I guess? Even today when you picked me up, you were perfect and I just . . . I don't know. I didn't feel anything," I admit.

He looks a little relieved when I say it. "It's fine, Charlotte. I totally agree. Friends?"

I nod. "Friends."

I wander out to the hallway for some air, stopping to take my heels off.

The painted brick wall of last year's graduating class catches my eye as I unfasten the buckle on the strap. The bricks remind me I still have to write the time capsule letter to myself for graduation next week.

In only a few days, I'll be saying goodbye to this school and these people forever. Mom once described high school as a "trip"—a passage of time that feels tediously slow, but also lightning fast. After chasing perfect grades, the next homework assignment, the next school event, it's hard to believe all those mini goalposts have culminated in four whole years.

As I amble barefoot to my locker, the click of dress shoes against tiles echoes behind me.

It's Renner. He's taken his suit jacket off, as well as his tie, and he's rolled his sleeves to his forearms. The disheveled-business-intern look is annoyingly sexy.

When I turn around, he clears his throat and says, "I want you to be happy."

I triple blink and lean closer to ensure I've heard him correctly.

He continues. "In the limo, you asked why I can't let you be happy. All I've ever wanted is for you to be happy."

I lower my chin, unable to compute. The sincerity of his voice doesn't match my recollection. "Then why would you kiss me if you had a date to prom already? What was your plan? To outdo freshman homecoming or something? To hook up with me and then take another girl to prom?"

Red-faced, he runs his hands down both cheeks. "No! For Christ's sake, Char. Stop being your stubborn-ass self for one second and listen to me."

I fold my arms over my chest. "I'm listening."

He levels me with his gaze. "You're the only person I ever wanted to take to prom. The only one."

"Since when?"

"The first day of school."

"How am I supposed to believe that?"

He runs his hands through his hair, the fluorescent light above casting a white glow over his face. "First period. Freshman year. I asked you for a pencil every single day as an excuse to talk to you."

I squint at him, blinking slowly. "You did that just to talk to me?"

"You thought I actually lost every pencil you gave me?" he scoffs, nudging me aside to open his locker. He reaches into its depths and pulls out a bundle of my mechanical pencils. They're tied together with a rubber band. I stare at them, breathless, as he places the bundle in my hand. "I kept them. Of course I kept them," he tells me.

How is this even possible? How has he kept every single pencil all this time? "But—but what about homecoming?"

"I think we both already know the answer to that."

A feeling of familiarity blooms. Does he mean what I think he means? Did we have this conversation before?

He watches me intently, waiting for me to respond. Right then, Andie rushes down the hallway. "J. T.! They're announcing the royal court!"

THIRTY-NINE

Ms. Chouloub looks like an announcer at the Oscars, proudly clutching the envelope with the results, officially tabulated by Mr. Hamilton, head of the math department.

She clears her throat into the mic, which gets everyone's attention. It's all-out anarchy as everyone crowds around the stage like groupies at a rock concert. Those at the front even bang their fists in a drumroll as Ms. Chouloub struggles to rip the envelope open with her acrylic nails.

From my perch on the sidelines, I search the swelling crowd for my predicted winners—Kassie and Ollie—but fail to spot them. Everything is a blur. To be fair, my mind is on overload. I still haven't finished processing my conversation with Renner.

Ms. Chouloub finally opens the envelope, and her face breaks into a wide grin as she reads the results. "And your prom king is . . . J. T. Renner!" she bellows into the microphone. The gym explodes with rowdy applause as Renner parts the crowd with his megawatt smile, sauntering to the stage like a rockstar accepting a Grammy.

I'll admit, I'm a little bit surprised. I mean, Renner was always a top pick. But I assumed it would be Ollie, given he's MHS's football star and Kassie's boyfriend.

Renner didn't expect it either, by the looks of things. There's a bit of shock in his expression as he accepts his new title and cheap plastic crown. It makes his acceptance even more charming somehow. The crowd doesn't quiet, even when he says a rueful thank-you. The guy really doesn't have a single enemy. And it's easy to see why. He's walking sunlight.

The crowd finally hushes when Ms. Chouloub clears her throat to announce the next winner. "Your prom queen is . . . Kassie Byers!"

My heart explodes for Kassie as the confetti bomb and balloons fall from the ceiling. She's dreamed of being prom queen since we were kids. Meanwhile, my goal was just to have a date. Andie looks a little miffed, but Kassie doesn't notice as she elbows her way to the stage. She looks radiant with the sparkling silver crown atop her head, like it was made for her.

It's tradition for the royal court to do a slow dance, which works most of the time, when the couple is actually an item. Renner and Kassie aren't obligated to dance, but they're both good sports about it, laughing, doing dramatic twirls and spins for the crowd. Ollie doesn't appear annoyed that he lost in the slightest. He whistles from the sidelines, trying to embarrass them.

I think about all those years ago, when Kassie came over after dinner, vibrating with excitement over the first time she met Renner.

"We made out for like . . . two hours," she bragged, handing me a globby container of chip dip.

"Two hours?" I asked, in awe, dipping my chip. Making out with someone for that long seemed physically impossible.

She shrugged, fluffing her hair. "Okay, probably not two hours. It might have even been two minutes. Who knows? He's the best kisser. And the best part? He's going to MHS."

She seemed so excited that evening, clutching my pillow to her chest, starry eyes glimmering as she rattled off every detail. That's why it struck me the next day when she said the kiss was meaningless—no feelings attached.

My mind drifts back to Renner's words in the hallway. *I think we both already know the answer to that.*

My fingers tingle with a creeping sense. I think back—well, forward—to being thirty. To the night at Walnut Creek, when Renner told me that he turned Kassie down, despite Kassie telling me otherwise for all these years. I think about the look of confusion on Adult Renner's face when I accused him of ditching homecoming for another girl. About how there never was another girl. And I finally realize—Kassie lied.

When the song is over, Kassie flops into the chair next to me to rest her feet. "Can you believe I actually won?" she asks, slightly out of breath.

"Of course you won. You're Kassie freakin' Byers. That crown looks good on you," I say on best friend autopilot. I reach to straighten it on her head, but take a shaky breath when I realize what I'm doing. What I always do with Kassie: dismiss her shortcomings and forgive her instantly. But she lied. She's lied to me about Renner for four years.

This feels too big to ignore. I don't know why she lied to me, but I need to confront her. Now.

"It suits J. T. too," she says, as he chats with his adoring fans.

I inch my chair closer to her. "Hey, speaking of J. T. . . . Remind me. What happened with you two?"

She fidgets with her rose corsage, plucking off a dead petal. "Nothing. We made out forever ago. That's all."

"Right. It's coming back to me now. And you never had feelings for him?"

She presses her mouth into a thin line, eyes wide, as though she's a thief caught midheist. "Why would you think that? Of course I don't have feelings for J. T. You know how much I love Ollie." I don't doubt her love for Ollie. I've been reminded of it every minute of every day for the past four years. But that's not what I asked her.

I sit up straight, spine steeled as it all falls into place. "That wasn't my question. Did you ever have feelings for him?"

"I . . . um . . . I . . ." She looks flustered. Kassie never looks flustered. "Hasn't everyone had a crush on him at some point?"

"You didn't actually turn him down, did you?"

She scratches her arm nervously. "Um . . . well." Her face says it all.

I storm out of the gym. The air in the hallway is fresh. I sag against the cool brick wall, face in my hands, trying to make sense of this.

Kassie lied to me. For four years she lied. The question is, Why? And the bigger question is, How is all this possible? How could Renner have told me before? Was our conversation—our entire time as thirty-year-olds—actually real? There's no way. Is it possible I knew, deep down, that she was lying to me? Possibly.

Kassie bursts into the hall, and I finally get the guts to grill her. "Why would you lie about that, Kassie?" I ask, standing to match her height.

She bites her lip and looks down. A crystal from her dress has fallen at her feet. "Because I was embarrassed. And you liked him."

The image of her face when I told her Renner asked me to homecoming flashes through my mind. Her expression was unreadable. "That's why you were mad when he asked me to homecoming."

"I—I . . ." Her voice trails away, at a loss for words.

I shake my head and cross my arms. "And when he ditched homecoming, you lied and said he was with another girl."

She gives me a knowing look. "I'm sorry, Char. I panicked. And in my defense, I did hear that rumor. It's not like he was some saint."

"But you were with Ollie. Why did it matter?"

"I don't know . . . It was stupid. I was still jealous and bitter that he turned me down. It wasn't even that I liked him, I swear. But no one had rejected me before and it got to me. I got over him pretty much right after that, especially when Ollie and I got more serious. I always felt like shit for lying about it. Believe me, there were so many times I wanted to tell you but there was never a right moment and—"

"I've hated Renner ever since . . ." I think about how mad I was at him. How loyal I've been to her even though she blatantly lied to me all these years. I can't even look at her. I can't believe she'd lie to me. And most of all, I can't believe Adult Renner was right.

"You can't blame me for hating Renner. How many times did I beg and plead with you to stop holding your stupid grudge against him?

And don't act like you hated him all because of me. You have an entire list of reasons you hate him, do you not?"

"Only because of homecoming!" I make an effort to lower my voice. "I just can't believe you'd do something like this . . . You were supposed to be my best friend."

She lowers her chin in what appears to be genuine remorse. "I'm so sorry. It was beyond wrong and immature to let a guy affect our friendship. I know that now."

I don't doubt she's truly sorry. Kassie has never been one to apologize, even when she knows she's wrong. And while I can try to forgive her for the past, I don't know that it's enough to repair us.

"What can I do to make it up to you?" she pleads.

"Stop lying," I demand. "You lie to me, all the time. Not just about big things, but about insignificant things too. And I know you don't like conflict, but it hurts because I know you're lying. Change plans, do whatever it is you're going to do, but at least give me the respect of telling the truth."

She winces. "I know. I really do need to work on that. I'm sorry for hurting you. I never meant to. I swear. We just have really different ways of dealing with things and sometimes it makes it hard."

"Tell me about it," I huff.

"In the end . . . we've always been different, haven't we?" She's not wrong. We've always been polar opposites. And without a common town, a common high school, and a common group of friends, who are we really to each other?

"We were always opposites," I agree. Yin and yang. That's what Mom calls us.

"Well, from here on out, it'll be one hundred percent honesty. I promise." She reaches for my hand and squeezes. For a flash, I see Adult Kassie in yoga-wear. While I appreciate the gesture, I think we both know something has changed. Something irreversible. It's like the tiniest hairline fracture that will inevitably deepen with time.

Maybe Mom was right. Maybe not all friends are meant to be in your life for the long haul. Not being friends anymore doesn't have to involve a catastrophic fight. No one means to hurt the other person. People just move on with life. Sad as it is, it also brings me a sense of peace.

"Well, for the sake of honesty, I need to tell you something too." I contemplate telling her everything. But I settle for the heart of it. "I have feelings for Renner."

Her eyes bulge. "No. Way. What? Since you guys kissed at the sleepover?"

That doesn't seem right either. I can't pinpoint the exact moment it happened. Was it that first smile he gave me on the bleachers the first day of school? The hours of bickering? That kiss on the rooftop? It doesn't really matter. Somehow, Renner took hold of my heart and made it whole. Fuller. Happier. "For . . . a long time. I think."

And while Kassie doesn't know everything, she can interpret the look in my eyes. Somehow, she just knows what I need, because she's still my best friend, for now at least. "Go find him," she says with a nudge.

With her approval, I march back into the gym, head held high—only, the mood has slowed. And that's when I hear it. That familiar tune.

The *Dirty Dancing* song.

FORTY

The lighting is low, and glittering dots of yellow swirl around the dance floor.

It's like wading through a starry galaxy as I pass through the crowd, the rhythm of the music thrumming in my ears. You know it's the end of the night when the girls' hair is plastered to their foreheads with sweat, and guys' dress shirts are wrinkled and partially unbuttoned. It's nearing eleven o'clock, but everyone is holding strong on the dance floor. These are the last precious moments of high school.

As I round the refreshment table, I spot a tall figure chatting with the DJ. I know it's Renner. No one else has that self-assured stance. He beams when he spots me, handsome face backlit by the blue lights near the stage. Human sunshine.

When our eyes meet, the crowd seems to part, opening a direct path to him. There's a knowing look in his eyes. A look of realization, fear, adoration, all wrapped into one. Without even saying a word, I know he's experienced it too. I know it deep in my soul.

It's only when my feet start to ache that I realize we're walking toward the middle of the star-filled dance floor.

We stop and he holds his hand out. "Dance with me?"

"I'm scared you might drop me," I say.

A smile dances across his lips. "Touché. No fancy lifts this time. I promise."

I pretend to look around. "But what about your date?"

He smiles ruefully. "She's over there . . . making out with Cliff."

I crane my neck. Andie and Cliff Johnson are making out against the bleachers. "Oh? I didn't know they were a thing." In fact, I'm fairly certain Cliff had a date from another school at the beginning of the night.

He shrugs. "Guess they are now."

My eyes flare. "But I thought . . ."

"Andie and I went to prom as friends."

"It didn't look like you were just friends. Andie likes you."

"She does." Renner's Adam's apple dips. "And I told her I wanted to stay friends."

"You did?"

"Yeah. I told her I had feelings for someone else. And have for a long time. I told Andie I wasn't sure if this girl felt the same way, but I had to see. That I'd regret it if I didn't." He makes a come-hither motion with his hand. "Now come here before our song ends."

My stomach loosens and I finally feel like I can breathe. "You requested it?"

He dips his chin and nods.

"Why didn't you say anything?" I ask. "Why didn't you tell me it happened to you too?"

He smirks. "I could ask you the same thing."

"I thought you'd think I'd lost my mind," I say, peering up at him.

"We both have. Clearly. And you seemed too angry when we woke up in the gym . . . I thought there was no way."

I blink, confused. "I could say the same to you. I mean, you did tell me I looked like shit."

He gives me a sheepish smile. "I'm a dumbass. What can I say? I don't think that's ever gonna change. Even when we're thirty."

"Fair."

"How did you know for sure?" he asks.

"Kassie. She told me the truth about homecoming. You?"

"I kinda put the pieces together when you jumped me on the roof. And you said that thing about my sister and taking the burden for my parents and I just . . . I hadn't told anybody that before."

"I can't believe this. It's so weird."

He nods. "It would be slightly less weird if you'd dance with me." He extends his hand again and I take it. He gently pulls me into him, one hand splayed on my waist, while the other tucks a ringlet behind my ear and then wraps around my lower back. "I like your hair."

"Ugh. Don't lie. It looks awful."

He chuckles as he twirls me. "Any style would suit you. I promise."

"Good, 'cause I was thinking of getting an angled mom-bob."

He cringes. "How do we even begin to explain this to our grandchildren?"

"Wow. Now we're having grandchildren? We haven't even broached the topic of kids yet."

"Hey, you're the one that went there, talking about mom hairstyles."

"Was it . . . real?" I ask, burrowing my head into his neck.

"I don't know. It felt real. Everything I said to you was real. To me. And those feelings haven't stopped since we've come back. And I can't just continue pretending it never happened because real life doesn't feel real without you. I can't pretend I don't love you."

I'm filled with a warmth I'll never forget, like a soft, fizzy drink. I tilt my eyes to his. "You love me? Are you sure?" I ask, leaning closer to confirm I've heard him correctly.

His thumb sweeps along my jaw in a gentle rhythm. "Surer than I've ever been."

"I love you too," I shout over the music, though it comes out more like *iloveyou!*

His shoulders sag in what looks like relief. "I didn't know if you were gonna admit that."

I relish the low vibration of his voice. "I had to. We only have one week left," I remind him, unable to hide my disappointment.

There's only one week left to walk these halls, see these familiar faces, lament the torturously long distance between Class A and Class B. Only one week left to fight to the death, *Hunger Games*–style, for a coveted table in the cafeteria. Just one single week.

It's strange to think that all of high school is a way of preparing to leave it all behind. You work so hard to establish yourself. Grades. Friends. A reputation. These four years feel like they'll never end—until they do. It's like I've channeled the great Usain Bolt, full-on sprinting my way to the finish line. But instead of finishing victoriously, I come to a dead stop, only inches before crossing it. It's not just because of Renner that I don't want to cross it. It's everything. I'm going to miss it all. All the little things, even struggling with my combination lock between every period. Suddenly, one week doesn't feel like enough. Not nearly.

"One week, huh?" Renner cups my chin and tilts my head up again, eyes blazing. "Then we better make the most of it."

How is it fair that of the 720 days of high school, Renner and I get five? Five. Life is cruel. Then again, five days is better than zero.

"What does that entail?" I ask, letting the fantasy take over.

He bounces his brows suggestively, tightening his grip on my waist. "What do you want it to entail?"

I bite my lip, scared to admit the truth, that I want it to entail everything. "You tell me."

"Unlimited access to your pencils."

"So long as you don't wait four years to return them."

He gives me that cheeky grin, and his eyes search mine. "In all seriousness, I think it entails holding hands, definitely."

"Holding hands? Like in public?" I mock.

"Oh yeah. In the hallway. Walking to class. In the library. Until your hand gets tired, loses all circulation, and falls off." Morbid visual aside, I let myself imagine what it would be like to walk down the hall in front of everyone, hand in hand with Renner. Finally.

Everything in me wants to leap into the air and let out a giddy screech. But for the sake of playing it cool, I just smile up at him coyly. "Yeah? Where else would you hold my hand?"

He reaches for my hand on his shoulder and squeezes for added effect. "Graduation. Grad party. When I pick you up after work at Two Cows. When I visit you at the lake house. Every day. All summer."

I see all of it so clearly in my mind. Because I already know how it feels to ride in the passenger seat of his van. To have him smile at me. Hold me in his arms.

"What's wrong?" he asks.

I rest my head against his chest and squeeze him tight, as though he's going to disappear again. "I just . . . I'm scared. To lose you. Already."

He pulls me closer, placing a soft kiss on top of my head, then pulls back slightly. He places both hands on either side of my cheeks, and specks of light dance across his face. "Look, I don't know what's going to happen in the next thirteen years. I don't even know what's going to happen tomorrow. But what I do know is, right now, all I want is to be with you, Char. And that's all I've wanted since I saw you on the first day of school. So please stop planning ahead for five seconds and just be with me in this moment."

"I can do that." Happy tears fill my eyes when I realize maybe this is what it's all about. Maybe this is true happiness. Being in Renner's arms, surrounded by our closest friends.

I take it all in. The lights, transforming the gym into the magical place it is. Kassie and Ollie dancing and laughing a couple feet over. Nori in conversation with Tayshia near the door, head back midlaugh.

Sure, I may have seen all our potential futures. I may know exactly how it's going to unfold. And yet, here, right now, I'm present. In this moment, this is the youngest I'll ever be. While I can't control what will happen or who I'll lose in my life, I know I can make the most of right now.

And I want to live in this moment.

Letter to myself at thirty—by Charlotte Wu

For the MHS 2024 Time Capsule, to be buried after graduation

Dear thirty-year-old Charlotte,

I'm writing to you moments after crossing the stage at graduation. I'll make this quick because Mom, Dad, and Renner are waiting to take cap and gown pictures.

Let's be honest, you're still a goal-chaser. There's no way to stop that. And that's okay. Goals are good. Goals propel us forward.

But I hope that with every milestone you achieve, you take the time to appreciate it. Don't let future goals get in the way of enjoying present happiness. Teenage Charlotte spent too many days dwelling over things she couldn't control. Don't let the stress of college exams, jobs, or relationships ruin your ability to experience life to the fullest. Hold on to every moment. Be present. Take it all in, second by second, untainted by plans and logistics. Treasure the now forever, because in the blink of an eye, it'll be gone. And on that same note, don't let the past dampen your present. Don't let fear or anger stop you from what you truly want.

Let go of the past and stop waiting for the future.

Love,

Teenage Charlotte

ACKNOWLEDGMENTS

Like Charlotte Wu, I was the person in the group project who took over because they didn't trust others. I've always aimed high. In fact, I've spent most of my life chasing the next thing: good grades, university acceptance, the degree, the dream job, the dream house, and so on. In all those years of goal-chasing, I've learned a couple things:

1) Satisfaction after hitting a milestone is only temporary. The secret to happiness (for me) is being at peace with the "now." It's not to say you can't have dreams, but don't attach them to your self-worth.

2) You can't do everything on your own. It takes a village to publish a book. And in fact, having a talented and passionate team behind me has produced results beyond what I could have comprehended. *Woke Up Like This* would not exist without the hard work and support of the following people:

My literary agent, Kim Lionetti, and her amazing assistant, Maggie Nambot, at Bookends Literary for being the very first to see this book's potential; my film agent, Addison Duffy, at UTA; Carmen Johnson, for being the best champion this book could ever ask for; the hardworking team at Amazon Publishing, Mindy's Book Studio, and Amazon Studios: Laura Chasen, Tara Whitaker, Emma Reh, Tree Abraham, Chrissy Penido, Erica Moriarty, and Ashley Vanicek. To the wickedly talented and incomparable Mindy Kaling herself: as a staunch advocate of showcasing stories from the perspective of women of color, you are an inspiration to us all. To my family and friends, who have been so supportive throughout this wild ride; and to my readers, who make it all worth it.

ABOUT THE AUTHOR

Amy Lea is a Canadian bureaucrat by day and contemporary romance author by night (and weekends). She writes laugh-out-loud adult and young adult romantic comedies featuring strong heroines, banter, mid-2000s pop culture references, and happily ever afters. When Amy is not writing, she can be found fangirling over other romance books on Instagram (@amyleabooks), eating potato chips with reckless abandon, and snuggling with her husband and goldendoodle.